"We've got you."

Zu's reassurance warmed her and settled in her chest.

"I believe you." For the first time in days, weeks, she steadied, and maybe a few of the broken pieces of her confidence slipped back into place.

She took a few steps forward, closing the distance between her and Zu. He didn't back away. She leaned up on tiptoe, resting the palm of one hand against his chest for balance, and gave him a quick kiss on the cheek before returning to where she'd been standing.

Or she meant to return. As she backed away, she encountered something furry right behind her legs, and she almost fell. Zu's arm wrapped around her waist, catching her and bringing her back against him. Suddenly, she was pressed against his very muscular body, and something was tapping the side of her calf. Tock-tock.

She looked up, way up, into Zu's face. This close, she could see the deep brown of his dark eyes. "I..."

Zu was murmuring something at the same time. "Buck..."

Neither of them finished their thought. Zu leaned closer and she tilted her face up. His lips brushed against hers, and she gasped as the slight contact burned through her. She rose up on tiptoe again, meeting him across the barest distance between their lips for the kiss she wanted more than air.

"This whole series is a great concept. If you're an animal lover and want a hero story, this book is for you."
—WritingPearls.com on *Absolute Trust*

"Top pick! I'm not sure what I can read next that will compare to *Ultimate Courage*!"
—HarlequinJunkie.com

"If you're looking for something sexy, strong, yet sweet at the same time, then *Ultimate Courage* will not disappoint."
—HeroesandHeartbreakers.com

"I didn't want to stop reading…I thought the characters, storyline, and tension were just about perfect. I give *Ultimate Courage* an A."
—TheBookPushers.com

"Drake's sharp storytelling shines with an engaging plot that's thick with tension…"
—*RT Book Reviews* on *Extreme Honor*

"*Extreme Honor* by Piper J. Drake is one sexy-as-hell romance novel. Readers won't be able to stay away from this juicy yet well-written plot."
—Romancing-the-Book.com

"Overall, if you want a fast-paced romantic suspense with a military hottie who trains dogs and a heroine who is likable, this is a great choice. I am really looking forward to book 2!"
—TheBookDisciple.com on *Extreme Honor*

FOREVER STRONG

PIPER J. DRAKE

FOREVER

NEW YORK BOSTON

Copyright © 2020 by Piper J. Drake
Excerpt from *Total Bravery* copyright 2018 by Piper J. Drake
Cover illustration by Michael Heath. Cover design by Elizabeth Turner Stokes. Cover copyright © 2020 by Hachette Book Group, Inc.

Forever
Hachette Book Group
1290 Avenue of the Americas, New York, NY 10104
read-forever.com
twitter.com/readforeverpub

First Edition: January 2020

Forever is an imprint of Grand Central Publishing. The Forever name and logo are trademarks of Hachette Book Group, Inc.

The publisher is not responsible for websites (or their content) that are not owned by the publisher.

The Hachette Speakers Bureau provides a wide range of authors for speaking events. To find out more, go to www.hachettespeakersbureau.com or call (866) 376-6591.

ISBNs: 978-1-5387-5960-8 (mass market), 978-1-5387-5961-5 (ebook)

Printed in the United States of America

OPM

10 9 8 7 6 5 4 3 2 1

To Katee and Åsa,
Your support and encouragement helped
me through some of the most frustrating,
challenging times and this book
wouldn't be what it is without you to
steady me.
Thank you.

ACKNOWLEDGMENTS

Thank you to Courtney Miller-Callihan for your encouragement and support, for protecting me from myself when I could be my own harshest taskmaster. Thank you for understanding me, seeing me, hearing me, and standing with me when I felt the need to step forward.

Huge thanks to Joy Harris and Sabrina Flemming for reading through this book for issues of representation and for instances of bias on the page. Your observations and commentary were invaluable. Thank you so much for your understanding and professionalism.

Thank you to Madeleine Colavita. Working with you has been a learning experience.

Thank you to Christopher Baity, executive director of Semper K9 Assistance Dogs, for your insight and advice regarding working dogs. Any errors are my own—because sometimes we writers need to stretch a few truths to make things work or dial back on the detail to keep the story moving—but hopefully the canines in this story are plausible thanks to you.

As I've written the books of the True Heroes series, my address has changed from the Baltimore area in Maryland to the Phoenix area in Arizona and now to Downtown Seattle in Washington State. Home for me has always been Matthew. Daisuke.

And finally, thanks to my readers. Many of you have been with me throughout the True Heroes series and some of you have joined the adventure with this book. I hope you all enjoy.

FOREVER
STRONG

CHAPTER ONE

hank you, Miss Jiang. Your statement has been very helpful. You'll be contacted if you can be of any further help."

Jiang Ying Yue closed her eyes and allowed herself to fully exhale. Sure. Relive the most terrifying time of your life, not once, but as many times as needed to dredge up anything she might have seen that could possibly be of help to the authorities. She'd thought her first statement had been detailed, but she'd found herself adding more today as the police asked her to clarify portions of what she remembered of her kidnapping and captivity. The only thing stopping her from cracking into a million pieces and laughing, or crying hysterically, was the desperate thought that she'd been helpful to someone. Maybe it'd been helpful to her, too, but it didn't feel that way at the moment.

As she took in her next breath, she opened her eyes and lifted her chin. "I'd like to be kept up to date on the progress of your investigation."

She clung to the calm she heard in her own voice. If she sounded sane, she could stay that way.

Officer Kokua nodded. "I'll be honest. We can't give you all the details from an ongoing investigation, but I will keep you apprised as much as I can. We'll find the people who kidnapped you."

She gave him a smile because it was what was expected. Truly? They both knew her kidnappers might never be found or brought to justice. She'd been plucked from the streets of Singapore on her way home from overseeing a charity event. When she'd regained consciousness, she'd been in a tiny cabin on a cargo ship crossing the Pacific Ocean. She hadn't even known that much until she'd been rescued just yesterday and gotten a look at the ship as her rescuer hustled her to a huge helicopter along with a large group of other captives.

After a night at Queen's Medical Center on the island of Oahu for observation, she'd been escorted to the nearby police station. Even with the detail she'd been able to add this morning, she'd only been able to give the police information on the appearances of her kidnappers. She hadn't heard any names. It'd be an impossible search without more.

"In the meantime, we've contacted your father." Officer Kokua might have been trying to sound reassuring, but bits and pieces of rationale were crumbling inside her head now that she was done giving her statement. She struggled to breathe past the fluttering in her chest as she fought to remain steady for a little longer.

Thankfully, he didn't reach over to pat her hand or make any other comforting gestures. She could keep it together if no one made sudden moves or tried to reach for her. Going through her kidnapping over and over again in increasing detail had left her wrung out and exhausted. Mentally, emotionally, and physically. She wanted to cry, but if she did, she'd also be embarrassed. Then she'd yell at herself for having any kind of shame for a perfectly justified reaction, and she'd feel even more out of control as she fell into a spiral of logic versus... all the feels.

There was more. Intellectually, she knew her captors could have done unspeakable things to her. They hadn't, at least not by the time her rescuer had burst through the door to the cabin. But the people who had taken her could have. Her living nightmare could've been a hundred, a thousand times more awful. Part of her was relieved. Another part of her felt guilty for being so lucky. She'd gotten a look at the other captives rescued from the same ship. They'd suffered far worse.

"My father was scheduled to be here, in Hawaii." She clung to the remembered detail from her father's itinerary, something she only knew because he'd mentioned it in passing during a perfunctory phone call. Their monthly chat was a habit started years ago, carried on through undergrad and graduate school and now maintained as she established her career. It was a fortunate coincidence it'd happened right before she'd been taken, and she was thankful. She was fully capable of returning to her apartment in Singapore on her own, but she'd like to at least see him before she tried to go through the process of returning to normal life. Whatever that was going to take.

It wasn't going to be as simple as getting on the next available flight, and she hadn't yet begun to figure out what she actually needed to do. Her father was the closest family she had, geographically speaking. Her mother was touring Europe while her father was on business. She wanted to see him, wanted to be held and know he'd been worried for her. A terrible fear lurked in the pit of her stomach, and she tasted bile as she considered the possibility that he'd been too busy to miss her.

"He's right here on Oahu," Officer Kokua confirmed with a broad smile. "We reached out to him as your emergency contact. His personal aide has made arrangements for you at the same hotel as your father."

She clenched her teeth but kept her smile frozen in place. "Of course."

The officer had spoken not to her father, but his aide. Her father hadn't had time to speak to the police, not even after she'd been kidnapped and rescued. A familiar blend of hurt and anger churned in her stomach to mix with her fear. Perhaps she should have made his aide her emergency contact rather than her next of kin, the head and patriarch of her family. Bitterness joined the twisting mess of emotions until she wondered how terrible she could feel in a single moment.

Something wet and cold pressed against the back of her hand. She blinked and relaxed her curled fingers. She hadn't realized she'd clenched her hands into fists on her lap. The black nose belonged to a large dog, who looked up at her with soulful golden-brown eyes. He withdrew and sat beside her, apparently satisfied he had her attention. He was a deep brown all over, almost burnished red, and his long tail brushed the ground once in greeting. Such a somber dog.

Recognition blossomed in her chest and spread through her in a cool, soothing wave. She was inordinately happy to see the dog. Her nausea eased as her lips curved into her first smile in forever. She reached out and gingerly patted the side of his neck, then crooked her fingers to scratch the base of one ear as he leaned into her hand. He'd been with her rescuer yesterday.

"Hey, Buck." Officer Kokua rose from his seat behind his desk. "I guess Zu is around here somewhere, then. Funny, usually Buck doesn't leave Zu."

Maybe her heart beat harder at the mention of the man, the owner of this dog. Maybe. She wasn't about to admit it if anyone called her on it. All she was experiencing was a natural reaction to the person who'd helped her get out of her dangerous captivity. She remembered someone larger than life, powerful and full of vitality, the memory influenced by the stress of her situation.

Still, she stood and turned, intending to follow the police officer in search of Buck's human. She wanted to thank the man who'd saved her. She also wanted him to see her calm and collected after a night's rest to restore her so he wouldn't have the memory of her afraid and captive. She wanted that version of her gone from existence, replaced by the real her, even if it had existed just in the mind of one man.

"Zu, there you are." Officer Kokua stopped short, and Ying Yue halted to avoid walking into the taller man's back.

She peered around the officer and caught sight of Zu, Azubuike Anyanwu. He'd told her his full name yesterday, when he'd found her. He stood in the doorway to the open office area—filled it, really. It wasn't just about his height, either. His shoulders and even his chest and torso were wide and heavily muscled, easy to see under the simple T-shirt he wore. He was a wall of intimidation.

Or, he was the first time she'd seen him. Now, she took in the sight of him like another dose of the same relief she'd experienced when she'd seen Buck. Here was someone who could manage to look at her without the pity that set her teeth on edge when she'd been dealing first with hospital staff and now with the police. She felt sure he'd take in the calm she'd gained and recognize the progress she'd made in processing what she'd been through. If she was surrounded by these other people for much longer, all of their careful sympathy would drag her down and keep her from moving forward.

Zu's gaze took in the room first; then Officer Kokua dropped lower to Buck as the dog returned to his side and then rose again to find her. She swallowed hard. His eyes were so dark they seemed to trap light, like polished obsidian, set below a heavy brow, and his lids were dropped halfway down in what might have been mistaken for a sleepy look if not for the sharp intelligence that sliced through her as he studied her.

"Miss Jiang." He nodded as he addressed her.

She'd lost her words despite all the thoughts running around in her head, so she opted for a nod in greeting rather than have something crazy pop out of her mouth.

"Ah, yeah." Officer Kokua stepped to the side so she could walk forward unimpeded. "We were taking her statement, now that's she's been released from the hospital."

Zu made a sound of acknowledgment.

He hadn't said much on the helicopter ride back from the cargo ship, either.

Questions bubbled up. She still wanted to know why he and his team had been out there in the middle of the ocean in the first place. Had her father sent them? Had someone else? Who was he? Here was something—or rather, a very interesting someone—to focus on rather than the questions people had been asking her. "Are you here at the police station often?"

She snapped her mouth shut. Of all the questions she had in mind, that hadn't come out sounding anywhere near as composed as she wanted, or even relevant.

His severe expression didn't change. If anything, he seemed to scowl. "No."

She stared at him. He stared back. Okay, then.

"I checked in at the hospital with the other people rescued from the cargo ship," he said finally, "and the hospital said you'd come here to give your statement and wait for family to pick you up."

"You came to check on me? That's appreciated." Tingling warmth filled her chest. She didn't want to make more of it than it was, though. "Did you check on all of the people you rescued from the cargo ship?

"Yes."

Disappointment extinguished the warmth in a tepid splash. She tried to rally, caught by surprise as she realized she'd wanted him to be interested in her. She'd been fishing. Heat burned her cheeks. He was a good—actually amazing—looking man with a chiseled jaw and close-cropped black hair, dark-skinned and built like a legendary warrior, but she didn't need to fall in a puddle at his feet. "Can't imagine the kind of people who hire you pay you for following up on people, too."

After all, he didn't serve his country or any noble cause. He was a private contractor, a mercenary. She'd realized he wasn't law enforcement or military last night when he hadn't stayed as the police took over the situation at the hospital with all of the rescued captives, including her.

"No." He didn't seem bothered by her reference to money at all. "It's just the right thing to do."

She lifted an eyebrow. "Do you always do the right thing?"

He lifted an eyebrow in response. "When possible, yes."

She mentally checked herself, hard. She'd been headed down a haughty, judgmental path to hide from her embarrassment. Not only was she not attractive to him, she wasn't liking herself much, either. She felt worse than off-balance. She was oscillating in unexpected directions, emotionally and mentally, and what was coming out of her mouth either didn't make sense or wasn't what she intended. She was a better person than this, not that he'd find out at the rate she was going.

Officer Kokua cleared his throat. "Hey, Zu. Can you escort Miss Jiang over to her hotel? Her father's people said accommodations had been reserved there for her."

Of course, not only was her father too busy to come and check on her, but his aide was, too.

"Considering what she's been through, they didn't want to send a car, so I was going to drive her over," the officer continued. "But they wanted to personally thank you, too. Her father's aide will be waiting for her at the hotel with some things for her comfort."

Zu wasn't looking at Officer Kokua as the man spoke. Instead, Zu was watching her.

She lifted her chin. "I can go to the hotel on my own."

She was thirty-two, and before this insane kidnapping had happened, she'd been an accomplished community investment professional with a background in grants administration and nonprofit capacity building. She'd been establishing herself as one of the best in the fields of philanthropy and social innovation. A simple taxi ride to a hotel was no big thing.

"You could," Zu confirmed. "But given recent events, it makes sense for me and Buck to give you a lift."

She opened her mouth and closed it again, undecided. Now that he'd said more than a couple of words at a time, the deep resonance of his voice distracted her. She felt it all along her sternum, pulling at her, and she wanted to hear more. And even if she could do just about anything she needed on her own, she didn't particularly want to just yet. It didn't hurt to accept a ride. "Thank you."

* * *

The drive from the police station to the hotel was only a couple of miles, but at this time of day, there was a lot of traffic. Zu didn't enjoy the stop and go of downtown Honolulu ever, and it made him irritable behind the wheel. Buck had curled up in the back of Zu's SUV readily for a nap. Normally, the two of them would've made a trip like this in relaxed quiet.

But their passenger might find the silence awkward. A lot of people did, in Zu's experience, and he didn't know enough about her to know whether it'd be more helpful to leave her to her thoughts or provide some kind of entertaining conversation. He was also a terrible conversationalist.

For her part, Ying Yue had sat quietly in the passenger seat for the past minute or so. As far as Zu could tell, she was people watching.

"Is it just me, or do you not talk much in general?"

He chuckled. She wasn't the first to point it out, but he liked hearing it from her better than others. She sounded genuinely curious and not accusing or in search of a fight. "It's not just you."

"Okay." She paused. "Do you not like talking or is it that you don't usually initiate conversation?"

Good question. He hadn't thought about it. "It's easier to answer questions when I don't know a person."

There were too many ways a conversation could go sideways or be misinterpreted. If a person asked him about what they wanted to know, he didn't have to do any guessing about what information they needed from him. Then, it took less time to decide what he actually wanted to share.

From the corner of his eye, he saw her square herself in the passenger seat and nod. "So, I'd like to know a few things."

He'd bet. She'd probably spent the time at the police station doing all the answering. It couldn't have been a pleasant experience, no matter how nice the officers tried to be. He'd been there a few times himself, and it was frustrating not to receive answers in return. If it helped Ying Yue, he'd be glad to share what he could. "Ask. I'll answer if I can."

"Tell me about your team, please."

"That's not a question." Damn. And he wasn't being helpful, but the observation came out before he thought to stop himself. This was one of the reasons why he kept his talking to a minimum.

She wasn't deterred, though. She even fired back. "But your response will answer quite a few at the same time, I think."

Fair. He came to a stop at a traffic light and checked all approaches. "Search and Protect is a private contract organization."

"Freelance? Like the kind governments hire to supplement their military?" she asked. "Or the kind large corporations and wealthy people hire for private security?"

"Both, yes, but we have focused skill sets." He liked that she was going for the nuances right away, instead of trying to apply broad definitions to things. "I and my team work with canines trained for a type of search and rescue. We specialize in infiltrating difficult areas and extracting high-value hostages."

"So political figures or their families." She sounded thoughtful.

"There are a lot of possible scenarios." He navigated the stop-and-go traffic, keeping an eye on not just the vehicles around him but also the pedestrians on the sidewalks. Ying Yue's rescue hadn't been released to the news, but whoever had been expecting her had to know the cargo ship had been intercepted. It would be good when she was safely with family and had private security in addition to local law enforcement. "Could be politicians or their family. It could also be journalists or scientists, executives or other key business representatives. A government or company might have a policy never to negotiate with terrorists or kidnappers but still want to take action to retrieve their people. So they hire us."

"But no one hired you to rescue me?" She turned her head to look out the passenger side window.

Ah. He shook his head. "No, Miss Jiang. My team and I were searching that cargo ship for other reasons."

There was a long pause and he started to worry. Sometimes the truth wasn't what a person wanted to hear. He didn't want to cause her hurt, even disappointment. She'd already been through enough. He might not have been around today for the full debrief, but he'd remained near her last night when they'd first arrived at the hospital and she'd given her initial statement to the police. He reached for something, anything, to say to ease the anguish he imagined might be on her face.

"Ying Yue," she said, quietly. "There's no need to call me Miss Jiang."

"Thank you." Awkward. He'd told her his name on the boat when he'd found her. She knew his nickname, even knew Buck. She'd offered him something in giving him permission to be familiar with her, and he didn't know how to reciprocate.

In every other aspect of his life, running Search and Protect or managing his private time, he considered himself competent. He had extensive experience in both the military and private sectors. He'd been a part of some of the most effective teams in the world and led more than a few of them. But one-on-one with civilians, particularly those who might benefit from more compassionate interaction, was most definitely not his forte.

"It won't be much longer to your hotel." Status updates always helped to move things forward. "You can see it up ahead."

"Okay." She straightened, looking forward, and from his perspective he saw no signs of tears.

Whew.

"One of the taller ones, I'm guessing." She didn't sound impressed.

The hotel her father was staying in was part of a resort commanding a serious chunk of prime location right on the beaches of Waikiki. The hotels on the property were some of the tallest in the area and designed to catch the eye from a distance.

"Not your style?" He wondered if she was jaded in some way when it came to hotels and resorts. He'd gathered her father was an affluent businessman with interests in quite a few countries around the globe.

"I love any kind of hotel, actually. Big ones, small boutique places, bed-and-breakfasts. I love seeing what they do to make the stay an experience." She let out a small laugh. "Staying with my father when he's on business tends to take some of the simple pleasure out of it."

Conversation came easier with her than anyone else he

could remember in a long while, but that was too complex to explore when this car ride was going to be over in the next couple of minutes. Except that he'd welcome the chance. He wanted to hear her laugh again and see a real smile reach her eyes. He tightened his hands on the steering wheel as he resisted the irrational impulse to turn off on a detour to get more time with her.

Yeah. He should not kidnap the kidnap victim as a means to get to know her better. Way to go, ancient part of the brain. No more great impulses for the rest of this mission, however informal.

The hotel had a curved drive to accommodate drop-offs and a taxi line. A few tourists walked down the middle of the drive, displaying some very low survival skills, so he slowed to let them clear out before he continued forward.

Ying Yue reached over and clamped her hand down on his right wrist. Energy zinged up his forearm with the contact, through his shoulder, and hit him in the chest. She had a solid grip and wasn't digging in with just her fingertips, instead exerting pressure from her palm and fingers. It felt good. He glanced at her and registered the way the shell-pink flush had gone from her cheeks and her eyes had widened. Even her delicate nostrils flared as she stared hard at something in front of them. Something was wrong.

His attention sharpened and expanded outward at the same time, assessing every available input to detect what might be out of place.

He followed her gaze and took in the very obvious contingent of private security waiting at the top of the drive, a handful of men, all dressed in suits, each projecting an air of fit intimidation. Very impressive to most, Zu guessed. "Your father's security detail, I assume."

She nodded in a jerky way, then shook her head side to

side too fast. "He's one of them. One of my kidnappers. He's there."

The words dropped like ice on Zu's skin. React now, ask questions later. "Down. Now."

He freed his wrist from her grip and reached out, cupping his hand behind her head and encouraging her to lean forward until she was out of sight. He dropped his foot down on the gas pedal and carried them past the security detail in a burst of speed before they could approach his vehicle.

"Hey!" One of the security people had shouted loud enough to be heard despite the windows closed. Good set of lungs on that one.

Zu caught sight of a suit in the rearview, hand to his ear, probably reporting in to his superiors.

Didn't matter. Zu focused on getting clear of the building. He shot down the drive and turned onto the main road, cutting off some poor car on the way out. There was a screech of brakes and a horn, but no sound of a crash. Lucky. He continued driving.

At the corner, a few suits ran out from the side of the hotel. One came to a stop and raised his weapon. Zu turned the wheel slightly in a controlled lane change as shots rang out. He made a sharp left turn onto a cross street, putting buildings between his vehicle and their pursuers coming on foot. He made several more turns, then shot across traffic and into the big mall parking deck.

When he brought the SUV to a stop, Ying Yue groaned. "What are we doing?"

But she didn't straighten, still bent over her knees with her hands over her head. He admired her intelligence. Too many television shows featured the plucky person who needed protection popping up in their seat at the wrong time, before anyone told them it was safe to do so.

"We're disappearing until we can straighten this out with Kokua. Best to leave behind the SUV. They had enough time to see the license plate." Zu stepped out of his car and circled around, letting Buck out of the back. Buck hopped out and sat as Zu hooked the big dog's short lead onto his collar. Buck didn't need it to know to stick with Zu, but having a leash on a working dog helped calm people who might otherwise be alarmed by a big dog walking through a public area. Then Zu headed around to the passenger side and opened the door. "Please come with me, and try to look like you're about to enjoy a shopping trip."

Ying Yue stared at him for a long moment, eyes narrowed and lips parted in an incredulous expression. "Shopping?"

"The first thing they'll do is search the streets to find us. Hopefully I got us out of the public eye before they reestablished line of sight on us. The next step will be to search for this vehicle. We don't want to be in it, so we'll go someplace where we can blend until another ride can pick us up." Zu held out his hand. Her gaze darted around the parking deck; then she placed her hand in his.

As they walked toward the mall with Buck, Zu pulled his phone out of his pocket. "Pua, this is Alpha. We're going to need a pickup at Ala Moana Center. Stat. Send Bravo for pickup and have Charlie cover. There might be a call from Officer Kokua, high priority. We've got a situation to clarify."

A burst of cool air-conditioning hit them as they entered the nearest clothing store with entrances both to the parking deck and to the mall. Might as well pick up a few things while he waited for his team to arrive. It'd only be a few minutes, but giving Ying Yue a task to focus on would help her more naturally blend with the shoppers in the area. Besides, it'd provide more cover than trying to walk through the mall to the other side in case their pursuers realized where they'd gone.

"You called for your friends to meet us? You don't want to grab a taxi or rideshare?" She pitched her voice to sound very close to a normal tone. Her question didn't sound unusual if someone passing close by overheard her. She'd regained her poise fast.

He leaned in slowly, doing his best to give her time to decide to let him close as she stiffened, and he whispered low near her ear. "I can't control a taxi driver if we end up in a chase on the streets. My people can pick us up and handle evasion with minimal danger to civilians on the streets if it comes to it."

She didn't speak, only nodded. She also didn't lean away from him, even though she could have.

He should straighten and give her space. He planned to, so he could keep watch on their surroundings. But before he did, he added one more thing. "I promise I won't leave you until you are safe."

CHAPTER TWO

Ying Yue stared at the racks of ladies' clothing, too numb and struggling to process what had happened in the space of such a short time. She'd seen one of her kidnappers, she was sure. The man had been there, among her father's security detail.

Security.

She wanted to laugh out loud, but if she did, she was afraid she'd start crying, too. Here she was, in a mall, shopping with a man she'd met yesterday under the most stressful circumstances of her life, while he was discussing the virtues of cotton versus linen shirts in hot, humid weather with a salesperson.

Well, if you could call it a conversation. The young man was going on at length and with great passion as he held out two different shirts in solid, bright colors as Zu grunted or flat out said no to suggestions. Honestly, the colors the young man was suggesting would be amazing against Zu's ebony skin tone. For his part, Zu's gaze still swept the store around them even as he paid enough attention to the other man to be polite.

She reached out and slid hangers on the rack to get a better look at a simple day dress. Zu had suggested she look at the clothing available and choose enough items for the next few days. He hadn't told her what to do, only gave her the option. And this was a practical thing, something to focus on and steady her while still giving her the chance to think through what was happening. She'd assigned similarly calming tasks to staff as she was coordinating large fund-raisers when personnel started to get overwhelmed by the stress of too much going on at once.

Her heart didn't feel like it was going to beat its way through her sternum anymore. Yes, she was still tense, but this situation wasn't as scary as running across the cargo ship yesterday and climbing onto a helicopter. Then and now, Zu and Buck had been within arm's reach.

Now, Buck sat at his master's feet, facing the opposite direction from Zu. She wasn't sure of anything at the moment, but she could've sworn the dog was keeping watch on whatever might be behind them. The notion was comforting.

"That's pretty."

She blinked and looked up into Zu's face, his dark gaze holding hers for one intense moment before he looked up and away, taking in their surroundings. She was left even more off-balance with the loss of that brief connection. She closed her hand around the smooth fabric of the dress, cool against her palm, to steady herself with something tangible and mundane. "I'm fairly certain it will fit."

"You could go try it on if you want. I'll keep watch outside the dressing room." He slipped his smartphone out of his pocket. "My team should be here in minutes, and we should get moving, but if you want that, we can buy it now."

"You should get that deep blue shirt he was trying to get you to buy, if it'll fit you. It's a good color for you." Not that he needed her to make clothing recommendations for him. She shook her head and snagged another dress of the same style in a different color and pattern. A basic white tank and a pair of slacks in her size came next. Then she grabbed a large, flowing scarf. "These should all fit me and be enough for a couple of days."

He raised an eyebrow but said nothing.

She shrugged. "I'm familiar with this brand, and all these might be a little loose on me but will definitely fit. I don't want to stay here."

He nodded and motioned toward the register. He produced a credit card and paid for the purchases, including the shirt she and the salesman had recommended. Then, he held out the bag to her. "I need to have my hands free. It'd be helpful if you could carry the bag, please."

"Of course." She doubted he planned to defend her with his bare hands. She wondered if he had a concealed gun somewhere. Either way, they were mostly clothes for her. She didn't have any issues carrying them. It had been awkward to watch him pay for them, but she planned to keep the receipt so she could reimburse him as soon as she could. Everything about her life needed to be pieced together before she could leave Hawaii and go home to Singapore. She needed her passport and access to her bank accounts and credit cards.

Funny, she'd been thinking one step at a time ever since she'd woke up in captivity, but now, standing next to Zu, she had the confidence to think ahead.

He lifted his phone to his ear. "This is Alpha."

Her breath quickened, and she tried to think through the sudden desire to hyperventilate. A phone ringing wasn't an alarm. She was jumpy but didn't want to bolt and draw attention to herself, so she tried to focus on his call. He didn't sound worried.

She supposed Alpha was some sort of code name. She wondered who Bravo and Charlie were. He'd mentioned them earlier, and she wasn't sure if each code name was for a single person or a team of more than one individual. They might have been people she'd seen yesterday on the helicopter ride from the cargo ship, or they might have been other members of the team. She wasn't sure how large his team was.

It wasn't until she rubbed her free hand over her arm that she realized she was chilled. The air-conditioning in the store wasn't turned up that high.

"Copy. Coming out the south exit into the parking deck on level two." His deep voice spoke so low into the phone, she barely understood what he'd said.

But he kept her at an easy pace, pausing here and there to point out an item or two but definitely making their way to the exit. It was smart, she thought when she shoved her panic to the back of her mind. They were blending with other shoppers in the store and not rushing in any specific direction.

Or at least she thought they would blend if Zu weren't a towering wall of devastating good looks. Women were stopping in their tracks to gawk at him. Buck was an unusual sight, too, his service dog vest standing out against the burnished red-brown of his coat. Even if Zu was taking precautions, he and Buck stood out in a crowd. She actually disappeared a bit in his shadow. And she was okay with that.

They finally reached the exit. She paused before going out the door, suddenly unable to make her feet move forward. She wasn't even sure why. Her brain just froze.

"Charlie has eyes on the exit," Zu murmured, leaning close enough for his breath to puff hot against her ear, sending delicious shivers down her spine in complete contrast to the fear she couldn't explain, even inside her own head. "No one is going to jump on us as we go out."

No criticism in his tone, and no laughter, either. He was calm and reassuring. She had the feeling he understood, probably better than she did, what kept her rooted in place. His words resonated through her, and she lifted first one foot, then the other. They walked out into the parking deck, and a car pulled smoothly up in front of them. Zu opened the back door to the vehicle and motioned her into the back seat. As she sat, Buck hopped in and settled in the footwell in front of her.

Before she could ask anything, Zu had gone around and entered the vehicle from the other side. The car pulled away and headed out of the parking deck. There was no music playing, but her heartbeat pounded in her ears. She looked all around for signs of anything out of place.

A warm weight came to rest on her left knee, and she looked down into Buck's golden-brown regard. She buried her fingers into the short, smooth fur around his neck, finding an anchor in the tactile sensation under her hands and outside her own head.

"Bravo here. I have Alpha and the package. Headed to HQ." The driver glanced up, and she could see his eyes reflected in the rearview mirror. "We meet again. I'm Raul Sa. This is Taz next to me in the passenger seat."

"Ying Yue." She hadn't even noticed the black and tan

dog in the front with him as she'd gotten in the car. The dog peered around the headrest at her, his tongue lolling out as he panted. His face was mostly black, and his tongue seemed very pink in contrast, or maybe she was noticing a lot of color contrast while she was under stress.

"Boss." The voice of a young woman chirruped over the car speakers.

"Go ahead, Pua." Zu didn't relax from his watching out the windows.

"I've got Officer Kokua on the line." There was a pause. "He sounds worried."

Zu grunted. "Connect him to this call."

Ying Yue considered their ease with Bluetooth technology. Her experience with her father's security people mostly involved them all wearing little earbuds and having microphones clipped to the inside of their sleeves. Communications were kept between the members of the security team and only relayed to her as necessary. She wondered what it said about the professionalism of Zu's team that they so openly included her in their communications. Then again, she considered what had started all of this.

She hadn't even been able to articulate her alarm at first, only reached out to grab Zu. He'd reacted immediately, going on nothing but her stuttered attempt to explain. As quick as that, he'd whisked her away and surrounded her with his people and his dogs. It was chaotic, yet extremely efficient. She couldn't imagine any security team she'd been exposed to responding faster.

Honestly, these people seemed less formal, but they were significantly more reassuring.

* * *

Zu glanced at Buck and the way Ying Yue had begun massaging the base of the big dog's ears with her fingertips. Buck was in heaven, eyes rolling with pleasure. The interaction seemed to be providing her with much needed comfort, but damn, it was unusual for Buck to allow it. Normally the hound was reserved with strangers to the point of being aloof.

Zu didn't often dig too deep into the rationale behind his dog's behavior, but his best guess was that since Buck had found Ying Yue in the first place, the dog had decided she was still his to protect in some way. Which was true for the moment, however unexpected. Besides, Zu was definitely not going to call his dog out for sentiments he himself shared.

Nothing about Ying Yue had been expected, from finding her to interacting with her today to literally swiping her right out from in front of the security detail meant to protect her.

"Zu, just what in hell are you doing?" Kokua's voice issued from the car's speakers and didn't just sound worried. The man was frazzled.

He'd also asked a good question.

"You asked me to get Miss Jiang safely to her father." Not Kokua's exact request, but Zu believed the spirit of a request meant more than the wording. Simply taking her to the hotel and leaving her there with one of her kidnappers had not been an option. Disappearing with her might not have been the best idea, either, but it'd been a split-second decision. He wasn't in the habit of second-guessing while he and his team were still in the middle of taking action, but he could explain. And now that he had Ying Yue in the relative safety of transportation managed by his own people, he felt this was a good time. He hadn't wanted to call earlier while they were still exposed in the mall. "As we arrived at the hotel, Miss Jiang identified one of her kidnappers within the security detail, so I removed her from the danger until you can take the suspect into custody for questioning."

Actually, Zu thought the entire security detail should be questioned, but there was no need to tell Kokua how to do his job. Zu waited as Kokua put them on mute to talk to someone else for a few seconds, probably to take action on Zu's news.

"So you're not going to bring her back." Kokua had lost the edge to his voice.

"Not until you have the suspect in custody." It was the logical thing to do, even if it put Kokua in a tough spot. After all, Ying Yue's father must be incredibly upset, worried. Zu had known Ying Yue for barely more than a day, and if she'd disappeared at this point? He would scour the island looking for her. All because he'd talked to her, heard her laugh on the car ride to the hotel, seen the fear in her eyes when she saw danger again, and been the one she'd reached out to in that moment.

Next to him, Ying Yue was watching him, her eyes the color of molten chocolate. Dark and unreadable. Light shone through the car window, and Zu wondered how her skin could be so luminescent. He squashed the urge to reach out and brush his fingers over her cheek, her shoulder, to find out if her skin was as silken smooth as he imagined. Touching her was a dangerous distraction, and he'd had to restrain himself from placing his hand on her back or his arms around her shoulders while they'd been in the mall. It would've been presuming too much, and her recent experiences only added to the reasons why he shouldn't touch her without her express invitation. He hadn't been able to resist leaning in close to her when he'd spoken quietly to her, though. It'd been necessary to talk to her without random passersby overhearing. He'd caught the almost floral scent of her and was fighting the urge to catch a hint of her scent again.

Now, even exhausted and still recovering from her prolonged duress and the traumatic shock of the last half hour, she was upright and listening carefully. She wasn't letting things happen around her; she was a part of the actions being taken. He might be concerned for her safety, considering what was happening, but his respect for her was quickly taking over the majority of his thought process.

"Most of the security detail is scattered on the streets in the immediate vicinity around the hotel looking for you," Kokua growled. "We're working with Mr. Jiang's aide to identify which security guard and get personnel records on him. But I'm having a tough time getting them to focus while Miss Jiang has been kidnapped again, as far as they're concerned."

Kokua had a point. Zu turned to Ying Yue. "Would you feel comfortable going back to the police station?"

"Miss Jiang, I insist you do," said Kokua. "Your father..."

Zu opened his mouth to cut Kokua off and give her room to make her own decision, but she reached out and laid her fingertips on the back of his wrist as she gave him a slight shake of her head. Then she looked straight ahead.

"My father will recognize the urgency of apprehending my abductor before he disappears on us all, if the man hasn't already taken advantage of the confusion." Her words were delivered in a clear, confident tone. "I understand there is concern for my safety, but as you felt comfortable entrusting me to Mr. Anyanwu in the first place, surely you can confirm to my father's people that I am indeed in safe hands. I assure you, Officer Kokua, that I will remain with Mr. Anyanwu and his team and cooperate with whatever precautions they deem necessary while you and your men take my abductor into custody."

Zu didn't bother to hide the smile tugging at the corners of his mouth. She was not giving any of them any room to make her choices for her—not him or his team or Kokua—and he was happy to sit back and let her make her wishes clear.

"Well..."

She didn't give Kokua a chance to come up with a counterargument. "Thank you. I really appreciate your efforts to capture this criminal. Knowing he's here, on the island, and who knows what other damage he's done to other people..."

It took a moment, but she continued before Kokua could speak again. "I am happy to stay out of the way until he's caught."

There was a sweet sincerity to her voice, and true anxiety when she'd hinted at what other damage her abductor could've done. Zu would've been hard pressed to go against what she was suggesting if he'd been in Kokua's shoes. Kokua definitely didn't stand a chance.

"We'll keep you informed as much as possible, Miss Jiang." Kokua might say so, but Zu was betting there would be plenty the officer couldn't share about the investigation. "Your father's aide—"

"Can contact the Search and Protect team to coordinate next steps in ensuring my safety." Ying Yue wasn't going to cede control to her father or his people, apparently.

Zu made a mental note to ask her for more details. He was happy to support her, but he also had a responsibility to his team to figure out exactly what they'd gotten into beyond providing a temporary haven for Ying Yue over the next several hours. He planned to have Pua do a check on Ying Yue's family and all of her father's employees. The kidnapper being a part of the security detail meant to welcome her back was a big-ass red flag. This aide or the head of security should act on the information, but there were few analysts as thorough as Pua, and most of them couldn't go as deep into the world of computers and data as she could to get the information they were looking for.

"All right, Miss Jiang," said Kokua finally. "The Search and Protect team will take over officially as consultants to the Honolulu Police Department, at least for tonight. Zu, I'll take care of the paperwork on this side. If this goes past tomorrow morning, we're going to have to come up with a few next steps."

There were a few beats of silence; then Pua's voice came over the speakers. "Officer Kokua dropped the call."

"Understood," Zu acknowledged.

"Why tomorrow morning?" Ying Yue asked. She sagged back into the seat.

Zu hesitated, but didn't have a good reason to withhold anything. It was just a habit, and he didn't think it would be a benefit to anyone in this situation. "Officer Kokua can state we're on police payroll as supplemental resources. But that has money tied to it, and his department budget can't handle the expense for an undefined period of time when they might have need to hire us or other consultants in the near future."

"You and your team are that expensive?" She remained slouched into the seat, but she'd turned her face to him and raised an eyebrow.

He lifted one shoulder in a shrug. "Depends on what you

consider expensive. Our services are not usually practical for an individual looking to hire us."

"Everything costs something." She made the statement with what sounded like quiet acceptance, as if it was a universal truth like gravity or death.

Yeah. Maybe so. But he'd designed his team and his business to have enough buffer in their income to accommodate unusual needs. He'd set up Search and Protect to respond with speed and flexibility depending on a given situation without waiting on the contract to be signed. They were able to act on what they felt was the right thing and act with compassion.

"I made you a promise. It doesn't expire in the morning."

CHAPTER THREE

Would you like some coffee? Or maybe tea? We've also got some lovely tisanes. Are you hungry? Let me feed you something."

Ying Yue watched Pua bustle around the kitchen area of Search and Protect headquarters, pouring a glass of water before turning back to a cabinet for a small plate. The other woman was all energy, warm and vibrant, with a nonstop smile and kind, dark, liquid eyes. After the insanity of the day so far, Pua's enthusiastic welcome and eagerness to make Ying Yue comfortable was really...nice. It was an odd time to realize how infrequently Ying Yue had encountered genuine kindness and sincerity in recent years.

"You seem to be really food and beverage oriented." Ying Yue honestly wasn't sure what she wanted, but Pua didn't seem to mind that she hadn't answered the question.

Instead, Pua placed the small plate on the long table in the kitchen area. "I am. A few bites of something delicious and a nice drink go a long way to making everything right in the world."

Maybe so. Ying Yue was willing to give it a try. She wasn't exactly sure what to do next, now that she'd arrived and had to wait to hear from Office Kokua.

She'd been tense when she'd first come into the head-quarters with Zu and worried as she'd been swept up by Pua, thinking Pua's high energy and tumbling words would exhaust her even further. There were some coworkers at the nonprofits Ying Yue helped who were bundles of nervous energy, constantly in need of direction and guidance. But instead, Ying Yue found herself relaxing into the easy flow of conversation. Pua had her own tasks in hand and took on the main burden of thinking of what to say. There were no overly long, uncomfortable silences, only a friendly prompt here and there for Ying Yue to participate in the conversation. It was blessedly low pressure.

"You are very kind." Ying Yue moved to the table and slid into a seat.

"Mahalo." Pua placed a platter full of what looked like sugared doughnut on the table. She took the compliment in stride, a blush coloring her tan cheeks. "The team, they go out and do scary things. This is how I cope with worrying about them and my way of taking care of them when they come back. From what I know, you've had a really bad day and an even worse recent history out on that cargo ship. So this might only be a little bit helpful, but, well, here it is."

Ying Yue stared at the doughnut-like things, blinking back sudden tears. She'd been holding herself together through all of this. Even before her kidnapping, she'd constantly been in intense, high-demand environments, keeping a level head and cool business demeanor. She'd never looked at food and thought so fervently of solace before. "What are these?"

"Malasadas from Leonard's Bakery," Pua answered quickly, turning to the fridge. The other woman might have been giving Ying Yue a moment to herself without actually leaving her. In a minute, Pua returned with another plate and a large pitcher. "And something savory, because Zu doesn't eat a lot of sweet things. Arin makes these skewers of grilled pork and chicken satay that we keep in the fridge for quick protein. She marinates them Thai style and makes the peanut sauce from scratch, too. They're better than any Thai restaurant on the island."

Well, Zu might not go for confections, but a malasada seemed perfect at the moment. Ying Yue took one, biting into the soft, fluffy goodness and letting the rich chocolate coconut filling flood her senses. The filling was decadent without being too sweet, with a hint of bitterness to counter the coconut, and the outer doughnut part was light, dusted with just the right amount of fine sugar.

"Mmm." It was all she could manage as she made short work of the malasada.

Pua smiled and filled a glass with a deep crimson beverage. "Hibiscus. It's refreshing and has a lot of health benefits, but what's more important right now, it has no caffeine, because I figured you didn't need the jitters. Unless you like caffeine. We do have coffee."

"No, this is perfect." And it was. Ying Yue hadn't had an appetite at the hospital, and even though Officer Kokua had offered her snacks and coffee at the station, she'd been too tied up in knots going over her kidnapping to eat then, either. Now, finally, having been brought here by the people who'd saved her from the cargo ship in the first place and being caught up in a flow of cheery conversation with Pua, Ying Yue was starting to breathe easy again.

She was also wondering where Zu had gone. He'd

promised he wouldn't leave her. She didn't expect him to be glued to her side at all times, but she felt off-balance not knowing where he was. Aside from the obvious safety he and Buck had been providing for her, she missed his presence. He was... she wasn't exactly sure. But she liked him near.

"Okay." Pua hovered for a moment, then must've realized she was doing it, so she sat in another chair at the table. "Where's home for you?"

"You mean where I live currently? Or where I'm from?" Home could have a lot of definitions. Journalists interested in what it was like to grow up with her father, the incredibly successful international businessman, had almost always meant the opposite from what Ying Yue thought during interviews, so she'd taken to clarifying in advance. It saved a lot of drama when people were looking for a juicy bit of shady gossip where there was none. She wasn't interested in being famous for being related to famous people, not even in the business world.

"Yeah, home." Pua flipped her smartphone around in her hands as she thought on it for a moment. "The place you go to take all your troubles off your shoulders. It's your place, where you're safe and don't have to be anything. You can just be. Home."

Well, that was a new way to put it. Ying Yue washed down another malasada with some of the hibiscus tea. "I live in Singapore currently. Where I'm from gets complicated."

"I'm all ears." Pua put her phone down, put her elbows on the table, and propped her chin on her palms.

Well, Pua had been doing all the talking. Besides, it'd been a long while since anyone had actually wanted to know about Ying Yue and her background as opposed to gaining insight on her father or the nonprofits for which she worked. "My family moved a lot. My father pursued various business interests all over the world, so I went to a lot of different primary schools or had tutors."

"Wow." Pua snagged a malasada and started in on it. "Did you like that? I mean, moving around all the time is interesting for some people and not so much for others."

Ying Yue shrugged. "It was okay when I was young. Exciting to see new places. But as I got a little older, I wanted friends more, and so I asked for a chance to make some lasting friends. Luckily for me, my tutors thought a consistent school experience would set me up for better success in university. So my father chose a private board-ing school for me. After that, I went directly into college, then grad school, so I never moved back in with my parents. Where they lived wasn't ever home for me, even when I visited."

Pua didn't make any judgments, only nodded. "I guess it doesn't feel like coming home if you've never been to a place before, huh?"

"Not for me." And that was about all Ying Yue was willing to say about that for the time being. She considered the satay skewers. Sure, she'd had dessert first, but now a bit of protein sounded like a good idea to keep her stomach settled. Besides, if Pua asked the usual question next, it'd be nice to have something more substantial to chew on to hide Ying Yue's frustration with the conversation always turning to her father.

But Pua didn't ask about him. "So what *is* home for you?"

Ying Yue hesitated. "My current apartment in Singapore, I guess."

But was it? Her apartment in Singapore was new, barely moved into. It was the latest in a string of apartments as

Ying Yue kept looking for a place she wanted to live in for longer than a year. It was more like a long-term hotel accommodation than a...home.

Pua didn't seem to notice Ying Yue's hesitation. "That's exciting. I've never been to Singapore, but I really want to visit. I hear the street food is amazing there. All the food is amazing. Maybe that's true of just about any place in the world. You can really taste your way around the globe if you want to, right? So what's your favorite thing to treat yourself to at home?"

Ying Yue opened her mouth to respond, then took a sip of hibiscus tea to cover her discomfort. She didn't have a favorite. Not really. She stopped to pick up food because it was convenient. Oh, she enjoyed it when it was good, and she noticed if it wasn't. But she didn't seek anything out specifically as a treat. It was about convenience and fulfilling a nutritional need. She watched Pua's unfettered joy as the woman bit into another malasada.

Fear had filled Ying Yue for the past days, weeks, however long since she'd been kidnapped. Now, the fear was receding, and she wondered what she was trying to get back to. Seeing Pua, Ying Yue had to admit she hadn't been happy. She didn't even begrudge Pua. Ying Yue had been busy, and she'd taken pride in her work.

But she couldn't remember the last time she'd done anything for the simple joy of it. She'd always pushed her wants to the side in favor of the major goals. To succeed, one had to sacrifice, or she had thought so. But would it really have hurt to love the bite she had to eat on those nights when she'd worked late? Ying Yue's stomach growled, and she snagged a chicken skewer.

Suddenly, though, she was hungry for more than just protein to fill her belly.

"So what's your apartment like?" Pua didn't seem to have noticed Ying Yue's hesitation or subsequent introspective moment. "I'm planning to move into a new apartment, and I'm looking for different ideas of how to decorate it and make it mine."

Just as well. Ying Yue didn't have the energy to explore what would be fulfilling right now. She'd think deeper about things when she got through the next couple of days and returned to Singapore.

"My flat is fairly simple. One bedroom, one and a half baths, all with wood or stone flooring. I should get some rugs in, but I mostly wear house slippers. Those kinds of floors are hard on your feet." Ying Yue liked her privacy and could afford a much bigger place, but then she'd be bouncing around in the space without any real purpose for it all. "I'm not a great decorator, so I think you'd be bored seeing it even if I had a phone to show you pictures. My taste is pretty minimalist. I have everything I need in my own space, but the building has very nice common areas, too."

Pua nodded. "Arin says the same about her apartment. She says if she had more space, she'd fill it with things, and she's on the move too much to have so many things to take with her."

Ying Yue wondered if she'd be meeting this Arin. Pua seemed to think highly of her. Then Ying Yue checked her thoughts. There wasn't any reason to want to get to know the team. Her stay with them was going to continue for a few more hours, or overnight at most. It didn't make sense to invest too much into getting to know people she had no reason to continue knowing over time. If they were in some business tangential to hers, maybe, then she could consider it networking. But Ying Yue hadn't ever had a reason to work with mercenaries in the past, and she could think of no scenario in which she would in the foreseeable future.

She cleared her throat. "Decluttering can be a painful exercise. Seems smart not to accumulate unnecessary things in the first place."

Had she always sounded like her father? It was a sentiment he'd voiced frequently as she was growing up, but she was fairly certain she'd come to the same conclusion on her own and made the words her own. Moving often meant packing, and packing meant holding each thing you owned in your hands and making the decision to carry it with you or to discard it. It hadn't been just about material items, either.

"True! I am so bad about starting to collect things, though. I just love the cutest sets of teacups and saucers, for example." Pua sighed happily. "So you don't collect anything?"

Grants. Professional victories. "Nothing cute. I don't have a good eye for that. I like to have jewelry perfect for any occasion, though. I guess you could say I collect that."

"Ooh. That's so sophisticated." Pua smiled, not a trace of envy or any of the emotions Ying Yue saw on other people's faces when talking about material things. Pua seemed to like to get enthusiastic along with the person she was sharing experiences with.

Ying Yue smiled. "Teacups and saucers have a very specific level of sophistication to them. You enjoy tea, then?"

Pua grinned. "Absolutely. I love different types of teas. I love how tea is served. I think my favorite is a simple cream tea, where you have a nice cup of black tea with a fresh baked scone served with butter and jam and clotted cream."

"Not afternoon tea?" Ying Yue tipped her head to one side. "I would've thought you'd love the variety in finger sandwiches and sweets."

Pua reached out and took one of Ying Yue's hands in both of her own, almost trembling with excitement. "I love that you call it afternoon tea! So many people think it's high tea, but it's not really because high tea has the meat and fish and egg dishes and is more of a...a light supper. The fancy tea and finger sandwiches and scones and maybe crumpets and the selection of sweets is really afternoon tea. But so many people get them mixed up, and now the hotels or restaurants that host any kind of service just call it what people are likely to recognize it as instead of what it historically was."

Ying Yue blushed as Pua continued to beam at her. The sheer excitement of this woman was close to blinding. At the same time, Ying Yue really wanted to know if Pua was always like this or if this was a temporary state. Did it take something to trigger this much energy? Caffeine, perhaps? Or maybe it was the hibiscus tea. If that was the case, Ying Yue made a mental note to get a few boxes of it to take with her when she left Hawaii.

"So why Singapore?" Pua's mercurial mood seemed to make topic hopping a characteristic of conversation.

"Pardon?" Ying Yue had gotten distracted because she'd caught the low tones of a familiar voice approaching from the hallway and Buck came in the door. That meant Zu couldn't be far behind. Ying Yue straightened and ran a hand over her shirt to smooth out any wrinkles.

"Singapore. You said you'd be going back to your apartment in Singapore." Pua didn't seem to even register Buck as the big dog walked past her, paused to give the woman a sniff, then continued around to Ying Yue.

"It's a good hub for my business travel." Ying Yue gave Buck a good scratch behind the ears as he came to stand beside her. He leaned his shoulder into her hip, and she smiled. "I wanted a place where I could do my work without being my father's daughter, and he mostly focuses his business in other cities at the moment."

Inwardly, she cursed. She'd been so tense anticipating Pua was going to bring up her father as a main topic of conversation because so many people did. And yet, she'd been the one to bring him up. In fact, she'd been doing it all day, hadn't she? It'd been a while since Ying Yue had significant interaction with people who didn't know anything about her. She was used to business networking and various interviews with media. This was a different kind of social interaction, and it made her think hard. How long had it been since she'd made new friends organically, through chance meeting and happenstance? Her life until recently had been so carefully planned out, her time consciously managed for maximum productivity, that she hadn't done anything random in as long as she could remember. No wonder she'd been easy to kidnap.

"Speaking of Mr. Jiang, he and Officer Kokua are heading up." Zu filled the doorway, giving Pua a nod before settling his gaze on Ying Yue.

She was used to direct eye contact, but the near electric quality of their gazes meeting kicked up her heart rate in a completely new way, and her cheeks heated just a bit.

"Are you sure it isn't just my father's aide?" She regretted her comment instantly. To her ears, it made her sound petulant or bitter or both, and she didn't want to return the kindness and consideration she'd been offered by Zu and his team with negativity.

Pua pulled out her smartphone and swiped the screen a few times with her fingertips. "Cameras show Officer Kokua and your father, if media images are accurate. There's a third man standing next to them, and I'm guessing that's his aide? Plus two more suits behind them."

She turned the smartphone screen so Ying Yue could see. There was Ying Yue's father on live streaming video, standing in the elevator. Not only were Officer Kokua and her father's aide with him, but two of the security team were there, too. Neither of those men was her kidnapper.

Of course, her father wouldn't be bringing her kidnapper with him. She had no idea why she was looking to make sure, except that she needed to make sure.

"Building surveillance right on your smartphone. Who needs a room full of monitors?" Ying Yue was impressed, and she hoped that emotion would come through in her tone instead of the tension she was experiencing looking at those security people. She knew the technology was available, of course. People could do it with webcams and baby monitors, and even live stream their pets when they were away from home. It was just the way Pua used it in such a matter-of-fact manner, like it was no big thing to have the entire building's surveillance feeds at her fingertips.

"Well, I have a room full of monitors, too." Pua grinned. "Makes it easier to multitask."

Ying Yue had to force her clenched jaw to relax in order to smile in return. "I am really glad to have met you. I'm not sure what's next, but I guess we should go meet my father at the door before his aide or one of the security team decides to shoot his way in."

She was joking.

"Oh no, they can't." Pua made the statement with cheerful confidence. "All the walls of this office space are made of ballistic glass. If you don't want us to let them in, we don't absolutely have to."

Ying Yue was tempted. So tempted. And she couldn't explain exactly why.

CHAPTER FOUR

Zu stepped into the kitchen area and leaned back against the wall directly next to the door.

Ying Yue's shoulders relaxed a fraction and her back straightened.

He wasn't sure if she was conscious of her reaction, but having him—or maybe anyone—blocking the only entrance to the room had been an issue. She had reacted defensively, hunching her shoulders and slouching to make herself less of a target. But she'd also placed her hands on the table, in plain sight, and held on to the glass. The woman was a fighter in her own way. There'd be a long series of battles ahead to process her experiences from the moment she'd been kidnapped to the current situation.

Anger on her behalf smoldered in his chest, and he inhaled slowly, careful to keep his facial expression neutral and soften his gaze so he didn't end up glaring at her. He didn't want her to think his rage was directed toward her. Even getting her here, to a safe space, hadn't been enough to ease his growing need to defend and protect her. She'd chosen to come with him and his team. She'd made it clear she was entrusting her safety to him, and her faith in him had weight.

He would keep her safe. His determination settled into the core of him.

"Pua's right. If you don't want to see them, you don't have to." He would put Ying Yue's needs first. But he had a feeling it was important to understand why Ying Yue had complex feelings about her father. He was identified as her emergency contact, and she'd seemed to want to go to him earlier in the day. There'd been some bitterness, though, on the way to the hotel and this aide could be a part of it. Zu hadn't wanted to touch the subject at the time, but that was before circumstances got complicated.

Now, to continue ensuring her safety, it was his business to know the contributing factors to her situation. The kidnapping wasn't a thing of chance if one of her kidnappers had inserted himself into her father's security team. That much was obvious. There were still a lot of unknowns, and to help Ying Yue, he was going to dig past the surface.

Ying Yue stared at him. It felt like she could look right inside him. Problem was, he wasn't sure what she was seeing. He had some dark shit in his background, and the person he was now wasn't any kind of fun. Besides, he had no idea how she was going to make her choice by looking at him.

He waited for her response, figuring it'd be best not to say anything to prompt her. She'd see her father or she wouldn't, and he'd back up her decision.

She lifted her chin a fraction, and he wondered if the gesture was a tell, a physical giveaway indicating her thought process. He'd seen her do it in the car, too, when she'd made a significant decision. "I want to talk to all of them and find out what the status is on apprehending that man. Otherwise, I want to answer any questions Officer Kokua might have to facilitate getting the man into custody."

Zu nodded. He'd have done the former anyway, even if she hadn't wanted to talk to them herself. It was good she was willing to make herself available for the latter. "You got it."

She gave him a small smile. It zinged through him, and he wondered how such a small expression could get such a reaction out of him.

Feeling a little high, he swept his arm toward the doorway next to him. "After you."

Pua giggled, and he shot her a withering glance, which she completely ignored. His mood lightened even further. One of the things he loved about this small team of extremely competent people was that none of them were intimidated by him. It kept him balanced. He wasn't often tempted to indulge in dramatic gestures, but why not? It made Pua and Ying Yue smile more. If Arin or Raul had seen it, Arin would've given him side eye and Raul would've joined in. It was their team dynamic.

As Ying Yue walked past him, a faint blush colored her cheeks, and he was very aware of her proximity. He couldn't help turning to follow behind her, but he checked himself, giving her a step or two head start so he wasn't directly on her heels. He wanted to be close to her, but now that it wasn't necessary, she might not appreciate it the way she had when they'd been evading pursuit at the mall earlier. Better to give her the space she deserved.

Buck fell in step beside him, and Zu reached down to give his partner a pat on the side of the neck instead.

Ying Yue seemed comfortable heading straight for the

front doors, and he didn't stop her, not inside Search and Protect HQ. If they'd been outside, he might work with her to move together in a way so that he could provide proper protection while she was still able to get to where she was going. He simply kept pace and watched for any red flags as they made their way down the hall to the small reception area and the front doors. He'd watch her for signs of any stress—and Buck, too, in case the dog detected any threats faster than a human could.

Their visitors were already waiting. Officer Kokua and the man Zu assumed was Mr. Jiang's aide had ceded to Mr. Jiang himself when it came to standing right at the doors. Behind the trio, Jiang's security detail had taken up a flanking position.

Just as they approached the front doors, Zu lengthened his stride, coming up even at Ying Yue's side. Pua darted past, neatly avoiding Buck, and beat them all to the door. Buck came to a stop. Taking his cue, Ying Yue halted beside him, and Buck sat.

Pua reached the doors in a graceful rush, making it look more like she'd been hurrying for the benefit of their guests rather than to beat Zu to the doors, opening them and leaning around the edge. "Welcome to Search and Protect, gentle people. We have a conference room ready for you. Mr. Anyanwu will show you the way."

Pua was much better at pleasantries than Zu. She had a more open, kind personality, with the ability to make people feel acknowledged and important. She managed with poise, never coming across subservient or submissive in any way, and had just the right amount of deferential consideration. The result was usually a guest more receptive to negotiation and listening to the recommendations Zu had for whatever situation was at hand.

Mr. Jiang was not immune. The older man stepped inside and inclined his head politely to Pua. "Thank you."

Pua nodded in response.

The other men entered, and Zu got a good look at each of them. The two men in the security detail were standard personnel. They were reasonably fit and alert, making it obvious they were looking around the premises for any hidden dangers. These two hadn't been chosen for subtlety. Dressed in black suits in Hawaii the way they were, they served as much for visual impression as for providing actual protection. They also had probably been melting outside before they'd come inside to the blessing of air-conditioning. Zu could do formalwear when necessary, and even enjoyed it on the rare occasion, but he wouldn't want it to be his daily attire.

Jiang's aide was more physically imposing, standing tallest in the group. The man was white and had light blue eyes and thin lips. He likely had been spending most of his time on the island indoors, since he didn't show any signs of sunburn. A complexion as fair as his would've burned even with the strongest sunblock applied. The man's blond hair and slightly darker beard were impeccably groomed and close trimmed. He wore a gray suit of the kind of lightweight, breathable fabric that actually made sense in a tropical climate.

There wasn't any need to call either Arin or Raul to join them, since he could handle these visitors solo if the situation escalated to pose any kind of threat to Ying Yue or his people. Besides, he had Buck with him.

"This way." Zu indicated the other hallway, taking them at a ninety-degree angle away from the team offices and kitchen area, toward the conference room and small office spaces they maintained for partner resources who needed to work at headquarters. As they proceeded toward the conference rooms, he turned back. "Thank you, Pua. I appreciate the help."

He could've waited until later to tell her, but she deserved to be told in front of people. He appreciated everything she did for Search and Protect, from her official role as their technical analyst to the less obvious details like smoothing the way for positive interactions with just about everyone.

"Sure, boss." Pua gave him a little wave and headed back down the other hallway toward her own office.

As he continued to the conference room, Ying Yue fell in beside him. "She's good people," she said.

He was glad Ying Yue thought so. "The best."

"I'm told all of your people are the best at what they do." Mr. Jiang spoke up, breaking into the connection Zu thought he'd been sharing with Ying Yue despite the presence of all the others.

"We are." Zu didn't hesitate to confirm, but he had to tear his gaze away from Ying Yue to address her father. "I handpicked every member of the Search and Protect team."

They reached the conference room, and Zu tipped his head, indicating they should go ahead of him. Mr. Jiang would have stepped in, but his aide touched Jiang's sleeve discreetly. Jiang's mouth tightened, but he waited for one of the security guards to step inside and do a sweep of the room.

"Is that necessary?" Ying Yue asked.

"Yes." Both Jiang's aide and Zu answered.

Zu glared at Jiang's aide, who didn't look amused, either. They might be in agreement in this instance, but Zu had a lot of questions for the man. He was betting the aide had some questions for him, too, if the aide was any good at his job.

After a moment, Zu turned to Ying Yue. "It's good practice when in an unfamiliar location when there's been no time to check the premises in advance. Taking these kinds of precautions is crucial to successfully ensuring the safety of the client."

"Clear." The security guard returned to the door and stood to one side so Jiang could proceed inside. "There's video and audio surveillance in this room."

"Of course." Zu didn't make a big deal of it. Pua could see and hear everything that went on in any room at headquarters. "Each room can be set for privacy if needed. Otherwise, we maintain surveillance on premises."

"I would prefer privacy for this discussion." Mr. Jiang selected a seat in the middle of the conference room table.

Zu waited until Ying Yue chose her seat. She chose a chair opposite but not directly across from her father, leaving that spot presumably for Zu. Jiang's aide sat at his boss's right hand, predictably. Kokua hesitated for a second before sitting on the other side of Ying Yue. It was always interesting to see how people chose to place themselves at a table. It told Zu a lot about what they were thinking, and while Kokua was in a position to be supportive to Ying Yue, her father and his aide were facing her in what could potentially be a confrontation.

Zu flicked his fingers and Buck slipped under the table to lie down next to Ying Yue's feet with a sigh. Then Zu stepped to the table and pressed a button on a center console set into the table. A light on the console changed from green to red. "We are set to privacy. If you look at the video conference camera on the far wall and the surveillance camera above the door, both have a similar red light to indicate all cameras and audio in the room are turned off."

"Fine." Jiang sat forward in an aggressive posture, leaning his forearm on the table with his hand spread palm down on the surface. "I am Jiang Li Wei. Who are you and why is my daughter with you?"

* * *

As introductions went, Ying Yue thought it could've been worse. Her father had been far more antagonistic in other situations. Still, he should be speaking to her as much as to Zu.

"I am here because it was safer to remain with the Search and Protect team than to meet with your men when one of my kidnappers was one of them." Ying Yue decided she'd take control of the conversation before her father gained too much momentum. "I'm happy to do introductions, since I know most of the people in the room."

Her father looked as if he was about to say something, but he must've thought better of it. The sadness in his eyes caught her by surprise, and he only nodded his agreement to her offer to conduct introductions. Next to her, Zu gave her a slight nod as well. Well, those were the two people whose agreement she currently cared about when it came to those present. There were a lot of leaders in the room, and she wasn't going to feel any kind of issues about facilitating this conversation to save them all from a pissing contest via formalities.

"Father, this is Azubuike Anyanwu, leader of the Search and Protect team. They are a private contract organization that sometimes works freelance in conjunction with the local police and US government. Mr. Anyanwu is also the person who found me, along with his partner, Buck, and his team during a separate operation. That's why Officer Kokua felt it was reasonable to ask Mr. Anyanwu to escort me to the hotel this morning." Best to preemptively answer a few questions in one shot rather than let her father dissect the decisions made earlier in the day and second-guess the people who'd made them. She faced her father but sat back and kept her posture open to include Zu and Kokua in the exchange. Body language in a conference room was an art in its own way and here, she excelled. "Mr. Anyanwu, my father has introduced himself. Next to him is his personal aide, Julian Nilsson. He's worked with my father for five or six years now. I think we've all been introduced to Officer Kokua, but I'm not familiar enough with the other two men in the room to provide introduction."

She had never bothered to get to know her father's security personnel in the past. They'd never been responsive to her as she'd grown from childhood into adulthood, and they had tended to come and go with regularity. It'd never occurred to her to get to know details about them in order to be able to identify them outside their roles as bodyguards. She could do better, at least getting to know a few personal details about each of the people involved in her safety.

Her father cleared his throat, probably surprised she'd left the window open to introduce the security personnel. She wondered if he knew the names of the guards accompanying him today.

It was Julian who answered. "Silbermann and Molchany have been working with us for the past two years. Silbermann is the current lead of the team, also providing internal oversight on the hiring process and vetting new members of the security staff."

Silbermann stepped forward. "Ma'am."

She leaned back in her chair, keeping her forearms resting lightly on the armrests, even though she wanted to wrap her arms around her torso and protect herself instead. "Mr. Silbermann."

He glanced at Julian, not her father, for confirmation to proceed, and she didn't like it one bit. Yes, Julian was probably more closely involved in the logistics for her father's personal protection, but her father was the ultimate person in charge. She kept her peace on her thoughts for the moment, but she wanted to have a word with her father privately for sure. Really, her father placed too much trust in Julian.

Silbermann tugged on the cuff of his suit before continuing. "There were six men assigned to accompany Mr. Nilsson to meet you at the entrance to the hotel this morning, Miss Jiang. Two of them were assigned to Mr. Nilsson specifically. The other four were intended to become your personal security for the duration of your stay in Hawaii."

"Four men, no one who identifies as a woman?" Zu's voice was low and neutral.

When Silbermann didn't answer Zu right away, Ying Yue glared at the man. "This is not the time for professional pissing contests. Mr. Anyanwu has far more knowledge than I do regarding the topic of personal protection, and we all know it. I am interested in both the answer and why the question was asked."

"No female personnel were assigned to the detail planned for Miss Jiang, no." Silbermann sounded like he might be straining something as he provided the answer. He looked straight ahead, not at Ying Yue or Zu or anyone else in the room as he answered.

"It's not a criticism, Mr. Silbermann," Zu stated in a

matter-of-fact tone. He turned to Ying Yue. "For your information, and your father's, it's a good practice to assign at least one asset who identifies as the same gender as the client, particularly one who has had a negative experience of similar magnitude to that which Miss Jiang has experienced. It can be less stress on the client. It also makes it easier to ensure someone is accompanying the client everywhere, including restrooms. I'd like to understand how many resources Silbermann's team had available on this trip and whether the choice was made because of a limited team or for some other reason."

Silbermann met Zu's gaze. He might've been a little less defensive, but Ying Yue didn't know him well enough to interpret his face. Mostly, he still had shaggy eyebrows pulled close in a dour expression. "We do not have any female resources with us on this trip, and adjusting to ensure a detail was assigned to Miss Jiang specifically was unexpected."

Ying Yue stared at Silbermann. Zu was right, she'd have felt better all around if at least one of the suits following her around the hotel had been a woman. The idea of going to her hotel room and having four men with her at all times bothered the hell out of her. Maybe her mother hadn't ever minded, but if Silbermann didn't plan for this consideration in the future for Ying Yue, she'd insist.

"Was my kidnapper part of the detail assigned specifically to me? Or did he just join the men standing there?" She had to know, even if she was internally screaming.

There was a pause. Then Silbermann met her gaze. "Yes, ma'am, he was an employee, and he was part of the detail assigned to you. He was employed with our company prior to your incident and had taken a week of personal time. He'd returned to work before you were found at sea."

Her thoughts didn't scatter. Instead, they scrambled around her mind in a panicked mess and crashed into each other until words tumbled around in a jumble. All she could do was keep her mouth closed to keep them from spilling out and revealing how very not okay she was at the moment. It was suddenly very cold in the room, and she resisted the impulse to wrap her arms around herself.

"Is the man in custody?" Zu directed the question to Officer Kokua.

Officer Kokua shook his head. "I sent Miss Jiang's descriptions of him to Nilsson and Silbermann. They identified the employee matching the profile immediately, but the man is already in the wind. He must've suspected he'd been made the minute you sped past, Zu, and took advantage of the confusion to disappear."

"What was the alternative?" Ying Yue demanded, staring first at Officer Kokua, then at her father. "Mr. Anyanwu had seconds to react when I spotted my kidnapper. He responded to my warning and got me away. Was he supposed to just drop me off and expose me, so the man could be taken into custody? What if he wasn't working alone?"

Her father met her stare for stare, his expression neutral and unreadable. That wasn't a surprise. She'd learned some of her boardroom behaviors from him.

Officer Kokua held up his hands, palms out. "You are right, Miss Jiang. Zu didn't have a lot of options or information. I'm not going to second-guess his decision in the moment."

Ying Yue glared at Julian and Silbermann in turn. Based on Officer Kokua's statement, somebody had done a fair share of second-guessing and probably tried to pressure Officer Kokua to denounce Zu's actions. It was a good thing they'd taken up positions on the opposite side of the table, or she'd be swiveling in circles making sure to give them all their own dose of hard looks.

"We're looking for him," Officer Kokua continued. "We've got eyes on all major modes of transportation off the island. Your description has helped, and we've got the personnel file Silbermann provided, too."

"We're also doing a deep dive of all security personnel, starting with the assets here on the island and extending to the companies that we subcontract to for our staffing," Silbermann added. "We intend to track down how this man was hired and any people related to the incident."

Ying Yue stared at Silbermann. "Why was I kidnapped?"

For the first time, the man looked at her with sympathy. It was ruined when he opened his mouth, though, because his tone included a heavy dose of pity. "These things happen, Miss Jiang. You are the daughter of a very influential businessman."

"Is there a possibility that Miss Jiang has been targeted on the basis of her current work?" Zu asked.

Silbermann looked at Zu in surprise. "I'd think the evidence of one of her kidnappers having infiltrated Mr. Jiang's organization points to her father, not her current employment, especially since the man returned to work."

"Maybe, but it's good to investigate all possibilities since we've gathered several organizations with the means to do so in one room." Zu shrugged. "The goal at this point is to first ensure Miss Jiang remains safe and then can also return to her life."

It hadn't occurred to her that she couldn't yet. She'd been thinking she could go to the hotel and start getting her life back together, return to her job. "My life is not going to stop because of this."

"No. It won't," Zu responded. "But even if police capture

this kidnapper, there's too much evidence that there was an organized effort to kidnap you specifically. You weren't grabbed at random off the street. So we need to dig out this threat at the root before you go back to your life and are potentially exposed to further attempts."

The bitter taste of bile crawled up the back of her throat. She didn't even know what she'd need to feel like before it was okay to go back to living now that the implications of what was going on were set out in front of her. It was too much. There were too many ramifications.

"With your internal investigation in progress to identify if there are any other people connected to this kidnapper, can you guarantee a security detail for Miss Jiang?" Zu's voice was still calm, beating back the waves of panic inside her, but when she looked at him, his eyelids were at half-mast over his eyes. Maybe she'd have thought he looked sleepy if she hadn't been around him for the better part of the morning. But no. She suspected the sleepy look indicated a very different state of being when it came to Zu.

Silbermann lost some of his composure and slammed his hand flat on the conference room table. "You think you can protect her better?"

Everyone at the table other than Zu jumped at least a little bit. Ying Yue definitely jerked back from the table. But not Zu. Zu didn't even flinch. "My team has so far, yes."

Silbermann froze. His eyes had dilated, and Ying Yue resisted an insane desire to stare at his forehead, looking for a vein ready to burst.

A sharp knock had all of them whipping around to look at the door.

Zu was up and headed to the door before anyone else could react. Sure they hadn't been sitting close enough to touch, but Ying Yue was used to being aware on some level when someone rose or sat in a seat next to her. Zu was a large man, but he moved with a fluidity she was only beginning to grasp. She glanced at Silbermann and his colleague. Both had straightened but didn't seem to have had time to react any more than that.

Through the glass door, Ying Yue could make out Pua's form even though a portion of the glass was frosted. As Zu opened the door, Pua glanced at Zu then looked into the room. "Did anyone order a press release on Miss Jiang's disappearance?"

There was a pause as all of them processed her question.

Ying Yue turned her whole chair to face Pua. "You mean my rescue?"

Even though Ying Yue would've liked to have had a more active role in her freedom, she truly had been helped. Maybe television and movies encouraged people to keep watch for every opening, however slim the chance, but she hadn't had any opportunity to make her own escape before Zu and Buck had found her. She cringed inwardly, guessing at phrases the press might use to describe the situation. *Damsel in distress* came to mind.

Julian sat forward at the table. "There was no press release authorized by any of Mr. Jiang's companies."

Pua rushed into the room. "Okay, I was scanning the newsfeeds. You all need to watch this."

CHAPTER FIVE

Zu let Pua bring up the big video screen in the conference room. Her fingertips flew across the console as she brought up the clip she'd obviously saved from the newsfeeds. An image of Ying Yue was being displayed prominently behind a newscaster reporting on her disappearance and the reward for any information on her whereabouts. It was an attractive enough picture, the kind taken for professional profiles, but the image fell flat compared to the vitality of Ying Yue in real life. Instead of watching the rest, he focused on Jiang, his aide, and the security personnel.

Judging from their expressions, none of them had known about the press release. Silbermann and his colleague were going for the neutral expression adopted by most professionals when they didn't want to give away any hints about not being aware of a situation. Julian Nilsson's face had flushed, and his lips were pressed together in a thin line. The man was tapping his forefinger against the surface of the table almost silently, a sign of agitation. Ying Yue's father had gone from his earlier poker face to scowling.

Kokua looked at Zu, meeting his gaze and giving him a tiny shake of his head. He hadn't known.

Ying Yue spoke first. "But this is inaccurate. I'm not missing anymore."

"And anyone who has seen this news bulletin is going to latch on to you and call the police." Pua brought up a second and a third news channel to display on the screen with the first. "This was broadcast across major television networks and via their websites. It's streaming everywhere. It's going to be a mess if you go anywhere in public right now. You're an overnight celebrity, and not in a good way."

Jiang's aide had pulled out his smartphone and was punching out angry texts. "We need to find the source of these news bulletins."

"Done." Pua turned to Julian. "It came from within Mr. Jiang's corporate headquarters within the last couple of hours. As far as anyone is concerned, this came from Mr. Jiang."

Julian put his phone down on the table. "You're certain."

Pua nodded. "I can show you the data, but if you call your people, you'll find out the same thing. Whichever is faster for you."

"I'd believe Pua, if I were you." Zu didn't care to waste time double-checking data unnecessarily. "The bigger question is why the press release was put out there."

"It doesn't make sense," Mr. Jiang said, finally. "Ying Yue has been missing for almost three weeks. We'd been keeping it quiet until we had more information. A search has been conducted for her through private channels."

Ying Yue flinched slightly at the impersonal phrasing her father used. It was there, and then a second later she had her composure again. Zu felt for her. The hits just kept on coming, and she was taking them like a champ. For his part, he'd do what he could to be thoughtful as he asked any further necessary questions.

"Really?" Pua cocked her head. "Someone choked those queries, because I was looking for information on Ying Yue and wasn't finding anything. If you had searches going through even discreet channels, I'd have run across them. I was trying to figure out who might have been looking for her—both friendly and not so friendly."

Reading between the lines, Pua had been trying to find out if there'd been a specific buyer waiting for Ying Yue. Here, in the conference room, Ying Yue was strong, but she didn't have anyone she should've been able to rely on at her back. It bothered the hell out of him.

"Good job, Pua. Thank you." Zu stepped back to the seat next to Ying Yue but didn't sit again. Instead, he rested his hands on the back of the empty chair and addressed her father. "I would recommend Miss Jiang remain out of the public eye until answers are found."

He and his team didn't have a professional reason to be providing recommendations to the Jiangs. But hell, he'd be lying if he tried to claim this wasn't personal, even inside his own head. He wanted to make sure Ying Yue had no further worries when it came to her kidnappers, and he had a growing desire to personally eliminate those threats from the face of the earth.

"I need to get back to Singapore," Ying Yue said quietly. "I have work, if I still have a job. I need to let my employer and my coworkers know I'm alive and able to return to work."

Every person in the room besides Ying Yue was shaking their head. Zu didn't want to gang up on her, but she might not be thinking clearly at the moment. Her words were quieter, with less authority behind them. Knowing her kidnapper had been employed with her father's security company and then hearing about the mystery news releases were probably piling onto the fatigue she was already feeling from earlier. While he wanted to respect her decisions, he also wanted to give her a chance to catch her breath from the events of the day and make her choices when she could see the situation more clearly.

"Miss Jiang, you should continue with some level of protection while my men are searching for the suspect involved in your kidnapping." Kokua was trying to sound reassuring, but Ying Yue was getting paler by the second.

Silbermann cleared his throat. "I'll structure our security team to provide the necessary protection for Miss Jiang."

Zu started to counter the man's statement, but Ying Yue sat forward, seeming to rally. She glared at the man. "The way you had a detail set up for me this morning, including my kidnapper? With all due respect, Mr. Silbermann, I do not feel comfortable with a security detail from my father's company at the moment, even if you handpick them yourself."

Zu agreed, though he made sure to adopt his own version of a poker face to keep his thoughts to himself. No need to antagonize Silbermann. Zu had been worried about Ying Yue's ability to think clearly, and he stood corrected. Maybe she was tired, and sure, some of this was outside her sphere of experience, but she was tracking all of the information as it was discussed, and he couldn't fault her for the way she felt.

"Miss Jiang, I understand you are upset," Silbermann began.

Ying Yue placed her hand flat on the table. In contrast to Silbermann's show of temper earlier, she didn't slam it down on the surface. She didn't have to. Her movement was eloquent enough. "My reservations are absolutely valid, and where my personal safety is concerned, considering my recent experiences and taking into account what I have been informed could have happened to me, it is absolutely within my rights to question your team's ability to ensure my absolute safety for the rest of my time here on Oahu."

Zu studied Mr. Jiang and his aide. The two men were thinking hard, if their dual scowls were anything to go by. Whatever their business was from day to day, these men spent a lot of time at conference room tables, reading the other people around them. Silbermann wasn't as familiar with being the center of attention in a conference room. Ying Yue definitely was. If Zu had to guess, he was betting Mr. Jiang was seeing a side of her he hadn't seen before, and maybe, based on the minute nods Mr. Jiang was giving, he was liking what he was seeing. Zu guessed that both Jiang and Nilsson were reevaluating the image of Ying Yue they had in their minds.

Regardless, Zu was impressed. When it came to controlling the conversation, she was undeniably the victor. Silbermann didn't stand a chance.

"I'm not rejecting your team, Mr. Silbermann." Ying Yue's mouth settled into a serene smile. Somehow her words were sharper when she looked so calm. "I'm asking you to provide me with specific evidence that there will not be a recurrence. Some change in process or procedure, the way you staff the security detail, or even background files on each of the candidates."

Silbermann actually let out a frustrated gust of air. "The amount of time that would take is not worth—"

"My life?" Ying Yue pinned him to the wall with those two words.

Mr. Jiang sat straighter in his chair.

"Search and Protect could supplement your existing security detail." The offer came out before Zu really thought it through. In retrospect, he didn't intend to take it back, either. They had no major contracts pending in the next several days. "How long do you need coverage for?"

Silbermann was turning red in the face. Best not to antagonize the man. Zu turned to Mr. Jiang and Julian Nilsson.

It was Julian who answered. "We'd planned for Miss Jiang to have her own room at the same hotel as Mr. Jiang. A flight has been booked for her tomorrow afternoon. She'll rendezvous with her mother, who has returned to the primary Jiang estate."

Ying Yue leveled her glare on Julian. "I have a job to get back to in Singapore."

Julian nodded. "And insufficient protection, obviously. Until the issue with the ill-advised press release can be addressed, you will find it far more comfortable visiting with your mother. It also allows Mr. Jiang's security teams to guard one location, rather than multiple targets in different parts of the world."

Ying Yue fell silent.

Julian turned to Zu. "What type of added protection can you provide? Is my understanding correct that you and your team specialize in finding the lost?"

Interesting way to put it. Zu stepped away from the table and brought Buck to heel at his left with a murmured command. "Search and Protect teams are highly effective at search, you are correct. Each of the dogs is a scent dog, excellent at locating and following trails. But they are also trained with certain behaviors found to be useful in military working dogs. Each of our human-canine teams is able to detect potential threats exponentially better and faster than the limited senses of a lone human could."

Jiang remained relaxed in his seat as he spoke up. "What do you propose, Mr. Anyanwu?"

Zu had to think fast here, based on the personnel he had available. "Buck and I are available to provide personal escort to Miss Jiang for the next twenty-four to thirty-six hours, long enough to see her safely boarded on her flight. I also have a female resource. Arin and King can accompany Miss Jiang where it would be uncomfortable to Miss Jiang to have me with her, a ladies' bathroom, for example. Arin and King can also keep watch while Buck and I take a brief rest break through the course of the night."

Jiang considered for a moment, then gave Julian a nod.

Julian didn't miss a beat. "Please have the proposal drawn up. Do you require any preparation before meeting us at the hotel?"

Fair question, but Zu had made the offer because he'd intended to ensure Ying Yue had comprehensive protection from the moment she set foot outside of Search and Protect headquarters. "Minimal preparation, all easily handled here. We intend to leave here with you and head over to the hotel together."

Mr. Jiang nodded. "Excellent."

Well, that was a done deal, then.

Ying Yue remained seated as her father came around the table. He stood there for a long moment, but when she made no move toward him, he leaned forward and patted her on the shoulder. "I can't explain my business here, and there's no time to speak privately yet. I am relieved beyond words to see you."

Ying Yue didn't answer, but she placed her hand atop his on her shoulder.

There were a lot of undercurrents in the room, from the frustration being projected by Silbermann to the intense focus Julian had on Mr. Jiang. Silbermann's other guard, at least, was doing exactly what he should be doing: becoming invisible unless someone needed him. Kokua had sat back and let the discussion move forward and off his plate as law enforcement. The police officer was the least of Zu's concerns.

Pua leaned close to Zu as the bunch of them exited the conference room. "Awkward."

Zu shot her a pointed look, but Ying Yue sighed. "Tell me about it."

"How about some more hibiscus tea?" Pua sounded desperate to cheer Ying Yue up, which Zu heartily supported.

"And some of those chicken satay skewers, too." Ying Yue stood finally. "Those were really good."

"Oh, sure."

Both of them stood and turned to stare at him.

Feeling like he was caught in headlights, he resisted the urge to stand taller and cross his arms across his chest to look bigger. He was already twice the size of either one of them. "What?"

Pua made a shooing gesture. "Why don't you see our guests to the door so we can go get a snack from the kitchen? It'd just be weird for us to walk past them right now."

Zu grunted. It was a reasonable request. He headed for the door, Buck at his side.

"Thanks, boss. I'll get the proposal drafted and send it to you for review."

He waved his hand to acknowledge her, but as he crossed

the threshold, he looked back to see Ying Yue leaning her hip against the table and smiling at Pua. For the moment, Ying Yue was in the best hands possible. He could take care of the rest to give her some peace.

*   *   *

Ying Yue paused in front of the closed door of Zu's office. From the outside, it looked to be identical to any of the others in the same hallway. They all had floor-to-ceiling glass walls, frosted in horizontal panels, with curtains inside that could be drawn for privacy. Raul and Taz were in an office on the same side of the hallway, two doors down. Arin and King were right next door with the curtains drawn. Inside Zu's office, she could see his silhouette as he moved around behind his desk.

She'd encountered this man how many times now? And she still didn't know much about him. Curiosity drove her as much as a need to be doing something other than waiting. She didn't know why she was hesitating. Lifting her hand in a loose fist, she knocked on his door.

It didn't set off Buck or any of the other dogs. She'd been in places where any knock on a door anywhere on the floor would set dogs barking wildly inside their apartments. Not here. The lack of alarmed barking from the dogs was uncanny. She hadn't thought about it earlier when it'd only been Buck in the conference room and Pua had knocked on the conference room door. But as she looked up and down the hall, she could see Buck watching her through the glass of Zu's office, and the other dogs were on their feet and looking through the glass in each of their offices. The dogs were on alert, just not out of control.

Zu opened the door and Ying Yue jumped, caught up in her observation of the dogs.

"Oh." Normally she didn't have this much trouble keeping her thoughts on track. It could've been the result of the last several weeks, but she thought the experience of Zu looking straight at her would've scattered the thoughts in her head no matter when she met him. "I hoped to have a minute, before we head back to the hotel with my father and all his people."

Zu studied her for a moment, and she resisted the urge to fidget. Considering recent events and the distinct lack of any chance to take a real bath or give any real attention to her appearance, she wasn't sure what he thought, but she was going with sheer presence and personality. That'd have to do. He didn't say anything, but he did shift his stance to allow her access to the office.

Buck stood there, and at least he gave her a tock-tock wag of his tail.

"Every one of the dogs here is highly trained, aren't they?" She couldn't stop watching Buck as the big dog resumed his position, lying near the door where he could see both Zu behind his desk and the hallway beyond the glass.

Zu grunted an affirmative.

She closed her eyes briefly. Damn, that was a stupid question. She looked back up at Zu.

"I haven't encountered many search and rescue dogs." Try none up close, ever. At least, not until she'd met the dogs of the Search and Protect team. "But what little I've seen of them working with police and at airports gave me the impression the dogs were a little more...laid back than the dogs you have here."

Yes. Laid back and relaxed was what she remembered.

She'd never been cautious around the search dogs at the airport in her travels for business. They always had a sort of friendly approach and attitude. In fact, she remembered seeing the people working with the dogs repeatedly telling travelers not to try to pet the dogs as they were on the job. She didn't think anywhere near as many people would approach Buck or the other Search and Protect dogs, cooing and intending to pet them.

Zu leaned his hip against his desk as he faced her. "Our dogs are trained with a number of skills you might not see in other search and rescue dogs. I mentioned military application to your father. There's almost no scenario where they'd hurt you here."

Almost. She stepped farther into the office so she could see both Buck and Zu. "It's not that I'm afraid, though I'm sure each and every one of them could be dangerous. I get the impression your line of work calls for a lot of skill sets people like me wouldn't consider."

He raised an eyebrow, and she thought there was a hint of laughter in the subtle creases at the corners of his eyes. "Are you talking about the people or the dogs?"

She shrugged. "Does it matter? I think what I said is applicable to both."

"You're right." He didn't say anything more, simply waited, his attention fully on her.

Heat bloomed in her cheeks. She couldn't remember the last time anyone had given her their complete attention for longer than a few seconds outside of a business presentation, and even then, most people split their attention between her as a speaker and whatever tablet or smartphone they used. Zu's effect on her, in particular, was new. She felt exposed, and yet she didn't want to lose the intensity of the connection. She wanted to . . . savor it.

"In what scenario would one of your dogs present a danger to a person?" She assumed it wasn't personal, but she also was curious to know. She was hesitant to ask Zu more about himself, so asking about his dog or any of the dogs in his organization gave her a way to know more about him without quite taking the plunge. She wasn't this hesitant in her normal life, but she was still struggling to find her equilibrium. Talking about when a dog could be scary was more reassuring than directly asking Zu about who he was.

Okay, maybe the whole reason she'd sought him out here in his office, before they became a part of her father's entourage, had been to learn more about the man Azubuike Anyanwu was. She was placing her trust in him, yet she didn't know much of anything about him.

"If the handler, or someone the dog was commanded to guard, was threatened, any of the dogs would have an aggressive response," Zu answered quietly. "If one of us were to give the command, our dog would also carry out the command to the best of their ability, no matter what or who the target was."

She couldn't help it. She glanced at Buck. The red-brown dog was watching Zu. Buck's ears didn't stand up like the German Shepherds' ears did. Instead, Buck's ears folded over, inverted triangles of ultra softness. When Buck was listening or paying particular attention, she noticed the broad base of his ears sort of perked forward a bit. At the moment, the dog was listening and ready for anything his master had to say.

And could she blame Buck? Zu might not be talkative, but when he did speak, she loved the tenor of his voice and the way it resonated in her sternum. She wanted to hear more.

"Did I upset you?" Zu seemed to fade back without actually moving. She sensed his withdrawal, rather than saw it.

"No." She shook her head. "I asked. I think it's important to understand the capabilities of any person or thing. It doesn't make sense to ignore unpleasant aspects of anything. It means we don't give it proper respect. The same goes for people or animals."

Zu nodded, relaxing a fraction.

"Honestly"—she laughed softly, surprised at herself for the thought occurring to her—"I'm reassured, the more I know Buck can do. He's a part of the augmented security for me, after all."

Zu chuckled and his face transformed. His full lips stretched in a smile, and suddenly she noticed lights catch in his eyes. "He is. I come along as part of the deal, too."

"That's a nice bonus, too, I guess." She tried to say it lightly, but she got caught up in Zu's gaze. It got harder to draw breath. "I'm very glad you'll be with me."

"We've got you." Zu's reassurance warmed her and settled in her chest.

"I believe you." For the first time in days, weeks, she steadied, and maybe a few of the broken pieces of her confidence slipped back into place.

She took a few steps forward, closing the distance between her and Zu. He didn't back away. She leaned up on tiptoe, resting the palm of one hand against his chest for balance, and gave him a quick kiss on the cheek before returning to where she'd been standing.

Or she meant to return. As she backed away, she encountered something furry right behind her legs, and she almost fell. Zu's arm wrapped around her waist, catching her and bringing her back against him. Suddenly, she was pressed against his very muscular body, and something was tapping the side of her calf. Tock-tock.

She looked up, way up, into Zu's face. This close, she could see the deep brown of his dark eyes. "I . . ."

Zu was murmuring something at the same time. "Buck . . ."

Neither of them finished their thought. Zu leaned closer and she tilted her face up. His lips brushed against hers, and she gasped as the slight contact burned through her. She rose up on tiptoe again, meeting him across the barest distance between their lips for the kiss she wanted more than air.

He sent her drowning in that kiss. Her senses reeled as they tasted each other. She savored him, aware of the strength of his arm still around her, the hard muscles of his chest under her palms. He was solid and warm and real, and she was so very hungry for him.

His other hand came up to cup her face as he lifted his head away, and she leaned into his palm. This was perfect.

"Buck, *af.*"

She opened her eyes at the strange command and craned her neck so she could look over her shoulder. Behind her, Buck lay down on his belly, his tail still wagging in a sweep across the carpeted floor. She hadn't even heard the dog get up when she'd approached Zu. Maybe she was lucky Buck hadn't interpreted her impulsive move as a threat to his master.

Zu's arm tightened around her waist again, and she squealed as he lifted her and turned, setting her back down on her feet a few feet clear from Buck so she could stand without tripping over the big dog. Then Zu released her and stepped back. The air cooled between them and his face went strangely blank.

"I'm sorry. That won't happen again."

She blinked. "Why not?"

"You've been under duress, and I'm the person most directly involved in bringing you back to safety." Zu backed even farther away. "Your emotions are compromised, and you are still vulnerable. I should not have done that."

The delicious heat tingling over her body cooled as she wrestled with simultaneous waves of embarrassment and indignation. "I started it. I have no regrets."

Zu's expression didn't change. "I shouldn't have crossed the line."

She clenched her jaw before she made a sound like a tea kettle boiling, even if she felt like everything was bubbling up at the same time. "Fine. You regret it. I don't plan to. The main reason why I came here was to thank you. So. Thank you for saving me, and thank you for seeing to my safety until I leave tomorrow."

She turned on her heel and headed for the door, thankful she made it out without smacking into the doorjamb. She needed to put some distance between herself and that very embarrassing moment. Going down the hallway wasn't going to be enough. If she turned back to look at him, she wasn't sure if she'd shrink in embarrassment or try to throw something at him for presuming she didn't know she'd wanted to kiss him.

And whoa, it'd been a great kiss.

CHAPTER SIX

P lease wait outside."

Ying Yue glanced up and down the hotel hallway, at the security guards on either side of her, then finally at Zu. "Seriously? You want me to wait out here."

Zu nodded, his expression completely neutral. "Buck and I will clear your suite first. Arin and King will stay here with you and the rest of the security detail."

As he spoke, Arin and King came around the corner from exploring the other hallway. The woman was a couple of inches shorter than Ying Yue but had the kind of presence that filled any space, big or small, and her black-and-tan dog was the biggest Ying Yu had ever seen of his breed. As they neared, Arin gave Zu a sharp nod, then looked at Ying Yue and smiled. Arin's smile brightened the hallway somehow, and Ying Yue let go of the tension she hadn't been aware of building. Arin seemed to be finding a whole lot of things amusing since she'd joined them for the ride over to the hotel. Maybe it was because it was obvious, at least to Ying Yue and probably to Arin, that Zu was taking every chance to put distance between himself and Ying Yue.

Kiss a man and make the whole rest of your evening awkward. Who knew?

She should've known better. She didn't make overtures or even flirt with men often because it had never ended well. At this point in her life, everything seemed to have gone on immediate fail mode. So of course giving in to her natural impulse had resulted in new levels of embarrassment for her.

She'd spent some time considering what he'd warned her against. He wasn't wrong. She was the proverbial damsel in distress, more than once between the initial kidnapping and seeing one of her kidnappers among her father's men. But you know what? She'd done the best she could in her situation. She was truly grateful to him for his actions in each of those moments. So it was reasonable to be concerned about her becoming infatuated with her knight in shining armor. But she didn't think of him in that way so much as recognize him as also being a truly beautiful man. Yes, she was attracted to him, but it came from a different place than what he was assuming.

Ying Yue craned her neck to peer inside the suite even though Arin and King were now standing directly in the door frame. She caught sight of Buck walking through the area, sniffing the floor and then various chairs. A door somewhere in there slammed, and Ying Yue jumped.

"Sorry." Arin smiled at her apologetically. "We approach each closed door and slam it open to induce an involuntary jump out of anyone who might be hiding behind it or nearby. Most people just can't help reacting to it. It's standard when we methodically go through and clear a set of rooms."

"Ah." Ying Yue couldn't remember any of her father's men doing the same sort of thing throughout her childhood or any time she happened to be visiting her parents. Then again, it seemed like the kind of thing her mother would've protested because it would upset her. Maybe Ying Yue would've questioned how necessary it was, too, before. Now? "Anything you need to do to be absolutely sure there are no threats in the area."

Arin's smile widened. "Much appreciated. We'll have you inside and in a space where you can relax any minute now. If you want, you can even take a bath. These towers have really big tubs in the suites."

"You've been here before?" Ying Yue saw a flash of Zu's reflection in a mirror on a wall in the entryway as he walked around the suite. He moved so quickly, an imposing shadow. Maybe it should frighten her, but it was actually reassuring. Then she thought twice about what she'd said. "I'm sorry. Not to imply you wouldn't be staying at this kind of hotel. It's just that you live here."

Arin waved away her apology. "No worries. There are a lot of hotels, and I do live very close by. But I have a thing for the occasional staycation where I enjoy a hotel experience, and I plan to indulge in a stay here again with my SO, when he's in town eventually."

"SO?" Ying Yue struggled to figure out what the abbreviation was for. Obviously, she didn't have her full mental faculties yet. She needed a real night's sleep.

"Significant other." Arin didn't seem to mind clarifying. "Jason was with the team when we searched the cargo ship the other day. He and King and I were addressing the situation with the other captives we found when Zu found you."

"Ah." Ying Yue struggled to think of an appropriate

response. "I'm thankful to all of you. The trip from the cargo ship to Oahu and coming to the hospital is all sort of a blur."

She'd been exhausted and dazed, more than a little confused, and a little worried she was stepping out of a bad situation into an even worse one. But she'd been hopeful, and things had turned out mostly well. This time tomorrow, she'd be on a flight back to Singapore. In less than two days, she'd be able to put her life back together.

Arin nodded in sympathy. "A lot has happened for you in a short period of time. You might find you remember more details later."

Ying Yue smiled but said nothing. Remembering more details could be both a blessing and a curse. She didn't want to remember her kidnappers in more detail. They'd be featured in her nightmares for a while to come.

Arin didn't prompt her for a responding comment, instead returning to the lighter aspect of their conversation. "Since then, Jason's taken a contract in East Asia, so I'm not sure when he'll have the chance, but when he can come back, we'll kick back and relax here for at least a couple of nights. We have a few other places in mind, too."

It was nice not to be pressured to talk more about her kidnappers. She was sure she'd have to meet with the police again. For now, she was glad for the chance to chat about good things coming out of the last couple of days.

"But you don't know when. He's got a really unpredictable job?" Ying Yue wondered how any of the Search and Protect team managed relationships.

Arin shrugged. "He does. But then again, so do I. It's more likely that I'll be in Asia on contract through Search and Protect, and I'll take a few extra days before coming back. We'll be flexible about the time."

"Do you find long distance a challenge?" Ying Yue remembered long evenings, weeks, even months in her childhood when her mother would be waiting for her father to come home from business trips.

"This is still very new for us. I'm honestly not sure." Arin's smile softened and her eyes unfocused. "I think this gives us each the space to continue our own lifestyles and miss each other at the same time. We're committed to making us work, so our lives will evolve to fit our relationship as we go."

There was so much conviction in Arin's words. Ying Yue wondered if she'd ever had such certainty in the relationships in her life, any of them. But then again, Ying Yue did remember her mother saying how much missing a person could make the time together even better. Her parents had made long distance work as she'd been growing up. The time apart had varied, and while it'd probably been a few days here or a couple of weeks there, it'd always seemed like forever to Ying Yue's childhood self.

"Clear." Zu had returned to the entryway of the suite. He held the door as Arin stepped out of the way with King and motioned for Ying Yue to enter. "The master bedroom is to the right and has its own bathroom."

Entering a new hotel room was always Ying Yue's favorite part. An added flutter hit her in the chest as she passed close to Zu. She was very aware of his proximity, a little embarrassingly so as her nipples tightened, and she ducked her head to hide the sudden rush of heat to her cheeks. Her memory of their one kiss was going to stay with her a good, long while.

Basking in the pleasant memory, she turned her attention to the hotel suite. She loved the first impression and noticing what things, major or minor, made staying at a particular hotel special. The current situation being what it was, she figured it was even more important to embrace this simple pleasure. She hadn't been sure she'd ever experience it again.

The suite was basically a two-bedroom apartment, tastefully decorated in deep brown woods and cool sea colors. It was equipped with a full kitchen and dining area as well as a living room and a private balcony. There was even a tiny washer and dryer unit. A person could literally live in a place like this for an extended stay.

"Your security detail will take turns sleeping in the other bedroom when off duty through the night." Zu followed her into the suite but stopped at the doorway to the master bedroom. "The on-duty personnel will remain here in the kitchen and living room area. Arin will be coming into your room to check on you periodically."

He'd been serious about having a person of the same gender checking in on her wherever she went. "Not a lot of privacy."

He shook his head once. "No. Unfortunately not. Not with the current risks. Changing your room to the towers is something, but it would've been more advisable to change resorts completely. Until Officer Kokua has the suspect in custody and your father's people complete their internal investigation, my team will operate with the assumption of high risk. Please bear with us."

She studied his very serious countenance. All professional. It was impressive, and now that he'd executed the first of his objectives—getting her situated in this place— she thought maybe he could relax, even a bit. She wanted to say something, do something, to crack his careful exterior. She couldn't care less about Arin or her father's men being there to witness her challenging Zu. But most of her ideas involved confronting him about their recent kiss or trying to kiss him again, but those options didn't feel quite right to her. She was a patient woman. She'd bide her time and come up with something that felt right to her.

"Fine. I'd like some privacy to take a bath, though, and I don't feel comfortable with anyone—not even Arin—coming into the bathroom to check on me. If someone has to be in there with me, can I just take Buck?"

Both of her father's men suddenly found the wall incredibly interesting. Arin coughed and stared at the ceiling. Buck and King sat there, both of their mouths open as their tongues lolled out in doggie grins.

Zu's neutral face cracked as his eyes widened in surprise. After a moment, he recovered, and his eyes narrowed instead. "No one has asked for that before, but it's a valid option."

"Good." She turned and sallied into the bedroom.

Behind her, Zu gave a quiet command and shut the bedroom door. She looked over her shoulder and found Buck sitting just inside, looking at her with his head tilted a little to one side. She huffed out a quiet laugh. Well, this was way better than having a stranger peek in on her in the bath.

* * *

Zu stared at the closed door. She really had kept Buck with her.

Arin laughed. "You should see your face."

Zu scowled at his colleague and sometimes friend, but right now he wasn't inclined to think charitably of her. "Yeah?"

Jiang's security personnel were opening a laptop in the breakfast nook near the kitchen, opposite the dining area.

Both had headphones on as they set up their communications, so they weren't likely to be paying attention to Arin and his conversation at the moment.

"Oh yeah." Arin reached down and ruffled King's ears. She didn't have to reach far. Even sitting, her German Shepherd Dog's head was level with her hip. "I've known you a long time, Zu, and very rarely if ever have I seen someone put that disgruntled look all over your face."

Zu didn't say anything, and he wasn't going to admit he was wishing for a mirror, because he most definitely didn't like it when people could read him so easily. Even a colleague considered close enough to be a friend. And those were rare.

"You want first watch?" Arin asked.

Zu nodded, still working to pull his expression back to neutral, but Arin's dark eyes sparked with humor. She was not going to forget this for a long time, and she wasn't going to let him forget it, either.

Damn, but Ying Yue was under his skin. The woman just did things to unhinge him, keep him off-balance, and he didn't think she was doing it on purpose. Simple things, like taking Buck with her, caught Zu off guard. The things she did weren't crazy, but she managed to put her own twist on her decisions, and he couldn't quite anticipate them. She was just unlike any other woman he'd ever encountered. He wanted her, and he shouldn't.

Arin shrugged out of her backpack and tossed it on the couch. "I'm going to make a run down to the gift shop to get a little something for her bath. It'll give her some stress relief. She needs a real night's sleep."

Not a bad idea. It brought along with it a few choice images of what Ying Yue might look like in a bath, and Zu shut himself down right there. He needed to be focused on the mission at hand, not letting his mind wander where his libido wanted to lead him before he'd finished establishing the safety precautions he wanted in place.

Still, Arin must like her, too, or she wouldn't be going out of her way to help Ying Yue feel comfortable. Going to any place besides this hotel room meant taking a round-about path there and a different route back, plus checking to be sure she wasn't seen or followed. Generally, it was easier to settle in and stay put once they'd reached the room for the night.

"When you get back, can you give her this bag, too?" Zu removed his own pack from his back and fished out a much-compacted shopping bag.

Arin raised her eyebrows. "Or I could bring back what I planned to pick up and give it to you to give to her, along with what you thought to bring in advance."

He glared at her but didn't respond, because he liked her idea better. He just thought it was the less wise of the options.

She stepped closer and lowered her voice. "All joking aside, you're being way more considerate than you normally would be for a client."

Maybe so. He wasn't going to allow himself to think more deeply about it because it was a moot point. "Key consideration: she's a client. I don't go there."

"Mmm." Arin nodded. "You never have in the past. But there are no absolutes in this world. There are just situations and variables worth evaluating to make the best decision you can at the time. You taught me that."

Some people would say there were a few absolutes out there. Getting involved with your client or a teammate was definitely going to get you into trouble, for one. Hell, Zu had put too much trust in a romantic interest and a good friend in the past. He'd gotten himself stabbed in the back, figuratively, and his entire livelihood hijacked out from under him, literally. Mixing business and personal life was complex and messy as hell no matter what. Rebuilding his life and starting Search and Protect had been established on a foundation of those lessons learned. It'd taken years to save up the money and almost as many to hire the people he wanted.

Meeting Ying Yue had been one surprise after another, sure, but he wasn't going to give in to temptation—and yes, he did need to admit there was a whole lot of temptation when it came to Ying Yue—just when he was finally getting Search and Protect solidly established. Besides, they were on a hotel property he hadn't chosen, at a resort they all already knew had been compromised by at least one threat to her. There were too many risks to allow for him to get distracted. He and Buck, Arin and King, needed to be at their sharpest.

"I'm going to leave King here." Arin was talking to the security personnel, but the information was for him as well. "I'll be less conspicuous if I'm not walking around with a working dog. I'm headed down to get a few things, including food for us all. Anything I can get for you?"

Short of making the food themselves, the safest bet was for Arin to go out and pick up food for them. Ordering room service was convenient but brought attention to the room they were in, and while it was hard to connect a room service order to a target, it was far from impossible. If they had the extra person out anyway, why not? King, of course, had a different opinion about being left behind. The big dog parked his furry butt to one side of the door and stared, like he was going to be there, exactly like that, until Arin returned.

Zu remained rooted in place in the middle of the room until Jiang's two men nervously turned back to their laptop surveillance. Sure, he was making them uncomfortable. He had zero fucks to give about it. What he was considering was why he was inclined to take so many precautions when it came to Ying Yue. Every job had its associated risk level. On the surface, Ying Yue seemed to be a simple kidnapping victim. Her father's people were going with the obvious assumption that she was taken to be held hostage against her father. So Zu's first line of questions went along the path of what her father was doing in Hawaii that was worth kidnaping his daughter for leverage against him.

He wanted those answers, but something was off. Yes, she'd been kidnapped and left relatively unharmed. It was good fortune and maybe something more. Her kidnapper had ties to a human trafficking ring and had expected her to arrive in Oahu along with the rest of a shipment of captives. The man had time to insert himself into her father's security team, which just happened to be on the island. But there were a couple of possible reasons why the suspect had done it. There was also plenty of room for something he hadn't thought of yet.

Zu stared at the closed door to the master bedroom and considered Ying Yue, did his best not to imagine her undressing and stepping naked into a steaming bath. It was only a split-second thought, and his body was responding, heating up fast with need.

Shit. He yanked his thoughts back to the danger Ying Yue was in. A lot of the current situation could be attributed to who her father was, but Zu couldn't help but wonder: Who was Ying Yue, and what had she been doing just before she'd been kidnapped?

CHAPTER SEVEN

Zu scowled as travelers hustled from shuttles and cars across the walkway to the ticketing and check-in counters. Most of them gave him a wide berth, but there'd been one or two absorbed in their smartphone or distracted by something else who almost walked into him and stopped short, then stumbled around him. Maybe he could've stood farther to one side, out of the flow of foot traffic, but he was in a mood to be conspicuous.

"Alpha, this is Charlie. I'm in position," Arin's voice murmured over the comm in his ear.

He had Arin tucked away, out of sight. As far as anyone knew, including Mr. Jiang's personal security team, Arin had gone back to Search and Protect headquarters when Ying Yue had checked out of the hotel and headed for the airport. Instead, Arin had found a vantage point to provide cover outside as an extra layer of precaution for Ying Yue right up to the moment she stepped inside the airport. There were few snipers of Arin's caliber, and Zu made sure to use her to best advantage.

Ying Yue stood with her father, facing a wall of reporters. The photo op had been a last-minute addition to the itinerary, and it was another thing Zu didn't like about the entire situation. Yeah, he understood Mr. Jiang's perspective and the desire to reassure the public that Ying Yue was no longer missing and was safely reunited with her family. Zu also saw the benefit of doing it before she headed back to her life in Singapore. It'd save her a lot of grief from law enforcement and random strangers thinking she was still missing and possibly taking her into custody to return her to her family.

But her kidnapper still hadn't been found. Zu didn't think the man had left Oahu yet, nor did Zu think he'd been acting alone. It took connections to insert oneself into a security team like Jiang's. Too many issues were unresolved, and the police and her father's internal organization had too many things still to do for the investigation. Zu was certain she wasn't safe any moment she remained on Oahu. Things were going too smoothly.

"Alpha, are you going to talk to her before you put her on a plane?" Arin had shot him nagging looks throughout the night and early morning.

"There's nothing left to say. I explained to her why I needed to keep my distance." It'd driven him almost insane, especially when she'd opted to sleep with her door open—for safety, she'd said—and he'd been able to watch her sleep through the night.

"You sure?" Arin wasn't buying it, obviously. "From what I gathered, you explained to her she was vulnerable, which she knew. And you didn't want to take advantage of her, which she appreciated. But I don't think she knows you actually like her."

"Like her" was such a pitiful description for the torture

he'd been going through. He was incredibly attracted to Ying Yue, his body responding to just the thought of her, much less having her within arm's reach every minute of the last twenty-four hours. But more, he'd been listening to what she had to say. Ying Yue was a woman with a mind of her own and the ability to assert herself when necessary while still keeping the people around her amenable to working with her. She didn't grate on peoples' nerves. She didn't step on toes. She picked her battles. She was strategic. She spoke with irrefutable logic in a respectful, pleasant way to pull everyone along with her before they even realized they'd followed her lead. And every moment he'd listened to her, he wanted to hear her express herself more and more. He was hungry to get to know more of her personality as she regained bits and flashes of her confidence despite everything she'd been through. All that and he'd spent only a day in close company with her.

"She has a life to go back to." And he wasn't a part of it. "She has a job and a home. Maybe a relationship. She didn't say."

He didn't know enough about who she was or the life she'd led before she'd been kidnapped and ended up on that cargo ship, captive. Her past was hers, and she was going back to her life. In the meantime, he planned to look into what future was planned for her by her kidnappers, because there, at least, Zu had the ability to plan some karma for the individuals responsible for creating havoc in her life. Pua had already been running queries and would alert him the minute she had any new intel.

It would've been expensive to arrange for a kidnapping like hers. It didn't make sense that they hadn't made any further attempts to reacquire her while she was still on the island. Maybe the man she'd recognized was gone, but an organization like the human trafficking ring always had more assholes ready to do the unspeakable in the name of money.

"Tch. Alpha, with all due respect, you're taking the easy route." Arin had gone from mildly teasing to actually sounding irritated. "I see how you react to this woman. All of us do. You let her leave without saying something to her to let her know she's hooked you, or giving her some reason to stay in touch with you, and she is going to be your what-if for the rest of your time on this earth."

"My what?" He almost growled as a reporter stuck a camera too close to Ying Yue's face. She fended it off with a gracefully raised hand to push it out to a more respectful distance and a serene smile as her father continued to address questions.

"Your what-if." Arin sighed in exasperation. "She's going to haunt you for the rest of your days as you wonder what would've happened if you'd given it a chance."

"There is no chance." The reporters fired off a new wave of camera flashes as Mr. Jiang and Ying Yue posed again. Despite the strain of the photo op, she managed to look calm and project a sweet countenance. She was beautiful.

"Because you didn't make one." Arin was not letting this go. "There is no fate or luck or whatever. There's potential, and you give it a chance to become whatever. Or you don't. Unless you're the ninja master of dating, I'm pretty sure you haven't given any person the opportunity to get close to you in years, but this woman is under your skin. And you're just going to let her get on a plane and leave your life?"

The memory of Ying Yue in his arms came unbidden, the length of her body pressed soft against his. He hadn't been able to resist her invitation in his office and had lost himself for a few seconds—or forever—in the taste of her kiss. He'd wanted way more than she would've been able to give him. And he'd been wrong to cross that line. It didn't mean he hadn't been thinking about it nonstop since it'd happened.

Okay, so he would be thinking about Ying Yue for a long time to come.

Whether he was thinking about her or not, he was taking in as much of everything around her as was humanly possible. When keeping watch over a client, you don't actually watch them. Banter with Arin aside, he'd been scanning the area for anything out of place. He had confidence he could spot the average threat in plenty of time to react. The problem was, he suspected that the person who kidnapped Ying Yue and whatever colleagues or backers the man had were beyond the average.

So Zu quickly assessed every person: how they walked, what they were looking at, what they were wearing, and what they could possibly hide beneath those clothes or in the bags they carried.

"This photo op is looking like it's going to end on time, but it was a terrible idea in the first place," Arin's voice murmured in his ear.

He gave her a guttural sound in agreement. It meant a lot of people were looking at Ying Yue and Jiang, simply out of curiosity. It was a spectacle, even if it was on a fairly small scale.

"For what it's worth, Jiang's head of security looks like he hates this as much as we do."

Arin was being generous. Zu knew he should play nice

with Jiang's security team, but the fact that Ying Yue's kidnapper had managed to insert himself into the detail here in Hawaii at all bothered the hell out of Zu. He wasn't cutting the head of security any slack. A leader took accountability for his team, even if it wasn't his direct mistake. But Zu didn't voice his opinion. Arin knew him well enough by now, and currently she was being the wiser of the two of them from a collaborative perspective. It was best if they, as the supplemental resources, could work with the established team rather than in spite of them. Zu did his best to keep his opinion to himself and not undermine the good work Arin was doing.

But something, something around them was starting to set off his mental alarms. He scanned the area again, blowing out the air in his lungs in a slow, deliberate breath and letting his muscles relax into a loose and ready to move state.

"Alpha." Arin's earlier bantering tone was gone. She'd gone all business.

"You see something." He made a slow turn in place, looking for what was bothering them both.

"No. That's the problem." She hesitated. "There's a lull in the steady car traffic going past the area. Something's not right."

It was the hush before a predator, or pack of predators, pounced.

"Be ready." Zu tightened his jaw.

Enough was enough. He walked toward the group. Hell, he was prepared to step on photographers to get to Ying Yue.

* * *

"Miss Jiang needs to check in for her flight."

Ying Yue turned to face more cameras as the reporters started a fresh round of picture-taking at Julian's mild time check, shifting her expression from one smile to a slightly different one. It was the way she'd learned to give her facial muscles relief without slipping into any kind of non-smiling expression that could be caught on camera and taken out of context. No one could be perfectly camera-proof one hundred percent of the time, but she'd learned a few tricks through childhood and into adulthood. Her family wasn't at celebrity status, but even when there weren't reporters, there were always business partners and networking friends who wanted to have a picture to commemorate a business deal.

She'd grown up projecting an appropriate image for her parents, and she'd learned to value the ability to navigate such moments for business ventures. Besides, her mother enjoyed having pictures taken of them wherever they were, whether for Father's business or family vacation or just a nice time at home. For her mother, photographs were memories, keepsakes, and Ying Yue didn't mind them.

Speaking of things to be remembered, Ying Yue glanced at Zu. He and Buck were a distance away, walking toward her. She'd been able to sleep last night, knowing Zu had been only a room away. Now, she didn't feel as exposed as she'd thought she might out in the open. They were right there.

Just a few more minutes and she'd be able to leave the whole nightmare of her kidnapping behind her. She could piece herself together during the flight to her parents' home and let her mother fuss over her for a short time while her father's people completed their investigation. It would take some time to extract herself and return to her work, but she was going back to her life—even if she got back to Singapore and decided she wanted to relocate to a different city to move forward.

She should be excited, but she was wrestling with a reluctance to leave the new acquaintances she'd made here in Oahu. She'd genuinely liked both Pua and Arin and thought she could be friends with them in a way she wasn't with her coworkers. And then there was Zu.

Maybe she could reach out to Zu, keep in touch. She snuck another glance at him, but he never seemed to be looking quite at her even though he was coming closer. Perhaps not. A fresh wave of embarrassment burned her cheeks as she thought about the way he'd rebuffed her in his office. She'd probably misinterpreted his kindness toward her as attraction he didn't actually share.

"Hey!" a man shouted as a car jumped the curb nearby and almost ran into him. Several men burst out of the interior, brandishing guns. Very big guns.

Silbermann issued terse orders, and the security personnel behind them grabbed her father, surrounding him. She was bumped a few steps sideways as they pulled her father toward the cover of the terminal. Then a woman screamed as men emerged from the terminal, holding up handguns. Instinctively, Ying Yue crouched down.

More orders were shouted. The security team changed direction, heading back toward the street and farther away from Ying Yue as her father's driver backed their rental car toward the curbside to meet them.

Ying Yue's heart beat hard in her chest as she gathered her nerve to follow them or bolt around the men who were after her father and into the cover of the terminal. Someplace, anyplace safe.

Zu.

She turned to look for him. He had pulled his gun out. She started to rise, go to him; then a hand wrapped around her upper arm in a viselike hold. Fear seared through her as she threw all her weight forward, toward Zu. Whoever had her was stronger, and she was dragged back instead. Panicked, she looked around and saw another car, the back door thrown open. Arms were reaching out, toward her.

Zu shouted something and lifted his gun. Buck charged forward, moving so fast he was a streak of red to her. Shots rang out and a man fell at her side as Buck launched himself at the person holding her. Her attacker yelled in alarm; then the yell turned into a scream of pain amid loud snarling. The grip around her arm disappeared, and she fell forward. She caught herself on all fours and didn't waste time looking back. Instead, she scrambled to her feet and ran for Zu.

He was walking toward her, his gun up. As she made it to him, he herded her behind him with his left arm, still keeping his gun up. Only then did she peer back around him to see Buck. The big dog had her attacker's arm in his jaws and had yanked the man to the ground somehow. His growl was fierce and loud to her, drowning out the man's cries of anger and pain. Two more men came at her and Zu from opposite sides, and Zu backed her up to keep them in front of him. He shot one in the leg and the other...fell on his own. Bleeding and clutching his shoulder, weapon dropped on the ground. She looked around wildly. Someone had shot him.

"Charlie, this is Alpha. Kokua just arrived." Zu's terse message must have been meant for his communication link.

Charlie was Arin. Ying Yue had figured that much out over the last day. She'd thought Arin had left this morning, but she was here, somewhere. Zu had made sure his team was here. Relief blossomed in her chest. She could hold herself together, listen, be ready to follow Zu's instructions so he could keep her safe.

Zu hadn't said anything to her yet, but he backed up more, and she did her best to move with him and keep from tripping him. She realized there were police sirens and turned to see a police car pulled up onto the curb behind the initial attackers' car. Office Kokua was here, car door open and pointing his gun at the chaos.

"Buck, *los*!" Zu shouted.

Then Zu had her next to Officer Kokua's police car. He was opening the door and shoving her into the back seat. Buck dove in next and jumped over her. Zu remained crouching outside the door. He glanced at her over his shoulder. "Keep your head down."

She complied, because it made sense, but she had to ask. "My father?"

"His men have him in his car." Zu gave her the rushed answer in clipped tones, his broad back all she could see filling the opening to the car door. "He's not injured, as far as I saw. Sit tight and we'll get you both out of here."

He closed the door then, leaving her in the car with Buck. She wanted desperately to look out the windows, but if she could see out, someone could see her, shoot her. So she stayed down and waited.

Buck loomed over her in the seat, pressing against her back. Somehow, the dog's presence helped her stay calm. If she'd been alone in the car, waiting, with the shouting and chaos going on outside, she'd have wanted to bolt. She'd have wanted to run away, even knowing her legs couldn't take her farther or faster than a car could. But inside the police car, she had time to think. Being able to think didn't mean good judgment.

There weren't any more gunshots. That was a good thing, right?

More police sirens approached. More shouting. Through it all, Buck stayed right there with her and Zu's shadow remained outside the car window. Officer Kokua was on the other side, she hoped, by the driver's side door. No one was going to get to her in here.

CHAPTER EIGHT

Zu stood in the doorway of Kokua's office, arms crossed and barely able to hold himself back from raging at Jiang's head of security and his aide.

Jiang sat in one of two chairs, next to Ying Yue. They both were visibly shaken. Ying Yue had lost all the color and energy her night's sleep had given her, and slight tremors betrayed her ongoing fear. Seeing those refreshed Zu's anger over and over, so he stayed back, in the doorway. He probably should've given her even more room, because the office was already crowded with people, but he couldn't make himself leave her.

Arin tapped his shoulder, and he turned aside to let her into the room, too. Her glare had Silbermann and Julian Nilsson stepping prudently out of her way. She crouched by Ying Yue's chair, deftly avoiding stepping on Buck at Ying Yue's feet.

"I brought you an herbal tea," Arin said, quietly, holding out a mug. "Maybe it would've been better to put some whiskey in there, too, but I wasn't sure if you drank whiskey."

"Pua would call it a tisane," Ying Yue whispered, reaching out and taking the mug in both hands.

True. How closely had Ying Yue and Pua bonded? Not that it was a bad thing.

Arin only smiled, but when Ying Yue reached out to touch the mug, she withdrew quickly with a soft hiss.

"Careful, it's hot." Arin pulled the mug back and waited for Ying Yue to rub her palms on her pants legs before taking the mug back more gingerly.

Ying Yue shook her head ruefully. "It's just that my hands are freezing."

Zu wanted to check Ying Yue's palms, her fingertips, all of her. Hell, he knew she was unhurt. EMTs had said she seemed to be unhurt. No visible injuries, and she'd declined going to the hospital, insisting she felt all right. Shaken, but fine. He still wanted to check over every part of her. He couldn't stand the idea of her hurt in any way.

Jiang's head of security wrapped up a call with some resource. "We have the hotel secure again, sir, and we can head back as soon as we're done here."

Officer Kokua sat behind his desk, his expression dour. "We have forensic teams at the airport. The suspects taken into custody are being treated at the hospital under police supervision; then they'll be questioned. As soon as we have answers for you, we'll give you an update."

Uh-huh. "Those men weren't after Mr. Jiang."

Jiang and Ying Yue twisted in their seats to look at him. Kokua gave him a tired nod of agreement.

"Of course they were," Julian snapped.

Silbermann shook his head. "Anyanwu, am I saying that right? Anyway, Anyanwu's assessment is correct. The attack only put enough pressure on us to force us to get Mr. Jiang under cover and out of danger. They didn't try hard enough to come at him. My team assumed the target was Mr. Jiang and didn't properly cover other possibilities. We should have let Anyanwu stand guard with Miss Jiang instead of at a distance."

Zu's desire to bury Silbermann eased a fraction. But only the barest of fractions.

"What are you saying?" Ying Yue's eyes were dark pools of quiet, her outward demeanor so carefully calm, Zu wondered how long it would be before she shattered with the effort.

But he answered her with the truth, because she'd asked, and she deserved to have it. "Whoever these people are, they know your father's security team's first priority is him. They knew the security team would move to protect him first and get him out of the way, leaving you exposed for a few seconds until the security team could come back for you. It worked. You were exposed and vulnerable. They had another car roll up, and they would've pulled you into it, taking you away while the other attackers provided cover. It was a hastily put together operation and not as coordinated as it should have been. That is the only reason they weren't able to take you."

He glanced at Buck. It'd been a split-second decision. He'd wanted to run to her when one of the attackers grabbed her, but he wouldn't have gotten there fast enough. Either that or he'd have been gunned down as he tried. Buck had the best chance of getting to her while he provided cover, and his decision was why she was sitting here now. "You were the target. You're still the target. You can't get on a flight or a boat or anywhere without serious protection until these people are stopped."

There was silence in the room as his words sank in.

"So Miss Jiang remains here on Oahu until the investigations are complete." Silbermann shifted his weight forward. "Our team..."

"Has been compromised." Ying Yue's gaze pinned the man. "I do not feel comfortable entrusting my personal safety to you and your men until you can provide me with conclusive results from the investigations you already have in progress, plus the additional inquiry into what is going on with that misguided set of press releases. How did they know to attack at the airport during that photo op? I'm not sure about much right now, Mr. Silbermann, but I am absolutely clear on my feeling in that regard."

Even Zu rocked back on his heels. She wasn't wrong in any way. He'd have raised the same concerns. Julian Nilsson looked like he'd swallowed a very bitter tonic, but he wasn't arguing with her, either. "Perhaps Officer Kokua can provide protective custody of some sort."

It was a valid option and one Zu planned to be a part of. Zu could offer extra support to Kokua's team, however they decided to establish protection for Ying Yue. They had a standing contract to provide supplemental support to the local police force when their skill sets, usually the search capabilities of the dogs, would be helpful. This was an odd fit but still justifiable.

"Unfortunately, all of our established safe houses are involved in other investigations." It was Kokua's turn to be extremely uncomfortable, apparently. "Due to various investigations over the past year, our resources are stretched thin. We don't have a safe house location appropriate for Miss Jiang."

"I don't need the height of luxury." Ying Yue made the statement in a low tone, sounding slightly incredulous.

Zu knew Kokua, though, and Zu was sure he meant there wasn't anything available at all, rather than simply not something appropriate. He considered what he could say to help Kokua out, but this wasn't his sphere of influence, either. As much as he and his team provided support, it'd been made clear in recent months that they had to be careful to respect the jurisdiction of law enforcement. They had come dangerously close to the line between aiding the law and taking it into their own hands a couple of times.

But it was Mr. Jiang who came to his feet. "Ying Yue. Do you trust these people?"

Ying Yue looked from Buck to Zu, to Arin and King. "They've proven they are responsive, capable." She pushed back her chair and rested her hand on Buck's back. "They found me and have been there for me since."

It wasn't her formal words that touched him. It was the conviction in her voice. Her trust warmed Zu from deep inside, radiating outward in a gentle wave. He wanted to be worthy of it.

The older man tore his gaze from his daughter to look at Zu. "Mr. Anyanwu, I would appreciate if you and your people could provide an additional proposal to my aide for the protection of my daughter for the rest of our stay here on Oahu."

Whatever the words Jiang used, the anguish in his eyes and the quiet pride in his tone told Zu everything. Despite any issues the two of them had, the man truly loved his daughter. He wanted her alive and whole, safe.

"How long is that going to be?" Zu wanted to say yes, immediately. But he also wasn't going to promise what he couldn't commit his resources to one hundred percent.

"A week," Julian supplied. "I can provide you with contact

information for reaching out to me or Mr. Jiang during that time."

Zu looked directly at Ying Yue's father. "Mr. Jiang, why are you here on Oahu? What is it about your business here that would be worth throwing so much effort and so many resources into stealing your daughter to distract you from your business? I think it's too coincidental that she was kidnapped in Singapore and was shipped here along with captives of a human trafficking ring when she could've ended up in other places."

Other markets, sold to the highest bidder. The thought frayed his already strained temper.

"You do not need to know that information." Julian spoke a little too fast, with more than a little heat behind it.

Jiang raised his hand and shook his head. "I am here on business concerning several of my manufacturing sites in China, Mr. Anyanwu. There is always extreme scrutiny on such sites. I do not know why someone is willing to go to these lengths, but I believe in preparing to counter any threats to my business or my family. Julian will provide you with timelines and information appropriate for you and your team to know. Will you accept the contract to assume responsibility for the personal protection of my daughter?"

Zu nodded.

"Thank you." Jiang turned to his aide. "We will return to the hotel and my pressing business. Ying Yue will stay with the Search and Protect team. Please see to the details and coordinate with Officer Kokua."

Julian stepped back, nodding his agreement. Jiang moved past him and addressed Silbermann. "I want updates on the results of your investigations twice daily. Personally. This needs to be resolved before my business on Oahu is finished."

Jiang faced Zu again and this time, Ying Yue's father looked straight through him. "One last thing. You are my daughter's bodyguard, Mr. Anyanwu. Please tell me you have a plan."

Zu shot a glance at Silbermann and Nilsson, then nodded. "Buck and I are going to take her and disappear."

* * *

"This is a safe house?" Ying Yue slid off the Jet Ski and waded the rest of the way up the small private beach in the fading light. The sun had set below the ocean horizon, and it was getting dark fast. She could make out trees and the outline of a two-level house, but everything around it was shadows.

"How is your night vision?" Zu was a darker shadow in the dusk, his presence warm at her side. "You can hold on to my left arm if you want. We're headed to a small gate ahead. The sand transitions to grass."

She could make out the gate but none of the details of the house. "I never really thought about how dark it could get with no lights around a property. Don't you have neighbors?"

The nearest lights she could make out were several hundred yards away.

"The properties on either side of this are currently unoccupied," Zu answered, moving forward and gently tugging her along with him.

"That seems convenient." How did he manage that?

"I own them." Zu's response was short. "This is my home. I rent the properties on either side to business connections or old friends. People I trust."

"Oh." His home. He'd brought her to his private space.

There was a beat of hesitation, and maybe he guessed what she was thinking. "Search and Protect doesn't maintain safe houses. This was the best I could think of on short notice that will be secure. No one has been here. Not even the other Search and Protect team members."

"What about Buck?" She'd been confused when Zu had called a taxi service to the police station. In the shelter of the parking garage, he'd opened the door and had Buck hop inside, but then had sent the car away with just Buck sitting in the back, the dog's silhouette clear in the rear window.

"He'll be along in a while." Zu sounded unconcerned.

So Buck just went on road trips all the time?

They arrived at the small gate and Zu reached to one side, taking more than a few seconds to unlatch the gate. Once he did, he held the gate open and nudged her forward ahead of him. "There's a code on the gate linked to an alert system."

"Couldn't people go around?" The grass he'd mentioned was cool and thick under the soles of her bare feet. He'd slipped her shoes in the bag slung across his back before they'd gotten on the Jet Ski. Here, within the gate, it was even darker as trees and a tall wall bordered the property.

"They could." He was there beside her again, guiding her to one side when she would've tried to walk straight forward. "But the sand transitions to sharp rocks as a retaining wall for the lawn, and I've got motion and infrared sensors set up on the perimeter."

Ah. Well, then. "I guess video cameras aren't enough for you, even at home?"

"We each set up what we need to make our homes secure." Zu didn't sound the least bit self-conscious about his precautions.

Maybe before, she'd have considered him paranoid. Before she'd been snatched away from the illusion of a safe life. Now, she was interested. "Is it expensive to set all this up?"

Once she got back to her life, she'd probably want to do something to let her relax inside her own space, too.

"There's a step here." He paused as she lifted her foot experimentally and placed it on cool stone. "I can help you research systems while you're here. We can design one for your home."

He led her through a door and into a dark building. Once they were inside, she wondered how much darker a place could get. It was pitch black compared to the deepening night outside. The crashing waves were muted, and the silence of the house was almost tangible.

"We're clear. I control the setup from my smartphone, and there have been no alerts. I'm going to turn on the lights now."

She closed her eyes, figuring the lights would be super bright and blind her. But no, he surprised her again with gentle, soft glow against her eyelids. She opened her eyes and looked around.

"This is beautiful."

And it was. She stood in a large kitchen that was wide open to a large informal dining area and an even bigger living area. Its light-colored walls and indirect lighting contrasted with dark leather and wood furniture in warm shades. It managed to be contemporary and spacious with an earthy, island feel at the same time.

"While you're here, it'd be safest if you stayed inside." Zu wiped his feet on a woven mat next to the door, and she backtracked to do the same. Most of the sand had come away as they'd walked across the grass, but she thought it best to follow his example. "But you can go anywhere inside this house and the inner courtyard."

"Okay." Then his words sunk in. "Courtyard."

He smiled at her, and she was struck again by the warmth of it. He didn't smile much, or at all, in front of Officer Kokua or any of her father's employees. She realized she hadn't seen him smile since they'd been back at Search and Protect headquarters. "The house was built around a mature tree. I'll show you."

He led her from the kitchen through another sitting area to the opening to a small courtyard. It was carefully land-scaped with white gravel and a few lush plants arranged around a central tree rising up to tower over the two stories of the house. Its branches stretched out and sheltered the tiny courtyard, giving the area a whisper of the outdoors while still feeling hidden from the world. "It's like a secret garden."

And in the garden, the space was close enough to require Zu to stand right next to her. She could feel the heat of him behind her and was tempted to lean back into him. They stood in silence for a few long moments and she reveled in the way this place and this person put her at ease.

Zu cleared his throat and stepped back, a branch snap-ping as he did. It was the first time she'd heard him make a noise like a normal person in the dark. "I should show you the rest of the house."

Zu led her to the other side of the courtyard and through another door.

They climbed the steps, and she got a glimpse into a huge master bedroom. It must've taken up half of the upstairs. The entire far wall was a strange mosaic of horizontal segments. The bed had to be a California king. It was huge. Then again, Zu was a big man. She shut herself down before she imagined tumbling onto the bed with him.

Too late. Her imagination was too quick for her, and the idea of tangling with him was too tempting.

"I've got two guest rooms." Zu kept walking down the hallway. "You can pick whichever you like better. Just please keep the curtains shut while you're in either of these."

The windows were small in the guest rooms. Each had a queen-size bed, she guessed. The decor in these rooms was minimal, the bedspreads and sheets in simple whites with accent pillows in shades of yellow and red ochre. The rooms were cozy with warm colors but had a cool feel to them. She couldn't explain why, other than the pristine state of the sheets. The rooms didn't feel lived in, the way other spaces in the house did.

"You don't come into either of these often, do you?" She turned to look at him where he stood waiting, a few steps back in the hallway, between the doors to each of the rooms.

He shrugged. "I don't get guests often."

So he basically came into each of the rooms to dust. Not that it should matter at all. She was lucky he had guest accommodations. Otherwise, she had the feeling they'd be fighting over who slept on the couch. She was sure, given the chance, he'd insist she take the only bed in that kind of situation. He came across like the type to rough it on the floor, since his height made normal couches too small to be comfortable for him.

"These are both more than comfortable." She went for the room with the red accents. Red was a lucky color. "Thank you."

He stepped up to the threshold of the room but didn't

actually come inside. He pulled his backpack off his back and pulled out her shoes and the plastic bag of the clothes she'd bought with him at the mall yesterday. "We'll get you more to wear. In the meantime, you're welcome to raid my closet if you want."

Oh, the idea of running around his house in nothing but one of his shirts should not make her so gleeful. But she totally wanted to. She was betting his shirts would be huge and roomy and comfortable.

"I might just do that." She'd meant to be playful, to lighten the progressively heavy strain she was feeling as the day's events sank in with her. "It looks like my life is in limbo for the time being, anyway. At least until my father's business is finished here."

Sure she sounded bitter. She didn't think Zu would blame her for it.

"We'll see what we can do." His gaze met hers and burned into her. "I'll do what I can to make sure you can rest at ease while you're here, and maybe we can get some of your life back on track, too. No promises. But I might have a few options for you."

"Really?" She wondered what he could possibly do. Questions bubbled up.

He held up a hand. "Rest is priority. If I start talking about this with you now, you'll never eat. You need a meal."

"Oh." At the mention of food, her stomach burbled, letting them both know he was right. "Oh."

Embarrassing seemed to be a theme around him.

"There's a private bathroom with a shower here." He lifted his chin in the direction of a pocket door to one side of the room. "But I've got a soaking tub downstairs on the main floor. It's better for real relaxation and sore muscles."

"I wasn't hurt," she protested. Everyone kept checking her over for injuries, and she'd been lucky. So lucky. Over and over she'd fared far better than she deserved, maybe.

"You've had a lot of scares. Gone through a lot of stress." His gaze settled on her again, laid her bare. A man who looked at a woman the way he was looking at her wasn't just concerned with her well-being. No one had ever looked at her with that kind of need in his eyes. But his words were all kindness and consideration. "Your muscles have tensed over and over, and the strain wears you down. A long soak will help you unwind, sleep deep, get the rest you need. There's a whole lot bound up in what you've gone through. It'll be okay to start letting it go now, here. I'll stay away until you call me. Nothing will get to you through my security."

"What if I wanted you to join me?" The question slipped out before she had a chance to edit it, filter it, anything to keep herself from risking rejection and even more embarrassment.

"That's not appropriate." She thought he'd been standing still before. Somehow, he managed to become even more still. "You're my client."

Irritation snapped any caution or logic or patience she had left. "Stop hiding behind that. If you aren't attracted to me at all, I can accept it, and I won't mention it again. But please be truthful. Because I'm worn to the barest thread, and you keep offering me anything to make me feel better. But if you leave me alone in any room, anywhere, I'm going to go insane thinking about all the things that have happened and all the even worse things that could've happened. The only thing I can think of that I really want right now is wrapping myself around you."

CHAPTER NINE

She snapped her mouth shut. She'd said more than she should have. Sure, great. Extend an invitation that sounded more like a demand and totally force him to come out and admit he didn't want her attentions. Yup. Way to seduce the man she was more attracted to than anyone she could actually remember in the entirety of forever.

Zu stared at her.

She liked it when he did, actually. She'd seen the way he made the officers at the police department uncomfortable. He was a big man with a seriousness about him, and he wore it like armor. At the airport, he'd literally glowered at people until they'd walked around him, giving him plenty of room. But when he looked at her, he saw her.

After a long moment, he finally said something. "Would it help you to be held?"

It was her turn to stare at him. It was absolutely not what she'd expected. "A hug?"

He nodded. "I can hug. You've spent all day, and yesterday, too, being strong. No one's here right now."

She considered telling him where he could shove his impressions of strength and probable assumptions of her needing a chance to not be strong. But if she did, she wouldn't get a hug, and the idea of his arms around her was much closer to where she wanted to be. Conflicted. It was the definition of her current mood.

She took a step toward him, and he opened his arms to her. Tempting. Sweet Lord, the man was all height and wonderful muscles, and, okay, fine, strength was a theme for the evening. It was all she could do to hold herself back from rushing up and climbing all over him, instead crossing the distance between them like a sane person and letting him close his arms around her.

Pressing her forehead against his chest, she inhaled the scent of him. He smelled vaguely of woods and spicy cinnamon and sand. His hands settled at her lower back, and she sighed, letting the tension fall away. She didn't have to sit or stand straight, carry herself in any certain way, or even remain vertical if she didn't want to.

"Thank you." A hug was enough. She shouldn't press the issue she'd raised before. It'd been unfair of her.

"You're right." His words rumbled in his chest. "I'm hiding. You're my client, and I always keep things simple. But you make me imagine what I shouldn't."

He imagined things about her. Fantasies? Fantasies and imagination were good. She bit her lip, hopeful. Ridiculously so. But she'd had several recent brushes with life-threatening situations, and she wasn't inclined to give up any chance to live in the moment. No regrets.

She looked up into his face. "I imagine our kiss. I enjoyed it. Did you?"

He didn't look away. If anything, his gaze only gathered

more heat, and she felt his answer under her hands pressed against his chest as much as she heard it. "Yes."

"I want more," she whispered. "Do you?"

"Yes." Deeper, darker. His voice rolled through her, and she wanted so much more than a kiss.

But he still held back. He didn't lower his head to hers, and even if she went on tiptoe, the best she might be able to do was press her lips against his jaw. Which she'd like to do. But not until she was sure he wouldn't push her away again. Right now, both of them were being raw and honest, but no decisions had been made.

"You need rest." He sounded like he was looking for a reason to let her go, but his arms didn't loosen around her.

She growled in frustration. Even to her ears, the sound of it was tiny compared to what she figured he could manage. But the corner of his mouth lifted. She narrowed her eyes. "If I was one of your colleagues, a fellow soldier or teammate, would you tell them to go to sleep? After a crazy stressful mission, with bullets flying everywhere and adrenaline flowing. Would you tell them to go take a nap?"

"No." His gaze steadied her, drew her in. But he was holding back.

She raised her eyebrows. "What would you tell them? Be completely honest."

He seemed reluctant, but he also tightened his arms around her. "I'd suggest they go get laid."

She grinned. "Excellent suggestion."

Apparently, they were done hiding behind terms like *client* now, because Zu lowered his head and covered her mouth with his. The kiss was gentle at first, then deepened as she opened for him and pressed herself against him, trying to mold herself along his body. This wasn't a chance moment this time, an accident turned encounter. This was a choice, and she was going to enjoy every pleasure he gave her.

And it was good. As good as she remembered. Better.

She'd shared kisses with men in the past. They'd been polite. Restrained. Even sophisticated, if someone ever thought that word could be applied to a kiss. She'd thought she preferred them. But Zu's kiss, his tongue tasting her, exploring her, coaxing her own tongue to tangle with his, wrenched a groan from her, and she lifted her arms free from being crushed between them so she could wind them around his neck. This was so much better. And if his kiss was this good, the sex was about to blow her mind.

When his mouth left hers, she was gasping for breath. His breathing wasn't steady, either, and she was inordinately pleased about that. His lips skimmed along her jaw, tracing a line of heat to her ear. He whispered, "If you want to stop—"

"No." No stopping. Definitely no slowing down. She kissed the spot where his collarbone peeked out from the collar of his crewneck T-shirt.

"If you want me to stop at any time, tell me, Ying Yue. Any moment, you can tell me to stop and I will. Tell me you understand."

His self-control was everything. He held himself to rigid standards, didn't ever let himself loose. Not even like this. As much as she needed him, she wanted to give him a release he sorely needed, too. Because of that, they had to have absolutely no doubts about each other and this. She drew her head back and gave him a clear look, so he wouldn't worry she wasn't thinking clearly. "I understand."

He lifted a hand to cup her face. "Thank you."

He kissed her gently again, brushing his lips over hers in the lightest possible contact. Then he bent his knees and wrapped his arms around her legs just under her hips and lifted her. A squeak escaped her, and she grabbed at his shoulders for balance, then laughed.

"Which room?" Amusement lightened the rumble of his voice.

Which room, indeed. She was so very selfish. "Not a guest room."

She didn't want to be a guest. Even if this was the only moment they were going to share together. She didn't want to be a guest in his mind.

He didn't answer, only turned away from the guest room and carried her down the hall into his bedroom. He reached a hand up to cradle her head as they went through the doorway, making sure she didn't get a bump as he ducked them both through. He also kicked the door closed behind him. Buck wasn't home yet, but whenever the dog arrived, he'd have to wait. She felt a momentary blip of guilt but yeah, no. No observers, thank you.

Zu set her down on her feet next to his bed and she stayed as close as she could as he straightened in front of her. He helped her shove his shirt up his abs, tugging it over his head and tossing it to the ground. She took in the expanse of his upper chest and abs, all sculpted muscle covered by dark, beautiful, smooth skin. He had a dusting of hair, just enough to tease her palms as she ran her hands over him.

He made a rumbling sound of pleasure, then closed his hands over her shoulders, his thumbs catching on her bra straps under her dress. "Lights or no lights?"

* * *

"Lights. I want to see you, Zu."

He was thankful for Ying Yue's choice, because he definitely wanted to see every part of her. Something deep inside settled, too, knowing they weren't going to hide in the dark as they enjoyed each other. Everything about this was about her making choices, and he agreed with every one of them. He was glad she was choosing him, because he'd wanted her since the moment she'd sat in the car next to him and informed everyone she was going with him.

He slid the fabric off her shoulders, pulling her bra straps to the sides as well, and exposed her smooth shoulders. He bent and kissed the curve where her shoulder met her neck, first on one side and then the other. Beautiful.

She was exploring his body, her hands coasting over his waist and sides. He liked her touch. Then her hands dropped to his waist, and she tugged at the front of his pants. "We are wearing too much clothing."

"Agreed." He was glad she'd chosen loose, easy-fitting fabric for her dress, because it offered no resistance as he slid it down her arms and let the dress fall in a puddle at her feet. He reached around her back and undid her bra, freeing her from that piece of clothing, too.

She was working on the button to his pants and muttering dark curses in Mandarin. He chuckled. "I can curse in a lot of languages, and I think you have some to teach me."

Scowling, she finally got his pants open, and her fingers slid inside, wrapping around the length of his erection.

He sucked in air and took her face in his hands, bending to capture her mouth in a hungry kiss. Even as they drowned in each other, her hand squeezed and tugged ever so lightly. Control? What control? He was going to lose it right here, and he wasn't ready yet. He wanted way more.

He dropped his hands to his waistband and shoved his pants down, stepping toward her to get out of them because she'd decided not to let go of him, and he wasn't planning to ask her to. She was teasing and playing, careful not to hurt him, and he was very happy to be in her clever hands. Instead, he turned and sat on the edge of his bed, pulling her with him. He indulged then, running his hands over the backs of her knees and up her thighs. He gripped the curve of her behind as she stole breathless kisses from him. Her breasts rubbed lightly against his chest in the softest of teases. He got dangerously close again and tugged at the back of one knee, encouraging her to bend and lift her leg. When she did, he lay back in invitation.

Her smile was bright and delighted as she climbed over him. She bit her lip as she looked down and took in all of him, running her hands over his chest again. His cock jerked at the sight of her enjoying him. He skimmed his hands up the sides of her waist until he could brush the undersides of her pert breasts with his thumbs; then he reached higher and teased her taut nipples.

She gasped and her lips parted. She looked straight into his eyes and lifted herself on her knees, a silent request. Or maybe it was a demand. He liked demands coming from her.

He held her hip with one hand and reached for the drawer of his nightstand with the other. He fished for a frustrating minute before he came up with a foil-wrapped condom. He had to flip it between his thumb and forefinger to double-check the expiration date. There were several in there, but the occasion to use them didn't come up all that often, and he liked to be sure, especially to protect Ying Yue from any unanticipated consequences.

She'd been drawing circles over his chest with her fingertips, patient. But she took the condom from him, humming eagerly, and ripped the packet open. She placed the condom and rolled it down the length of him with care, then teased the underside of his balls with a soft laugh.

This woman. He wanted her so badly, he couldn't think straight anymore.

He reached between them and wrapped his hand around his erection, dragging the tip of his penis along her slit. She was wet. So wet. He held himself steady as she lowered herself onto him. It took everything he had not to grab her hips and thrust up into her. She was hot and tight, and he was about to lose his mind with how good she felt around him.

"Zu," she whispered his name has she took him inside of her, slow, inch by inch.

He did put his hands on her hips then, but he held still until she'd taken him to the hilt. He groaned.

Her breath was coming in short pants, and after a moment, she closed her eyes and rocked her hips. Pleasure crashed through him and blew coherent thought to smithereens. He tightened his grip on her hips and lifted his to meet her, letting her set the pace and meeting her with steady thrusts.

Her hair came loose from the knot she kept at the back of her head and fell in a curtain around both their faces as she leaned forward, adjusting the angle of his penetration. It was just the two of them, giving and taking and enjoying.

He let his hands roam over her smooth, silken soft skin, her back and sides, her ass and thighs, urging her.

She responded with a faster pace, and he lifted his hips to thrust harder inside her, hearing her call out as her spine straightened and then curved backward. He steadied her as they moved together, knowing she was on the edge and ready to spin out of control.

"Let go, Ying Yue." He breathed her name. "I've got you."

She came for him, the tiny muscles inside her tightening around the length of him and driving him the last bit of the way over the edge. He sat up, driving as far into her as he could as he held her against his chest. They rode their orgasms together like that, holding on to each other, their breaths ragged and their heartbeats slamming against their chests, against each other.

They were still trembling with the aftershocks for long minutes, maybe forever, and he lay back down, pulling her with him. She rested her head in the hollow of his shoulder with a sigh.

"No guilt."

He opened his eyes, lifted his head so he could look at her. "Hmm?"

She tilted her face up to him. "I'm guessing the minute you regain your senses you're going to feel guilty. I'm preempting. This was glorious, and I have no regrets. So no guilt from you."

Fair. She would've been right, except he'd reveled in every kiss and touch she'd given him. She'd made it clear she wasn't being taken advantage of, and she wanted him every bit as much as he wanted her. He might've been stubborn earlier, but he definitely planned to make up for it now. "You obviously came to your senses way too fast."

He rolled until she was on her back and he was crouched over the top of her. "I obviously have more work to do."

Her eyes went wide. "You..."

He laughed and dipped his head, sucking one of her nipples until she gasped. This time, he planned to taste and explore and learn as many of her sensitive spots as he could find before they both lost their minds. He lifted his head and smiled at her. "I'm going to spoil you, Ying Yue, and enjoy every minute of it. And when you are calling my name, begging me, I'll be ready for you."

CHAPTER TEN

Hh"ow many showers do you have?"

Ying Yue was in love with Zu's home. She hadn't been here long, hadn't explored every nook and cranny yet. But he'd led her downstairs wrapped in his shirt and into this room. He'd touched a panel just inside the doorway and more lighting revealed a room dedicated solely to a giant custom hot tub set into the floor. Across the room, an alcove lined with what looked like volcanic stone featured a rain water showerhead. He tugged her gently toward it, helping her out of his shirt as he turned on the water.

"It gets hot here on the island. I like to take multiple showers a day, given the chance." He sounded smug.

She didn't hold it against him. Not one bit. They rinsed off thoroughly, helping each other with enthusiastic caresses. "Can this get any better?"

"Mmm." He touched another panel as they left the shower and crossed the few steps to the hot tub.

The entire wall lifted to open the room to the backyard. The moon had risen now, and she could see out across the lawn and beyond. To one side, there was a cabana and a private pool they must've walked past when they'd arrived. And past the small gate, there was the ocean.

"Wow." She took in the gorgeous view as she stepped down into the heated water.

He steadied her with one hand until she was seated shoulder deep. Then he joined her, pulling her into his lap so she could lean back with her head cradled in the hollow of his shoulder, floating in water perfectly heated to soak all the aches from her body.

Of course, she'd forgotten about most of them while they'd been together earlier. And maybe she'd earned herself a few new aches with his help, but she had absolutely no regrets about those, either. "You were right."

"Hmm?" His wordless inquiry rumbled through his chest behind her.

"A hot soak is definitely doing me a world of good."

He chuckled.

"I thought I was supposed to stay inside the whole time." She stared out into the open night. It was beautiful, but she wondered about the exception to his rules. She couldn't help it. Her mind latched onto things and questioned everything, even when she didn't necessarily want to. It made sense to her to stay hidden.

"You are inside." He pressed his lips against her temple. "And you're with me."

There was a hefty dose of arrogance suffused in his statement, but she smiled. So far he'd been thoughtful and considerate. A touch of arrogance balanced him in her eyes. The more she spent time with him, the more she wanted to experience all the facets of him.

"You also asked me to keep the curtain closed in the guest room." Which made her sit up in his lap and turn so she could look at him, the incoming breeze whispering cool across her exposed shoulders.

He nodded, not a sign of guilt in his expression. If anything, a hint of a smile hovered around his full lips. "The guest room windows both face the front of the house. The front drive is gated, but you can still see the street, which means someone on the street can see you. It would take a lot more for someone to approach from the ocean. There isn't public access to this beach for a long way in both directions. You can enjoy the views from the back of the house while you're here."

While you're here.

The last phrase made her slip off his lap and sit more deeply in the water. It was a gentle reminder of how temporary this was. Probably. Of course this was temporary.

He didn't try to pull her back into his lap, only relaxed next to her as she pondered. Idly, she traced her fingers along his thigh beneath the water. The man had walked through the house stark naked without any hesitation. The idea of him walking around in all his substantial glory over the next few days was something she could cheerfully focus on, and maybe she could tuck away the question of what would happen next for the time being. She wanted to enjoy this. Right here. Because if she'd learned one thing through the course of the last forty-eight hours and more, it was that there was no telling what might happen from one moment to the next.

Movement caught her eye, out there in the night. A shadow emerged from the tree line, and she sat straight up again with a splash.

"Easy." Zu's hand caressed her spine. "He's a friendly."

Buck came into the light, pausing on the lanai to scuff his paws in a strange motion before trotting right into the room they were in. He had a brown paper bag in his mouth, which he placed on the floor within arm's reach.

She thought she saw a logo on the bag. "Is that... takeout?"

"Apparently." Zu stood and leaned over, momentarily distracting her as she admired the curve of his very fine behind.

He unrolled the slightly slobbered top and pulled out another bag with a note stapled to the front. Zu ripped it off the bag and held it closer for her to read. In neat letters the note read ZU. WE PUT THIS ON YOUR TAB.

She looked from Buck to Zu incredulously. "Earlier today, you put him in a taxi."

Zu crumpled up the note and opened the second bag, peering inside. "Yup."

"And the car took him around for takeout, then brought him back here?" It was crazy.

"No." Zu lifted his head and stared at Buck. "Where's the extra sauce?"

Buck sat and whined.

"You didn't eat it did you?" Zu's voice dropped an octave. "You know what happens to your butt when you sneak the sauce."

Buck pulled his head back, then whapped the first bag with his paw.

Zu leaned forward again and looked inside. "Okay. It's there."

Ying Yue closed her mouth. She'd seen people talking to their dogs before. She had. But never had it seemed so much like clear exchange as what she was witnessing now. "What happens to him when he sneaks sauce?"

Zu finished examining the contents of the second bag and put it back within the first. Then he pulled out a plastic bag, unwrapping it to reveal a sizable raw bone. He held it out to Buck, who took it carefully. "*Braaf*, good boy."

Buck took his prize out onto the lanai.

"It's too much for his GI tract. He regrets it when he gets the runs. I'm not real thrilled about it, either." Zu settled back into the water next to her. "To clarify my answer to your earlier question, the taxi didn't bring him back here. I know the driver. He took Buck on a ride up to one of the nearby parks with hiking trails and let Buck out there. He knows the way back from there."

Ying Yue slipped back to Zu's side. She liked the little touches and caresses they gave each other as they talked. "So, Buck just came home on his own?"

Zu shrugged. "Yeah."

Sure. No big deal. Ying Yue laughed. "I've dealt with personal assistants who couldn't act with so much independence. And he stopped to pick up dinner?"

Zu nodded. "It's a little shack on one of the main roads on the way back. We stop there once in a while. Buck stops in more often."

"The two of you have a system going." She admired the big red dog. As Buck lay on the lanai with his back to them, the ridge formed by the short fur growing in the opposite direction from the rest of his coat stood out along his spine.

"It's just been us a long time." Zu might have sounded lonely. But he moved on before she could ask about it. "Pua should have a loaner laptop ready for you by tomorrow. Raul will drop it off before he moves into the house next door for the time you're going to be here."

"Oh." Ying Yue perked up. A laptop would be extremely helpful. She might've thought about one once she'd had a chance to settle, but she'd have felt bad asking to use Zu's. "I'm allowed to use one while I'm in hiding?"

Zu tipped his head as he looked at her. "I've got a VPN established here. Anything you do will be untraceable to this location. There's no reason you can't get online with a few precautions and start putting your personal and business affairs back in order."

Happiness spread through her chest in a succession of small, excited bursts. She'd thought her life was on hold. He was facilitating a whole lot more than internet access for her. She'd be able to access her finances, cancel her credit cards, and maybe order new ones sent to the island somewhere for her to pick up when she could. She could reach out to her employers and try to persuade them to let her keep her job, maybe even resume some of her work. He'd given her a head start on getting back to everything she'd left hanging.

"Thank you." She thought about Raul. "You're bringing your team members close as backup."

Zu nodded. "I've got solid security designed around this place, but the longer you hide, the more likely they will be to find you. Before you go to sleep tonight, we'll talk about emergency precautions and what you do if certain scenarios come up. Tomorrow, we'll make even more plans together. In the meantime, Raul and Taz will be next door."

"Will Arin be coming, too?" Ying Yue had liked the fierce woman and her giant dog partner.

"Not where you'll be able to see her regularly." Zu frowned. "Your father's security team interacted with her."

"Ah." Ying Yue slumped until the water came up to her chin. There was the suspicion again. Someone on her father's security team could still be working to kidnap her. If they knew Arin and Zu were worried... "Is Arin in danger?"

She didn't want the people she was meeting, people who'd helped her, to be in harm's way because of her.

"Arin can take care of herself." Zu delivered the statement with the weight of conviction behind it. Ying Yue must've heard the same claim in countless television shows and movies, read it in books. But when Zu said it, it wasn't a dramatic line. It was a simple statement of fact. He reached out and hooked a finger under Ying Yue's chin. "Arin knows how to take precautions. We're actually hoping someone tries to come at her to get information on you. If we can capture them and question them, we can gain information on why they're so determined to get hold of you again."

"Oh." Ying Yue still didn't like the idea of Arin putting herself out there. But Ying Yue felt she'd be doing Arin a disservice in thinking of Arin as being out there as bait. More accurately, Arin was using herself as a lure for prey the woman was hunting herself. "You all have dedicated yourselves to an extremely challenging profession."

His gaze was dark and serious as he stared at her, unwavering. "It's worth it."

"Thank you." She had a whole lot of other words bouncing around in her head at high speed, but it all distilled to the single phrase. Everything he and his team were doing for her had all been started before there'd been any promise of payment. The contract her father had offered had been a formality, an acknowledgment, more for the benefit of her father's people than for the Search and Protect team.

They'd done this for Ying Yue, because of who they were and because it was simply what they did. Gratitude welled up and almost spilled over as tears, but it wasn't just that. She felt valued.

Her life had shattered the minute she'd been snatched from Singapore, but who she was had changed because of these people.

CHAPTER ELEVEN

Laptop arrived." Zu stood in his living room, looking out toward the ocean as a few clouds moved past. Wind was coming from the northeast this morning, and a few rain showers had passed by just after dawn. He'd raised the far wall facing the beach again to take advantage of the view and the ocean breeze. There was really no chance of a shooter getting any kind of angle into the house from that direction unless they were on a boat out on the water. He had too many sensors on the beach approaching the back of his property for someone to get that close. So it was reasonably safe to open up the house for Ying Yue to enjoy. The minute Ying Yue had it in her hands, she logged on. "No problems."

"Oh good!" Pua's voice was full of bubbly energy on the phone. "I'm glad my instructions were enough. If she needs any help, boss, she can call me direct or get on a web conference with me and I can walk her through it. I checked her financials yesterday and there's been no unusual activity since she went missing, so there's no need to dispute any weird charges or anything like that."

"It's appreciated." Zu paused and glanced back at Ying Yue.

She'd sat perched on a stool at the breakfast counter in the kitchen, her long black hair twisted into a knot on top of her head, secured with a couple of chopsticks she'd found in one of his kitchen drawers. She had a notepad at her side with a growing list of things she wanted to do. No question about it, she was happier being constructive and busy. Sitting and waiting would've driven her crazy. He was learning more and more of who she was as she had the opportunity to reclaim portions of her life.

And he had a small hope he had contributed to some of the happiness he was seeing in her, from the smile on her face to the light in her eyes. Her decision to share his bed was a gift he wasn't going to waste any more time denying. He planned to protect her and explore whatever this was between them for the short time they were together wholeheartedly.

"Any progress on our investigation?" He lowered his voice and stepped out onto the lanai. He wasn't planning to hide the information from Ying Yue, but he'd rather relay the information to her after he was finished speaking to Pua or set up a conference call if Ying Yue was going to participate.

"Sort of." Pua sounded uncharacteristically frustrated. "I can see plenty of reasons for someone to want to have leverage against Mr. Jiang. He's built himself a very extensive empire internationally with manufacturing sites scattered across the Asian continent, mostly specializing in the production of high-end personal electronics. He's diversified his business, though, with entrepreneurial ventures in a few tangential fields. He's legit in terms of business, with a few shady spots here and there, but no alarming loyalties to any one government or organization. He does a good job of being a neutral businessman."

"Okay." Zu could ask Ying Yue about some of her father's background, but he figured she'd have spoken up sooner if she thought she knew why anyone would be taking action against her father now.

"And he's definitely here for a secure business deal," Pua continued. "It's all sorts of hush-hush, with a few signs pointing to US government contract. Maybe NSA? I'm still poking around discreetly and doing what I can not to set off any virtual alarms anywhere."

"Seems like a good reason to kidnap his daughter." Zu could see why Julian Nilsson and Jake Silbermann had been so sure Ying Yue had been kidnapped to be held as leverage against her father. The both of them were very on edge. Still... "There's a 'but' in there, isn't there?"

"Yeah." Pua paused. "And may I say, boss, you are much more talky-talky than you usually are. Are you sure aliens didn't come and take over your body to live inside your brain or something?"

"Pua." He tried not to growl out the warning.

"Yeah, oh, that sounds like you now. Whew. Okay. Got it. Yes. Focus." Pua breathed in and out quickly. "Here's what's bothering me. There's no actual contract out there for one Jiang Ying Yue. There's no contract to kidnap any member of Mr. Jiang's family or household. Based on what's out there now and over the past several months, no one was looking to hire a freelance or private contract organization for the job. So while there's plenty of information to show why someone would want to kidnap her because of who her father is, there's no trail to follow for who ordered it done or even who carried it out. I got nothing."

Interesting. So either these people were good enough to

hide the information from the best, or there was a different approach to how all of this had come to happen.

"Any progress on identifying the suspect Ying Yue identified?" Zu figured Pua had been conducting her inquiries from multiple angles.

"Yes and no." Pua cursed under her breath. "I got the hotel security video feed. I have a few partial images of the guy's face, but he was fairly aware of where cameras were and never directly faced any of them. I'm running what images I've got through facial recognition databases, but it's not a fast process. Unless we get extremely lucky, this could take a long while before we get a hit, if we do at all. All I can tell you is he's not a major player. He doesn't have any outstanding accomplishments, so to speak, in the uber dark world of super-secret mercenary operatives, where there'd be an instant hit on his face. So that's sort of good news? But not enough information, and I'm still looking."

Fair. It was possible Kokua would apprehend the suspect before Pua found any more definitive information on him.

"I've also got what security feeds I could from the airport, boss." She had been very busy overnight, apparently. Zu made a note to ping Arin and have her check to be sure Pua had eaten a real meal. "This guy was there and part of the team who attacked her. I think you were right, based on how it all plays out on the camera feeds. The attackers herded her father and his security people away from her, then focused on covering the men who closed in to grab her. The guy she spotted was in the intended getaway car, and it pulled away as the police started arriving. He's got help, a decent amount of it."

Not reassuring. He might need to think about calling in some favors to supplement his people. He'd been careful to grow Search and Protect slowly, putting together a cohesive group with strong bonds and loyalty, not only to him but to each other. The drawback was a moment like this, when he was faced with a mission that required a bigger team than what he had now. He'd need to look at some of his files on potential candidates and maybe subcontract a few to come in for this.

"Boss." Pua sounded hesitant now. "I think you think the obvious answer isn't the reason all this is happening to Ying Yue. I'm going to run some random searches to see if I flush out something unexpected. Can we get some information from her on her work and what she was doing around the time she was kidnapped to give me a few places to start?"

"Yes." There was no need to think it through. It made sense, and he was already curious anyway.

"Is she ready to think about it?"

Well, that was a consideration. Ying Yue had been holding up amazingly well, but she'd also had a lot happen in the space of a very few days. He wouldn't have been surprised if a person needed therapy for any one of the number of things Ying Yue had experienced from the moment she'd been taken from Singapore to now. She could be unaware of the pressure building up inside her as she continued to move forward and not react to those things.

"I'll ask her." He thought he knew how she'd decide to proceed, but he wasn't going to make any assumptions.

"Okay. I'll be here. Just let me know."

"Thanks, Pua."

He ended the call and glanced at Buck. His partner lay half dozing on the cool stone of the lanai. If anything or anyone was approaching, Buck was likely to hear it first.

*   *   *

Ying Yue looked up from the laptop as Zu walked back in from the lanai. She'd tried not to pay attention, out of politeness, but she'd totally failed. He'd been talking to Pua, and not only had she wanted to express her thanks to the technical analyst for the use of the laptop, but she also thought Pua might've had some news. It might've been too much to hope her kidnapper had been caught and spilled all the information the authorities might need to track down anyone else involved in her kidnapping, but one could dream, right?

Zu gave her a warm, small smile as he walked over to her. He hooked a foot around the leg of the stool next to her and pulled it out so he could sit next to her. "You want to ask questions and have me answer them, or do you want me to just tell you what Pua told me and then ask any questions you have left?"

She smiled, relieved. Honestly, her experience with other security personnel had always been a lot of effort when it came to communication. In the past, they'd been invariably convinced she only needed to know key details to get her cooperation so they could focus on the broader situation. She preferred to make informed decisions with the big picture in mind.

"Tell me first, please." She closed the laptop so he had her full attention, but she kept the notepad close in case she wanted to scribble down any thoughts. "And I'll ask you as we go if I need clarification."

Zu started talking, and she tried her best to wait until she was sure he'd completed each thought before she asked any questions. He was pretty thorough, though, so she didn't have many as he shared what information Pua had found. Once he was done, she slouched on the stool.

"Are you okay?" He sounded solicitous as he rose from his stool. "Can I get you a drink, something else?"

She shook her head. "I was really hoping to hear that it was all over."

She looked up at him and tried to give him a smile, even though it might be a weak one. Then she thought about what she'd said.

"Not that I'm in a rush to leave you." She wasn't. But she paused and tried to give him a better understanding of what she was feeling. "I'd just rather be here with you because I want to be as opposed to waiting for whoever these people are to find me."

"Us." The one word was full of firm reassurance. "You won't be alone, even if they do find this place."

She nodded, grateful.

"It's okay." He moved around the breakfast bar to the counter area, where he had an Asian-style electronic hot water heater, the kind that maintained three liters or so at specified temperature. She had one in her own apartment. It was much more convenient than a kettle on a stove. He pulled two mugs from a cabinet and a box of tea from another. "Arin and Pua both say tea is a good thing to have when there's too much to think through at one time."

"Do you like tea?" She watched as he rinsed both mugs with steaming water first before filling each of them. Then he opened individually wrapped tea bags and set them in the hot water to steep.

"Yeah." He turned back to her and placed a mug by the laptop, safely away from the notepad. "It's black tea, so let it steep a few minutes."

"Okay." Interested, she looked at the tea bag and attached label. "What kind of tea is this? I'm not familiar with the brand. Is this some kind of papercraft label attached to the tea bag?"

He returned to his seat next to her. "My mother sends it to me. The label is made using dried banana leaves and each tea bag is hand tied with twine from dried banana leaves, too. Those little colored beads attached to the top of the label are made from recycled paper."

"Oh wow." For a moment, she let go of her immediate problems and let herself fall into the distraction of something new to her. "This tea have meaning to you? Or your mother?"

Zu shrugged. "It's a tea we enjoy from Africa, and some of the proceeds are donated to a good cause, so we like to support it in this small way. It's also a nice tea."

"It smells lovely." She thought it smelled a bit floral as the steam wafted up from the mug. "It's nice that your mother sends you a thing you like. My mother sends me little things, too."

He rolled his shoulders. Maybe he was uncomfortable talking about family? "I've been grown and gone from the house a long time. I try to stay away so I don't bring trouble home by accident. But I make sure she has ways to send me things when she wants, and I send her emails or postcards sometimes."

Ying Yue raised an eyebrow. "But not as often as she'd like."

He smiled in return. "No."

She wondered what kind of trouble he would be worried about bringing home, but then she considered his profession. In his line of work, she imagined he might make enemies. His home was beautifully designed and very comfortable, but it was also protected by multiple layers of state-of-the-art security. He'd walked her through some of them last night and additional layers first thing in the morning when there was daylight to see the precautions outside. She'd learned more about private security in those conversations with him than she ever had through the years of childhood and young adulthood within her father's household.

He plucked his tea bag out of his mug and placed it on a small plate he'd brought over as well. After another moment, he asked her, "Do you feel comfortable talking to me about yourself and your family?"

She followed his example, removing the tea bag from her own mug. "It'd be nice to pretend you simply want to know more about me, but this is part of the whole situation, isn't it?"

He nodded. "It'd help us if we understood why you were kidnapped."

She sipped the tea. He was right, it was definitely a good thing to have tea when there was so much to think through all at once. "You don't think it's because of my father's business."

"That angle is already being researched." Zu made the statement without heat or any hint of how he thought it was progressing. "We're exploring the angles that might be unexpected, less likely."

"Okay." She liked the tea, she decided. It was floral and fresh, with a natural sweetness to it. She normally added sugar to her black tea, but she didn't find herself wanting to ask for any for this one. "Where do I start?"

CHAPTER TWELVE

Zu leaned forward, taking in what she had to say. "So you work for nonprofit initiatives or businesses looking to donate some of their profits to charities."

Ying Yue's eyes widened. "Yes. Most people take what I do at face value and don't really care to get into the details."

Zu smiled. He liked the frank way she called out behavior others might politely ignore or excuse. She didn't have a sharp edge to her observations, either, no bitterness or resentment.

"I need to understand. It's not my area of expertise, but you might be surprised how often my work touches on what you do." Social change often meant making those in power uncomfortable. A lot of philanthropists went missing when they had too much integrity and became too good at making progress on behalf of their causes. Search and Protect hadn't been called in to find and extract such individuals yet, but he'd done it in past missions with another organization. "Is there an aspect of how you do your work that you're especially good at?"

"Well, I have a background in nonprofit capacity building, and..." She paused, then continued, "I have a PhD in international tax law and policy. It doesn't seem consequential at all to review my academic credentials, though."

He gave her hand what he hoped was an encouraging squeeze. Her hand was small in his, and when her fingers tightened around his in return...it meant more than he was willing to consider right now. She was his focus. He could analyze whatever was going on inside his own head later. "What specifically were you working on before you were taken?"

"Kidnapped?" She gave the word bite.

"You don't have to say it to acknowledge what happened." He didn't want her to flog herself with reality to face it. "You can be kind to yourself without hiding from what happened."

She pressed her lips together. "Thinking about it takes courage, and I keep thinking I need to rip the Band-Aid off or give the evil its name or some other convenient metaphor. I feel like I need to face it and call it out so I don't hide from it."

"It happened. I know it and you know it and we'll sift through the details together to figure out what we're facing." He wasn't a therapist. Hell, he was bad about handling emotions in general, whether it was his own or someone else's. Or so he'd been told by more than one ex. He definitely had enough people who'd called him an asshole in the past to believe it. But he gave her words that he hoped would help her know she wouldn't have to do this alone.

She nodded, fine lines smoothing out across her brow.

"I'd been in Singapore for almost two years already, working with a few nonprofit organizations to build their capacity. I spent a lot of time communicating directly to stakeholders."

There was a key word. What Pua did with internet and database searches, sifting through data and running searches on key words, Zu did in conversations. He picked out the thing that would lead him to more specific information on what he needed to know. "Tell me more about the stakeholders. What is a stakeholder for a nonprofit organization? What kind of communications did you have with them? Just email or remote? Or face-to-face?"

"It depends." Ying Yue gave him a brief smile and squeezed his hand back. "The term *stakeholder* is fairly general. It can apply to any given individual or even groups that have expressed interest in the nonprofit."

"Are they the people who donate money?"

"Yes, and more people, too." She opened his fingers and lifted her hand out of his, instead tapping each of his fingertips as she continued to elaborate. "There are people directly involved in the nonprofit, such as board members. Stakeholders could be the very people the nonprofit is intended to serve. They could also be foundations providing grants to the nonprofit or volunteers donating their time in place of monetary support. Take it a step further and stakeholders could be those indirectly involved, like vendors hired to provide supplies or services to the nonprofit, either for day to day operations or special events."

Well, maybe there was something there, but the field was still wide open with too many possibilities. They needed to narrow it down.

"Were you in direct communication with any particular stakeholders?"

She tipped her head to one side. "Several, but not too many to count."

"Can you make a list?" He could give those to Pua to do some poking around on their activities, things Ying Yue might not have been privy to.

"Yes." Ying Yue reopened the laptop. "They'd all be in my calendar, which I sync to the cloud. I keep my schedule up to date."

It was a solid habit for an organized, detail-oriented professional. It was also potentially a way her kidnappers had gotten familiar with her schedule and planned when they would take her. "Can I get a copy of your schedule?"

She shot him a questioning glance but didn't say no. "I can make a PDF. Do you want just a calendar overview or the details of each meeting, too?"

"If you feel comfortable, the details could be very helpful." He hesitated, then thought the openness Ying Yue was giving to him should be returned with honesty on his part. For her, he was going way beyond the need to know. "Or you could provide Pua with access to your calendar so she can conduct a direct analysis."

He normally wouldn't have mentioned what he'd intended to ask one of his people to do, but this was different. Ying Yue deserved more from him.

Ying Yue studied him for moment, and he thought he could see dismay, then a hint of fear, then acceptance flash across her face in fleeting changes of her expression. Her lips pursed and the corners of her eyes creased. Fine lines appeared and then faded from her brow. "Give me Pua's email address, and I'll give her temporary access."

He nodded, and then gave her the information. She tapped a few keys.

"Done. I suppose I should change the passwords to everything online?" Her voice wobbled briefly.

"Not yet." He hated to add further strain, but again, she deserved to know more about what he planned. "We'll be watching your accounts for signs of someone watching your activity. After we nail down who is trying to take you, then we can help you get your privacy back."

Ying Yue gave him a minute nod. Her posture had been getting progressively more and more tense, her expression becoming closed off.

Enough. This was enough for now. He didn't want to put her through any more than necessary. "Pua can get started on this. Why don't we do something different?"

"Like what?" Ying Yue narrowed her eyes at him, but her shoulders relaxed a fraction.

"Let's get you up and moving."

"What kind of moving?" Now her voice took on a note of play.

Delighted was not enough to describe the warmth and energy shooting through him as he stood and pulled her off the stool. He gave her his best devilish grin. "The kind to get the blood flowing and the heart rate up."

He kept her hand in his and headed for the lanai.

"Outside?" She came along with him, didn't pull back. But she did question him.

Ying Yue always questioned.

He liked that about her.

* * *

Ying Yue sucked in air as she glared at Zu, stepping to the side as he forced her to circle in the small area between his house and the high privacy wall of his property. She had to keep her attention on him even as she avoided the low-hanging branches of trees planted along the fence line to obstruct the view of the neighbors. If she could avoid getting swatted in the face by branches, they provided wonderful shade from the hot sun, for which she was extremely grateful. There was even a cool breeze coming off the ocean. Buck lay nearby, head on his paws, watching.

And there was Zu, wearing a huge curved mitt, swinging at her head.

She ducked under the swing the way he taught her and came up throwing a jab.

"Nice." He stepped back and held both mitts up so she could see the circles in the curved centers. Focus mitts, he'd called them. "Crisscross, ten of them. I'll count."

She took a breath and stepped up to him, punching each of the mitts in a crisscross pattern, right-left-right-left.

"Ten. Good."

Over the course of the last hour, he'd taught her the basics of punching, kicking, and even using her knees and elbows. She stepped back, dropping her hands and flexing them inside the wraps he'd helped her put on to protect herself. He was right—with them on, she felt like she could hit anything, and they weren't as bulky as the big boxing gloves she'd tried at the gym. She made a mental note to buy a set of her own.

"One self-defense lesson is going to make a difference, you think?" She watched as he put the focus mitts away on a small set of shelves sheltered from the elements.

He stepped around a stack of huge old tires strung up on thick chains, a makeshift punching bag like none she'd ever seen before. She wondered when he trained on those. She'd like to watch. There were PVC pipes put together in a sturdy frame for a person even as big as Zu to do dips and canvas bags filled with beach sand sitting to one side to be used as all-purpose weights. He'd made this area for himself. It was do-it-yourself, sturdy, and no-nonsense.

"One lesson? No." Zu held out a water bottle to her. "But the drills we just practiced, you can do by yourself at a gym or shadow box in the privacy of whatever room you're in at home or on travel."

She took a sip, slow, so she wouldn't upset her stomach with the cold water, as overheated as she was. "And the practice will help."

He nodded, taking a sip from another water bottle. "It becomes muscle memory. In an emergency, you might not have time to think, but your body will react, and that's what will make a difference."

Emergency, like a future attack. She shivered, and it wasn't because of the chill of the water she'd just swallowed.

"Panicked defense?" She was skeptical and more afraid than she wanted to acknowledge. It would be more comforting to try to leave her experiences behind like they were the worst thing that could ever happen to her.

"You're not ever going to want to get into any kind of drawn-out fight. No one wise ever wants to." He set down the water bottle and held out his hand. She placed hers into his and he began unwinding the wrap from her wrist and hand. "You strike for a chance to run away."

His touch was gentle and comforting. The fine tremors along her spine faded.

"What if I miss my chance to run?" she asked. Her words sounded flat, even to her. It was what had happened, after all. She gave him her other hand as he finished freeing her from one wrap.

He brushed his lips over her knuckles, then started to

unwind the rest of the wrap. "You go along and watch. Visualize what you'll do to get away when the opportunity comes. Keep it simple, and you'll have more chance of success."

His words were cool and rational. What he was suggesting sounded actionable. The fear building up inside her eased back. She didn't need to turn into a badass battle monster, just surprise an attacker enough to give herself time to get away.

"Visualize," she whispered as she rubbed her hands. They felt a little tacky after having been inside the wraps for their workout session.

"Yes." Zu caught her gaze for a long moment, until she started breathing easier. He was completely serious. He left the wraps hanging over the dip rack to air out. "You have a way better chance of remembering what you planned to do and executing if you bide your time and visualize what you hope to do before you do it."

"So you and Arin and Raul all visualize what you'll do?" She guessed he had a point. It was better than making it up as you went.

Zu nodded. "Anytime we go anywhere. We get into an elevator and we assess the people who get in with us and we consider what we'll do if one or all of them attack. Enter a room? Same thing. Walk down a street, we look for potential threats and consider how we'll neutralize them."

"That's a lot of visualization." The amount of awareness, readiness, the sheer energy it must take blew her away.

Zu only met her incredulous look with a bland stare. "We don't get bored."

She laughed then. Oh, she didn't think he was joking, not about the visualization and being ready for any threat. She believed he and all his teammates did exactly what he said. But he saw the overwhelming aspect of it, too, and she enjoyed his sense of humor.

"I'm all sweaty and I'd love to take a shower, but I'd hate to track sand into your house." She looked down at herself. He'd dropped her to the sand-covered ground several times over the course of the hour, showing her how to fall while minimizing the hurt. She was coated pretty much head to toe in it. Maybe the shower in the soaking room was the best bet, but she didn't like the idea of getting sand in there, in that glorious tub, either.

"Here." He took her by the hand and jerked his head for her to follow. He looked past her briefly. "Buck. *Blijf.*"

As they walked away, Buck remained where he was and simply heaved a big sigh.

Behind a bamboo screen was another nook. This one had huge, flat pieces of stone set into the ground to make a floor with a drain at the center. More stones lined an alcove set into the side of the house. Not one, not two, but three showerheads were set into the arch. Zu turned several handles and water rained down into the alcove.

She let him tug her under the spray, clothes and all. The water was wonderfully warm, not hot, but perfect for the outdoor area. He joined her, his big hands heavy on her hips, and she tilted her face up to him for a kiss. She was a different kind of winded when he let her up for air, and she smiled when he trailed kisses along her jaw. Even the ghosts of her earlier tension melted away.

He nipped at her earlobe. "Sand gets everywhere. We should be very careful to get the sand out of every nook and cranny, or it could irritate sensitive skin."

She laughed softly and tugged at the T-shirt plastered to his chest. "We should've undressed before we stepped in here."

He shrugged, unrepentant. "We have to wash the clothes anyway. I always rinse mine out here to save the washing machine from the sand."

Practical. He always made sense. She made a face at him anyway, her heart lighter as he grinned down at her. The hunger in his eyes woke an answering heat in her chest, too, radiating out to her extremities until her nipples tightened. She could blame the shower, but she was getting wet in other ways, too.

He kissed her and helped her peel the tank and the borrowed sweatpants off. Then he took off his own clothes. They stood for a moment, taking in the sight of each other. He was perfect, toned and sculpted, standing in that relaxed, ready-to-take-action way of his. And he had a glorious erection.

She stepped to him, running her hands over his shoulders and chest, helping the water wash away all the sand. He did the same, his hands roaming over her shoulders and back, pausing and gripping her behind. They each took their time and indulged, touching and caressing, following the water over skin. By the time he kissed her again, she was sure every grain of sand that could be possibly hiding in her hair, in the curve of her ear, or anywhere else on her body had been rinsed away. She wondered, wildly, what they were going to do next because the stone wall was rough and the floor . . .

He scooped her up in his arms, his full lips curved in a wicked smile. "Now, we can go for a hot soak."

CHAPTER THIRTEEN

Zu woke and immediately stretched out his awareness, struggling to identify what brought him out of the deepest sleep he'd had in a long time. The alarm cut through the silence of the household a second time, low but more than enough to bring him fully awake and alert. At the side of the bed, Zu could make out the dark outline of Buck, standing at the ready.

Emergency.

Zu untangled himself as gently as he could from Ying Yue, but quickly, so he could reach over to the nightstand and grab his phone. The screen showed bright despite the night setting, and as soon as he read the alert message he threw aside the covers and got out of bed. As he moved, he dialed the secure line.

"Boss?" Pua's voice was subdued and reduced to a whisper.

Ice shot through him. She shouldn't be at the office. Raul and Arin were positioned elsewhere. There would be no one else there with Pua at this time of night.

"You're inside?" He stood and put the phone on speaker so he could get into his closet. He flipped on the lights without warning Ying Yue. Gun. Harness. Backup weapon. And yeah, pants. He needed pants.

"Yes. I was here late, running a few more queries. Normal security measures kicked in when they broke in the front door, and I made sure to lock myself in my office. I followed procedure, just like the practice drills." The drive to move, to do something, eased a fraction when he heard her confirm her position. Her office was as reinforced as the most state-of-the-art panic room. She could wait out almost anything inside her office.

Pua didn't raise her voice. If anything, she got quieter. "They got to my door and shouted they were cops, and I gave them the answer we practiced. I said they had to wait for you. But, boss, I can see everything in our headquarters via the security feed. No way those are cops out there."

Ying Yue appeared in the doorway to the closet. "What is it?"

If it'd been anyone else, he'd have ignored them, but because it was Ying Yue, he hit mute on his phone quickly. "There's an attack on Search and Protect headquarters."

"What?" Ying Yue darted back to the bedside and re-trieved the shorts she'd worn the day before. She didn't demand any additional explanations from him. She didn't get in his way. She only came far enough into his closet to snag one of his fresh button-down shirts off a hanger. Then she was back out of the closet again.

He unmuted his phone. "What's your status now?"

"I'm still inside my office." Pua's response was chip-per, but the higher pitch and tremor in her voice told him more. Ah, Pua, fear wasn't supposed to be part of the job description. It was a risk, yes, always when working with a private contract organization and especially recently, considering the kinds of operations Search and Protect had been shutting down in conjunction with the Honolulu Police Department. But the visible targets were supposed to be him and Buck, Raul and Taz, and Arin and King. Not Pua.

She kept going. "My monitors tell me HPD is on their way, but, boss, those people, they're trying to get in here with some kind of laser, like this is a bank vault or something. I hit the ultimate panic safeties and the reinforced barriers came down around my office. I didn't lie to them. No one can get me out of here now but you, for real."

There was a pause.

In a very tiny voice, Pua continued. "I'm sorry."

"No worries." He patted himself down and did a mental check. He had everything necessary to move out. He needed to get there fast. Honolulu Police Department would beat him there, but she was right, HPD wouldn't be able to get her out of there short of taking the whole building apart. "Sit tight. I'm on my way."

"Okay, boss." There it was, the absolute faith his people had in him. Every one of them expressed it in a different way. Their faith in him gave him purpose and he wouldn't fail Pua when she needed him now.

Pua ended the call.

He needed to get to her. He turned and there was Ying Yue, standing next to Buck. "You need to stay here."

He touched the panel next to his bedside and reinforced plating came down across the windows. It wasn't just in this room. It was happening throughout the house. "I'm putting this place on lockdown, and you'll be secure in here."

Ying Yue shook her head. "I heard. What are you going

to do, rush over there? Then how will you get back here without them following you? You know this is my fault."

"It's not." It was his fault. Search and Protect was his organization, his team. Pua was one of his to protect.

"Pua's not made to be out in the field like you and the rest of your team." Ying Yue started heading toward the door to the hallway. She was forcing him to follow her out of the room. "She's going to need you, but your head will be here with me if I stay here. We're the two most vulnerable people under your watch, and it's going to stretch you too thin to have us in two different places. That's what they're trying to do, spread you out so you can't cover every possibility, and then they'll take advantage of a weakness somewhere."

She was right. He wasn't going to waste breath arguing with her about it. Instead, he stalked after her and thought hard about the unlikely options. The choices no one sane would make.

She hit the landing at the bottom of the stairs and turned to face him. "I'm going with you. You can't leave me here and you can't leave her there. I'll go and follow every instruction you give me, and we'll get her out, get her someplace safe. We can do that, right?"

He stared at Ying Yue. Her lips were pressed together in an expression of determination, and she held herself straight and tall. She wasn't just being kind or generous or brave. Ying Yue cared about Pua, yes. Ying Yue was also giving herself agency. This was her decision, and she was taking action. She wasn't about to let him make a decision that could lead to horrible things, not when they'd happened because of her. If something was going to be her fault, it was because she'd made the decision to do it herself.

He lifted his phone and dialed Raul.

"Bravo here." Raul was alert and his words had a snap to them. He would've received the alert, too, but procedure was for Zu to call the team. They didn't want too many calls going back and forth in this situation. Best to have a clear line of communication for maximum efficiency, minimal confusion.

"Are you geared up?"

"Ready, sir."

"Get here with your canine, now. We'll take my vehicle."

* * *

Ying Yue sat in the back of the SUV and struggled into the bulletproof vest Zu had handed her as they'd gotten into the car. She'd held her breath as they pulled out of the driveway and drove down several small roads with no headlights. Zu had been wearing some sort of goggles—maybe night vision—and taken the vehicle onto the roads with absolutely no running lights at all. Only once they hit the main highway did he turn on the headlights and drive normally.

Forget caffeine, the adrenaline rushing through her was enough to keep her alert for the night and the foreseeable future. Worry for Pua intertwined with Ying Yue's nervousness at being out in the open, and she held her hands in her lap to keep from fidgeting.

They sat without speaking, a police scanner chirping various updates Ying Yue didn't really understand. She figured Zu and Raul were listening to get the police status as they were on the way. Even Buck and Taz, riding in the far back of the SUV, were quiet.

Come to think of it, had she ever heard one of them barking?

A phone rang and she almost jumped out of her skin.

"Zu here." Zu sounded cool and calm, like he had when she first met him.

"Zu, you all safe?" Officer Kokua's voice came across the line with the sound of sirens in the background.

"We've got one person inside," Zu answered.

There was a pause. "The intruders dropped their equipment and got out before we got there. But there's a complication."

"What is it?" Zu's voice went grim.

"We're bringing in the bomb squad."

Ying Yue stared at Zu. A bomb squad meant there was a bomb, didn't it? Zu's eyelids dropped to half-mast, and he exchanged a look with Raul. This didn't seem to be normal procedure.

Pua.

"I'm the only one who can get my resource out of there." Zu's voice remained steady, but he leaned even harder on the accelerator.

"Zu, I can't let anyone inside. We've already cleared every other floor and pulled our units out of the building." Officer Kokua sounded truly sorry. "I knew you'd be on your way, and I wanted to tell you before you got here and forced half a dozen of us to physically stop you from going inside."

Ying Yue was reasonably certain it'd take more than six officers. Zu was bigger than most American football players, and he had a teammate inside the building.

But Zu wasn't the lead of Search and Protect for nothing. "I'm sure your bomb squad can handle the bomb you see. Buck and I are going in to investigate the presence of any additional IEDs."

What?

There was a pause. "Zu, I didn't think Buck was explosives detection. I didn't think any of the Search and Protect canines did explosives detection."

Zu didn't answer. He cut the call.

Raul looked at Zu. "Zu."

"Speak no evil," was all Zu said.

Ying Yue studied the two of them in the front seat. Raul's expression was serious but not surprised. She couldn't see Zu's face as he kept his face forward, eyes on the road, but she could see his eyes reflected in the rearview mirror, and his gaze was intense.

Maybe she should be more frightened. She was worried, yes, for Pua and for the team and for herself. But looking at Zu, she wouldn't ever be afraid of Zu.

"If you're going to do something on the questionable side of legal, I probably shouldn't know about it." She couldn't help it, she needed to break the tension, for herself and maybe for them. If it was an inappropriate distraction, Zu could tell her so and she wouldn't take offense.

But Zu let out a surprised chuckle. "Appreciated."

"I do want to know what you need me to do to minimize how much you'll be worrying about me." She figured it was the best she could do to help in this situation.

They were a small team. There was Pua, their data analyst, and their three field operative pairs. From what Ying Yue had gathered, they'd managed to do quite a lot in terms of missions completed and contributions to the local law enforcement or government initiatives. But they were still three humans and their corresponding canine partners. Pua was already isolated. For the same reason Ying Yue had come along to avoid splitting the team further, she wasn't sure how they would continue to watch over her and get in to help Pua.

"Hold that thought," Zu said, his gaze finding hers in the rearview mirror before he returned his attention to the road ahead.

He also reached out and tapped a button on the dash of the SUV. A call initiated, the audio coming across the interior speakers of the vehicle.

"Zu, brah, howzit?" A mellow tenor spoke on the call.

"Kenny." Zu lifted his chin in greeting. Ying Yue almost let out a giggle that was part nervousness and part hilarity, because it wasn't like whoever was on the phone could see Zu's gesture. Zu slanted a glance at her but continued, "You listening to the police calls?"

"You know it." This person, Kenny, sounded fairly cheerful about it. Then again, Arin had tended to sound upbeat when she'd worked with Zu the day before. Maybe it was a thing with all of them, the way they worked together. "I'm shaking my head here. Gotta be loclo to mess with Search and Protect headquarters."

"Pua is inside."

"What can I do?" All joking had gone from Kenny's voice, just like that.

He must be a friend, Ying Yue decided. He was at least close enough to the team to be concerned for Pua and that's all Ying Yue needed to know.

"I need you to take a package to Miller's." She glared at the back of Zu's head. Package? Was he referring to her? And who or where was this man taking her to?

"Rajah dat."

"Can you meet me in the city? I'm headed toward Search and Protect HQ now." Zu had slowed to a speed just above the speed limit.

"Dat you? Do me a solid and flash your high beams."

Zu and Raul exchanged glances, but Zu did as requested.

"Yah, brah, this is going to work out nice. Just come off the ramp and stop. I'll meet you there." Kenny seemed to be moving and the sounds of fabric rustling came across the audio. "I'd call this some kinda loco coincidence. But here we are."

Zu turned off the highway onto a curving ramp. "Where are you, Kenny?"

"Look to the side. You see that tent in the big tree?" Kenny laughed.

There was indeed a tent perched on a big branch nestled deep within the heart of an impressively sized tree. Ying Yue had no idea how one would climb up there, and she was sure a person would have to sleep very carefully because those branches were only wide enough for a single body to lie prone. All the mechanics aside, there was a tent in a tree. What the actual hell?

"I'm not going to ask how," Zu said, his tone dry. "I'm not even going to ask why."

"Hey, Kenny, you got Laki up there with you?" Raul's question was full of humor.

"Who is Laki?" Ying Yue couldn't resist asking. Was it another person who could help? Maybe a dog?

"Raul, brah, you know Laki is a talented individual, but no way he can climb all dah way up here." Kenny sighed. "He's mad at me for not staying close to the water tonight."

"Laki is a pig," Zu clarified.

Raul turned in his seat to look at her directly. "Laki is the best surfing pig on the island."

"Am I understanding this right?" Ying Yue asked quietly.

Raul tipped his head to the side, apparently listening, and Zu glanced up at her in the rearview mirror.

"There is a pig, who can surf, apparently not camping

out with a man who's pitched a tent in a tree. And he's the courier you're asking to deliver a package—me—to some-place called Miller's?" Hysterical giggles fluttered in her belly like a dozen butterflies.

Silence. Then Raul nodded. "Yeah. You're going to have to go on faith here."

Zu pulled over and came to a stop.

"I kept watch as you came in." Kenny's voice still came across on the audio. "No followers. Let's be quick, and you can go on your way."

"Ready when you are," Zu said.

"'K den." Kenny ended the call.

The city around them was quiet and thick with shadows. Zu had parked on a side street just past the ramp from the highway, and in the shadow of the overpass, there were few lights. It was creepy, honestly, and not a place Ying Yue would've wanted to walk through by herself. It wasn't a bad neighborhood, per se. It was just dark, and she found the dark unsettling. She was used to cities lit up after the sun went down and going from place to place in crowded areas with lots of foot traffic, even late at night. This was desolate, in its own way.

Two figures approached, their shapes taking clearer form as they got closer. One was a man, tall and lean with long legs, and the other was...a pig.

"You were serious about there being a pig." She couldn't help it. She'd thought they'd been joking, at least a little.

"Laki," Zu said, opening the driver's side door. "Pig's name is Laki."

After a moment, the other man stepped up and greeted Zu outside the car. Then, the man opened the back door, and a pig hopped into the seat with her. She shifted to make room, inanely relieved the pig didn't smell any more than a dog did—different, but not bad. The man folded his long-limbed self into the back seat, too, and shut the door. "Pleasure to meet you, miss. I'm Kenny."

"Hi." She wasn't exactly sure what was going on.

Zu got back into the front driver seat. "Let's make this quick."

"Because you dah brah for the epic long storytelling, yeah?" Kenny laughed.

Ying Yue smiled. The idea of Zu waxing eloquent and long-winded about anything bordered on the ridiculous.

Zu stared at Kenny until the man lifted his hands in surrender. "Sorry, brah."

"Raul and I are going to headquarters." Zu looked straight at Ying Yue. "I need you to take Ying Yue to Miller's."

"With all due haste. Rajah dat," Kenny agreed.

Ying Yue stared at Laki, the pig, sniffing noses with first Taz then Buck in the back seat. Then she glared at each of them. "That's it. That's the elaborate plan? You aren't going to go into any further detail? I'm just supposed to go with him to someplace else?"

"Miss." Kenny had a kind smile, and corkscrew coils framed his face. It was easier to make out his expression in the faint light inside the car. His skin was a copper brown, several shades lighter than the deep, flawless black of Zu's skin. "Complicated plans always go wrong."

She scowled. There were a few levels of faith. She wasn't comfortable with going blind since they weren't in immediate danger, but she also wasn't going to eat up precious time needed to get Pua help. "Fine. I'm guessing I'm going with you in some other vehicle. I'll follow you if you promise to answer my questions as we go."

Kenny gave her a grin. "More than fair. Come wit me."

Zu opened the door on her side of the SUV, offering her a hand as she exited. He pulled her close, bending until his lips brushed her ear. "Thank you."

Shivers skipped across her skin. "Go get Pua."

It was like pulling apart two strong magnets when she forced herself to step away and follow Kenny.

In moments, they'd transferred to a small, beat-up RV. Kenny helped her step up into the passenger seat at the front. He reached into the glove compartment in front of her and pulled out a satellite phone. He punched in numbers, then handed it to her. "Here. Zu's number is ready. You just have to hit this button to call him if you feel any kind of danger."

Oh. She cradled the satellite phone close, reassured.

Kenny shut the passenger side door carefully, then let Laki in the door behind her. The pig snorted quietly, and she turned to see it walk back into an ultramodern, high-tech interior and flop over on its side under a table covered in electronics.

"Forgive the mess, miss. We weren't expecting company, Laki and me." Kenny settled into the driver's seat and started up the engine.

"Please call me Ying Yue," she said faintly, taking in the clever design of the place. She'd been in an RV before, and this was beyond the already efficient design of the normal vehicle. It wasn't actually messy; there was just so much tech everywhere.

Kenny pulled onto the highway, headed back in the direction she thought she and Zu and Raul had come. "Right on. So, Ying Yue, hit me with your questions. We got about a half hour or so."

"Okay." She faced forward, looking out over the empty

highway. Out of sorts and still on edge, she pulled her thoughts together. "Who or what is Miller's?"

"Good a place to start as any." Kenny turned on the police scanner and set it to low volume. His calm and good-natured cheer settled her nerves a fraction. "Miller's is a place. It's a house belonging to Todd Miller and his wife, Kalea. We're gonna go a mile or two so I can make sure no one is following, then turn around and head toward the military base. Their house is near there. Any new Search and Protect members start there to get themselves oriented."

She relaxed a little more as she processed that. "So they're a part of Zu's team. And so are you?"

"Nah." Tight curls bounced around Kenny's head as he shook it. "I'm not. I'm a longtime friend of Zu and Arin's. We've seen some things together, before any of us came here to the island. But Miller? He's a member of the team. He trains the dogs for Zu, if the dogs didn't have training before they came. Kalea makes sure all of the human members of the team remember to eat, sleep, and wash their hands like civilized people before they come to the dinner table. They're good people, all of them."

The butterflies settled, and her nausea dissipated, too. Sending her there made more sense knowing that.

"You watch," Kenny said. "They gonna get Pua out of that oubliette she calls an office space and bring her right to Miller's. You and me, we'll wait there for the rest of the team and have good eats in the meantime."

He sounded very comforting. She appreciated it. But she stared out onto the highway and wondered what the team could do when a bomb could go off at any second.

CHAPTER FOURTEEN

Zu pulled his SUV up to the perimeter established by the Honolulu Police Department. The officers at the barrier recognized him and Raul and opened it up for him to drive inside. Kokua must've left word to keep an eye out for Zu and the rest of the Search and Protect team, because Kokua was striding toward them by the time Zu and Raul had disembarked and let Buck and Taz out of the back.

Kokua eyed them cautiously. "Bomb squad just finished suiting up and is heading inside. Remote robot didn't show a timer on the device, so we think we have time to get your personnel out of there."

Maybe so. Zu wasn't willing to take the risk.

"Now or later, I'm the only person who can walk in there and deactivate the fail-safes to let her out." Zu shrugged into his protective gear. Designed to protect his torso from firearm projectiles, his vest wouldn't stand up to an explosion, but it'd give him a better chance than not wearing anything at all. "This isn't a simple password, Kokua. The system is keyed to my biometrics."

Kokua shook his head. "You and your team should wait until the bomb squad has cleared the area.

Should. There was some wiggle room in Kokua's statement. "We're going in to check the building for other devices. We understand the risk involved. All I'm asking you to do is let us inside."

Raul handed Zu an earpiece. The minute Zu tucked it securely into place in his ear, Raul turned on the comms.

"Alpha, this is Charlie. I am in position." Arin's voice came across the comms clear and calm. Per established emergency procedure, Arin had headed straight to their crow's nest, a predetermined position high up, where Arin could have eyes on the building.

Zu simply nodded. No need to say anything out loud when Arin was watching him and Raul for the moment. Instead, he stared at Kokua, waiting.

Kokua returned his stare for a solid minute, then sighed and pivoted, heading toward the building. "Let's go before I second-guess myself for the fiftieth time since this alarm came in."

Zu followed, with Buck at his side. Raul and Taz were close behind them. Kokua exchanged a few words with the officers maintaining the perimeter closest to the building but still a safe distance back.

"Just how big do you think this bomb is?" Raul asked Kokua.

Kokua shook his head. "We don't know enough about it, so we're working conservatively here."

Well, *conservative* could be considered a relative term. There were bombs, and then there were bombs. Zu, his team, and every law enforcement person on site were hoping it wasn't the kind of explosive device that could wipe the city—or the island—off the map. HPD was probably treating this as the kind with the potential to bring down the entire building and maybe damage the structures adjacent to it. Zu, Arin, and Raul had seen worse in their time before becoming Search and Protect.

Regardless, Zu planned to get Pua out of there. She was his priority. The entire building could be blown, as far as he was concerned, and he could recover, but Pua was the heart of his team. A cold part of his mind was taking in details and storing them for a day when whoever was behind this would pay for endangering her.

He paused at the perimeter and took a long look around at the gathered onlookers milling around the outer perimeter, then up at the buildings around them. There were variables and factors to consider, too many unknowns. The intruders might have gone into Search and Protect with the intent to ransack the offices and take any data they could grab off the computers. They may or may not have expected Pua to be there, and they may or may not have known she could lock herself down inside her own office, which was essentially a reinforced panic room. This could've been planned as a smash and grab, or the intruders could've deliberately set off all the alarms to cause this situation and lure in the Search and Protect team. In which case, this could be an ambush. Just because the police had conducted normal procedures to clear the floors above and below didn't mean trained individuals couldn't have concealed themselves and remained.

From the moment he, Buck, Raul, and Taz proceeded into the building, their survival would hinge on both following Search and Protect procedures and acting unpredictably to anyone outside the team. He looked at Raul and received a nod.

Ready.

Zu walked into the building, his weapon drawn and pointed to the ground.

As soon as they entered, Arin checked in. "This is Charlie, all clear outside the building."

So their attackers weren't waiting on any of the rooftops for this or the adjacent buildings and weren't in the courtyard formed by this building and the neighboring two.

"Guys, I'm listening."

Pua. Zu paused, caught between frustration and amusement. He hadn't picked his team members to simply follow procedures. He shouldn't have expected her to just wait in silence. "You hacked our own secure channel."

"It's very nerve-wracking sitting here, waiting for the cavalry to arrive." Pua didn't sound the least bit repentant.

"Listen, then. Try not to break in too often." He wanted to give her the reassurance of knowing what was happening, but he and the rest of the team needed to communicate and react within split seconds of any encounter.

"Got it." She paused. "The elevator is operable."

"Roger." He and Raul didn't head for the elevator, though. Elevators were boxes of death in urban warfare. They headed for the stairs, which were not much better in terms of risk. But they were better.

Raul entered the stairwell first, sending Taz ahead with a whispered command. They proceeded forward and up, Raul keeping watch on where they were going and what was above them while Zu covered their rear and kept watch on what was below. Just because you passed safely through an area didn't mean a threat couldn't come up behind you.

"Cameras were disabled in the stairwell." Pua kept her report brief and concise. "The intruders came and left using the stairs."

"Roger."

"I'm glad you're all here, but be careful. Okay?" Pua's voice broke with the strain.

"Yes." Arin's response was gentle.

"Sit tight." Zu didn't want to give her any false reassurances, but he wanted to ease her worry. "Be ready to move."

"Roger, boss," Pua whispered. They didn't report on their progress at each floor. It would've helped Pua feel better, but there were operatives out there as good as, maybe better, than Pua, and it was best not to give anyone who might be listening too much information. Twice, Taz encountered something odd-looking on the stairs, and they all took pains to avoid disturbing what could've been booby traps as they passed by. In each case, Zu noted the position to report to Kokua once they had Pua clear.

With every potential trap they found, Zu's cold rage intensified. A lot of people could've died, and whoever this was thought it worth the body count to send a message to Search and Protect. Was Ying Yue worth so much to these people? This whole thing seemed designed to wipe Search and Protect off the map.

If anyone was looking at them, they might be truly disturbed because he smiled. It had nothing to do with happiness and everything to do with his promise to himself that whoever was behind this would pay. He was a patient man, and he had a long memory.

They arrived on the floor below the Search and Protect offices and exited the stairwell. The floor was empty, occupied on paper by another company, a shell company Zu had set up. He had purchased the space before he'd arranged for the purchase of the offices above for Search and Protect. He owned the office space on the floor above Search and

Protect, too. It'd been a precaution to reduce the chances of innocent bystanders being hurt in the case of an attack on headquarters. It'd seemed an unlikely and perhaps an extravagant precaution at the time, but here they were.

Raul and Taz swung wide, sweeping the entire floor as Zu headed directly to what looked like one of multiple furnished offices.

"This is Bravo, we're clear." Raul and Taz returned as he completed his report for Arin and Pua's benefit.

Zu stepped onto what looked like an ottoman and reached up, pulling down a sturdy ladder. Giving it a jerk once, then a second time, he set his boot on the first rung and started to climb. The trap door set into the ceiling required his fingerprint and a retinal scan, then it slid to the side, into a recess in the ceiling. Slowly, he climbed higher, scanning the space above.

"Hey, boss. It's really good to see you." Pua was tucked under her desk, dwarfed by the Kevlar vest and helmet she'd put on, with a laptop in her lap.

"Let's go." Everything else in the room was as expected, empty and turned off. All of the monitors on the walls around Pua's workspace were dark. She'd shut it all down and probably wiped everything clean.

Pua slid a backpack toward him, and he grabbed it, pulling it through the opening and dropping it down to Raul, waiting below. Minutes later, he and Pua were standing on the floor just below her office and the hidden trap door was closed again.

"Charlie, this is Alpha. Initiating phase 2."

"Roger." Arin responded cool and quiet, but Zu thought he heard a note of relief.

They'd all practiced this in the past, but not often. There was a difficult balance to maintain in having a secret escape plan and keeping it secret by not practicing it often. Arin and Raul, even the dogs, weren't the risk factors in this scenario. Pua, who wasn't experienced in these types of situations, was the unpredictable factor. Practice was still practice, without the tension a real situation had. People could make mistakes under that kind of pressure no matter how many drills they'd been through. So far, she'd come through with exemplary performance. More importantly, she was alive and unhurt, and he planned to keep her that way. Fortunately, the escape route was fairly easy to navigate. A few stairwells and a window out to the roof of a neighboring building, then more stairs. She could make it.

He placed a hand on her shoulder. "Good job. Let's go."

* * *

"Aloha. Welcome back safe. All of you."

Ying Yue stood in the living room as Kalea hustled the returning Search and Protect team members into her home. Kenny sat on a couch nearby with Laki at his feet. Ying Yue wanted to be calm, but she'd been waiting on edge since she and Kenny had arrived, despite Kalea's kind offers of refreshment and Todd's reassurances. When it came down to it, she needed to see Pua and Zu and Buck and all of them.

They flowed in the door in a controlled rush, Pua first. She had some kind of protective gear on that was way too big for her.

Kalea must've decided the same, because she turned Pua this way and that, looking at the armor with dismay. "Zu, what were you thinking?" She took the helmet off Pua and clucked disapprovingly. "This has to weigh half as much as Pua does herself."

Raul stepped forward. "There are releases..."

Before he could finish, Kalea simply got a grip on the back of the collar and hoisted the vest straight up. Pua lifted her arms in response and was freed from the vest in one expedient move.

"Or you could do that." Raul shook his head and got out of his own gear.

Pua was petite. Kalea, on the other hand, was a broad-shouldered woman comfortable in her curves with a solid presence that anchored wayward souls. The minute Ying Yue had entered the household, it'd been Kalea who had enveloped her in a warm sense of steady comfort. This was a safe harbor, a place one could come to rest. Now, Kalea literally wrapped her arms around Pua, murmuring comments in what sounded like Hawaiian. Ying Yue wasn't sure, but she wrapped her arms around herself, happy to see everyone on the team walk in on their own two feet.

Things could've gone so badly.

Zu scanned the room, and his gaze settled on her. The edges of the world around them blurred, and she was caught in the intensity. Relief and joy and a need to check every inch of him over for any kind of hurt pushed and pulled at her until she bounced on the balls of her feet. She didn't try to raise her voice over the chatter of various people in the room or the dogs. She simply mouthed a word. "Hi."

He didn't smile, but the corners of his eyes crinkled, and humor lit his gaze.

"Come. Both these girls should sit and eat. All of you should." Kalea had Pua tucked against her side under one arm and came around the couches to gather in Ying Yue, too. "I made breakfast. Come eat. You too, Kenny."

Ying Yue hadn't broken the eye contact connecting her and Zu. Zu lifted his chin in the direction of the kitchen, indicating she should let herself be herded. She wrinkled her nose at him but let herself be guided forward.

She hadn't been able to do more than nibble on an offered musubi when she'd first arrived. Now that everyone was here, she found her stomach was easing out of the knots of worry and was embarrassingly empty.

In the kitchen, Kalea encouraged Pua and Ying Yue to sit first. Then the rest of the team and Kenny filled in the seats. Todd and Zu hung back, exempt from Kalea's gentle managing, at least for the time being.

"Can I help at all?" Ying Yue half rose, but Raul's widened eyes on her made her pause.

"No, no." Kalea sang from the kitchen stove. "Sit. Eat. That's what will make me happy."

Arin snickered. "Raul tried to help once and ignored Kalea's orders to stay at the table. She's fast with a wooden spoon."

"It doesn't tickle," Raul grumbled.

Pua laughed. Her sweet face had shown strain, but sitting at the table, surrounded by people, she was quickly regaining the effervescent energy Ying Yue had come to associate with her.

Kalea placed a plate in front of Pua first, steaming rice piled high with a juicy hamburger patty placed on top and covered in a rich, brown gravy. A sunny-side-up egg sat atop it all, the yolk a beautiful, bright contrast to the brown gravy. Pua smiled wide. "You're loco moco is my favorite, Auntie Kalea."

Kalea chuckled. "You can get loco moco anywhere on the island."

"Yours is best," Pua insisted.

Kalea placed a similar serving in front of Ying Yue. It was gorgeous, the epitome of comfort. Ying Yue followed

Pua's lead and dug in as the others were getting their plates. There was no formality at this table, and no one wanted anyone to stand on ceremony, waiting for everyone to be served, letting the food get cold. Instead, everyone showed their appreciation to the cook by eating right away. And it was perfection. The burger was tender and savory, the gravy flavorful with a hit of pepper at the end on her palate. When Ying Yue pierced the yolk with her fork, it ran down over her rice in thick golden goodness.

"Delicious, right?"

Ying Yue looked up, meeting Pua's gaze. "So good."

Pua sighed happily. "You're one of us. I can tell."

Her statement suffused Ying Yue with warmth. Unsure what to say, Ying Yue only bumped her shoulder against Pua's and continued to eat.

Arin chuckled but kept her attention on her own plate.

This must be what it was like to have a big family. Ying Yue glanced around as she chewed and enjoyed the meal. Growing up, she'd been happy, really. Her family had been small and quiet, very restrained. Many meals had just been her and her mother at a dining table too big for them. Here, in Kalea and Todd's house, the kitchen table barely fit them all, elbow to elbow, and dogs were sitting hopefully outside the entryways to the kitchen. Besides Buck, King, and Taz were two more dogs in training. Todd Miller had introduced her to them when she'd arrived earlier with Kenny, and the dogs had kept her company.

Even the dogs didn't venture into Kalea's domain without her express permission. It was a home, for all of these people and dogs, even though most of them lived someplace else.

It was wonderful.

"Mm. Oh." Pua swallowed a particularly big mouthful. "I almost forgot."

She looked around and found Zu standing with Todd in the entryway. "Zu. While you were coming to get me, I was clearing the databases and saving down the results from my latest search strings. I got a hit, and it was almost random, but not, only it's very weird how this is connected to our current mission. I decided to double-check everything to be sure I was right."

Zu and Todd had stopped their conversation when Pua had called for Zu's attention. Now they both entered the room. Todd paused and wrapped an arm around his wife's shoulders, pressing a kiss to her temple. She laughed and nudged him toward the table. "Go on, then. Must be important."

"Go on, Pua," Zu prompted.

"Okay, I gotta rewind some for Ying Yue, or she might not know what I'm talking about, and it's important because she might be able to fill in some gaps we don't know about, or maybe she can't. I don't know." Pua picked up a glass of water and took a sip. "So months and months ago, Raul and Taz joined us. Arin's little sister was here on the island around the same time conducting research downtown. There was a kidnapping."

Ying Yue set her fork down a little too quickly. She kept thinking she was safe enough, rested and moving forward, but she wasn't. It was still too fresh for her, the terror and uncertainty. She tried to keep her face blank, unwilling to worry the people around her with her reaction.

Pua nodded. "Yeah. I'm sorry. It seemed best to mention it right away. Okay, so a bunch of scientists were taken right off the street, and only Mali managed to give them the slip, because she's Arin's sister and of course she'd manage it."

Arin lifted an eyebrow at that, but made no comment. Ying Yue squashed the pang of shame. She hadn't managed to evade her kidnappers.

But that's why Zu had been working with her on self-defense. She was better prepared, more aware. The tightness in her chest eased.

"The important thing here is that Search and Protect went after the scientists." Pua pressed on. "We exposed a small human trafficking operation on a plantation here on Oahu. A couple of months later, Arin and another freelancer, Jason, interfered with a new boss who came to the island to reestablish the human trafficking operation. Part of that was how we all ended up meeting you, Ying Yue."

They were all listening, waiting. Ying Yue was struggling to keep up. She did her best to keep breathing, in and out.

"We've been running searches on Mr. Jiang's business and even your career, Ying Yue. Those queries are ongoing. But I realized the one common thread I hadn't been researching was the human trafficking angle. So I checked into a few of the cold leads from Arin and Jason's investigation before the team went to intercept the cargo ship. I got a hit."

Pua started to wave her hands around as she got more excited. "I can't believe I didn't check earlier, but, Ying Yue, it wasn't a coincidence that you were on that cargo ship. There's a new boss coming in. A third one. He's maybe not just new management. He might be the big bad in charge of everything behind this human trafficking group repeatedly popping up here in the islands. And he specifically was looking to have you under his control."

Fear burst past the dams she'd been building inside herself, and Ying Yue stopped breathing.

CHAPTER FIFTEEN

Zu locked down the urge to destroy everything around him, his hands balled into tight fists locked to his sides. Ying Yue had gone very pale, and everyone had stopped eating.

After a moment, it was Arin who moved. She stood slowly and started gathering dishes. "We're going to need to talk this through. Raul, help me clean up. Pua, why don't you and Ying Yue go on into the living room."

Ying Yue didn't move as the rest got up from the breakfast table. Her gaze found his and the rest of the world fell away.

Zu leaned forward, placing his hands on the table. "Whoever this guy is, he can't have you. You're with us."

"He sounds like he has a lot of influence." Her voice was quiet, but her words carried through the room.

"We have our own resources." Zu put as much confidence into his words as he could for her. "I personally intend to put him where he can't threaten you or anyone on this team ever again."

After a moment, Ying Yue nodded. "I believe you."

She stood then and turned to Pua, who was waiting in one of the doorways. The two of them went into the other room.

A few minutes later, Pua was hooking her laptop up to the television to use as a large monitor. Zu rubbed his forehead, wondering how it was still only morning. He'd taken the time to compartmentalize his rage and get his anger under control so he could back away from the edge of violence for the first time since he'd woken to the alarm this morning.

Todd stepped over to stand next to him. "Good to have everyone in one room. This doesn't happen as much as it did a year ago."

Zu snorted. "A year ago, the team was smaller."

"Maybe we just need more chairs in the living room." Todd shrugged.

"Maybe so." Zu considered the group. Arin sat curled up in an armchair with King lying on the floor in front of her. Raul sat on a couch next to Ying Yue, with Taz and Buck between them. Two of the new search dogs were also vying for Ying Yue's attention, and she was trying to give pats all around. The dogs all liked her. Pua sat cross-legged on the floor by the television, doing her thing. Kenny had draped himself sideways over another armchair with Laki lying on the floor beside him. Kalea came and went between the living room and the kitchen, enjoying the company. "This is a good core team, but we might be facing more than we can handle soon."

Todd scratched the stubble at his jawline. "True. You wanted to keep this team lean, but maybe it would be best to pick up a few more resources."

Zu had been thinking along the same lines. "No time to

interview and recruit right now though. It'd bring too much risk into this situation."

He watched Ying Yue hold out her hand, and Buck obligingly gave her a paw. Desire to keep her with him clashed with the need to reach a resolution to her situation. On one hand, he wanted her to be happy, and a major part of her happiness would be her getting back to her old life. Maybe. Unless he could offer a new one. But this thing between them was so new, and he wasn't even sure what he wanted, so how could he even begin to know what he could offer her? A lot had happened in the space of a few days, and he wanted to give her the consideration she deserved. He also wanted to be careful not to hold her back.

"You have an alternative in mind?" Todd asked.

The question threw Zu off-balance for a split second, because his line of thought had taken a side trip from their conversation. Dragging himself back to the more pressing issue, Zu pulled a few ideas together. "I'm thinking about bringing in a few resources we've got ties with on the mainland. It'll take them some time to get here, though."

Todd nodded. "It's not like we've got a lot of connections conveniently here on the island that'll fit what we're looking for. If you think these people you have in mind can fit and integrate quickly, the sooner you can get them mobilized, the better. The two new dogs are about ready to start working with new handlers."

Zu smiled. "The people I have in mind are already established with their own partners."

"Huh." Todd gave Zu a sideways look.

Zu pulled out his phone. It'd be midafternoon where they were. It was a five- or six-hour time difference. They'd be around. He pulled up the info for his main contact, hit Call, and waited for the connection to go through. It rang twice and went to voice mail. Strange. He tried the secondary contact. Same. He tried the third and went straight to voice mail on that number. None of them was reachable. He scowled. Of all the damned times for all three of them to go off the grid.

"Oh, boss, I'm about ready." Pua unfolded herself and rose in a graceful motion. "Who are you calling?"

Everyone in the room was looking at him suddenly, and he realized his face must've caught all their attention. He worked to smooth out his expression. "I was considering calling in our friends at Hope's Crossing Kennels."

"Oh." Pua blushed. "They won't answer. They're in flight. I called them this morning."

Zu stared at her.

"Well, you had a note on your task list to contact them." Pua stood on one foot and scratched the back of her calf with the other. "I was looking for constructive things to do while I was locked down in my office, so I figured it was a good assumption you'd want them here sooner rather than later."

True. It was overstepping some, but in this case, he was glad she'd done it. "Next time, give me a heads-up."

"Sure. Yeah." Pua hurriedly pulled her laptop up and brought up a few screenshots. "So, should I get started on what I found?"

Zu hesitated and looked from Ying Yue to Kenny. Ying Yue was right at the center of all this, but Kenny had been dragged in. "You don't have to be a part of this, Kenny. You did us a solid, and I won't forget it. If you want to head out now, it's good."

Kenny waved off Zu's offer. "I'm here and I'm curious. Plus, this human trafficking ring grows roots like the worst kind of weed. I think every one of us wants to see this scoured off the face of the island. If Pua's right, now could be the best time to take this organization out right at the root."

Zu nodded. Then he looked at Ying Yue again. "This involves you. I won't say it doesn't. But you can stay here, and I'll continue to watch over you, or you can come with the team as we move against this new crime boss. It's your choice how much you want to be involved."

Ying Yue didn't answer immediately. She rubbed Buck's ears for a long moment, then met Zu's gaze. "It still makes sense for me to be where your team is. And if I'm here, I want to help in any way I can. I won't claim to have any skill sets you need, but I might be able to draw connections you wouldn't otherwise understand. I don't think any of us know until I listen. I'm very much hoping I can contribute."

Fair. And she wasn't overextending herself, expecting to suddenly be a badass operative. He appreciated her thoughtfulness, rather than reacting solely on emotion. He wouldn't have blamed her for wanting to hide or to go after this new boss in a rage. He nodded for Pua to proceed.

"Okay. Here we go." She folded back down into a cross-legged position on the floor and settled her laptop into her lap. "Last week, before the team intercepted the cargo ship, we interrupted the previous manager of the human trafficking ring at a hostess club. He was there making connections with certain political representatives here on the island. I'd started to monitor their phone and online accounts, but since the police arrested the manager as a suspect in the human trafficking case, I didn't check on those. There was a lot going on with the cargo ship mission and then Ying Yue's situation. I checked some of their outgoing calls and emails this morning while I was on lockdown."

She pointed to one screenshot, then another. "Turns out, at least two of the politicians are panicked as they're unable to reach anyone in the organization now that manager number two is in police custody. Seems manager number two had kidnapped family members."

"Charming." Arin spat out the word.

Pua nodded. "Right? So we have the human trafficking ring as a common thread through most of our missions in the last several months. Whether it was the initial manager or the second one, they both had a similar pattern of behavior kidnapping family members. That's why I think this third big boss is involved in Ying Yue's situation. One of the politicians reached out to a separate dummy email address and offered to use his connections with a private security vendor to bid on a contract to provide subcontracted security personnel to a client staying on the island. I'm tracking down the owner now, but it looks like a group inbox checked by multiple IPs."

"You think that's how my kidnapper managed to insert himself into my father's security team." Ying Yue's voice was steady, and she hadn't gone pale this time. Maybe she was becoming desensitized to the topic of her kidnapping, or maybe she felt she was safe in this company. Either way, Zu was glad this wasn't causing her distress.

"I do." Pua minimized the screenshots and pulled up a different window. "I think this new bad guy wants to do business with your father, and he's looking for whatever leverage he can get to ensure he gets his deal."

Ying Yue shook her head. "My father's business is all about manufacturing electronics and hardware. He doesn't deal in human trafficking."

"But manufacturing anything means factories." Pua pulled another window open. "This is a heat map of the regions most likely to have underpaid or forced labor. So far, your father doesn't have those kinds of employment practices, but a majority of his sites are in those regions. Your father would be very attractive as a new business partner, and this new big bad might want to find a way to pressure your father into it if he's declined in the past."

* * *

Ying Yue closed her eyes momentarily, thinking hard about whether what she wanted to say was actually true. It was the kind of thing that both had to be based in logic and have a lot of heart behind it. "My father is ambitious. He's always been driven. But through it all, he's done it with a strong level of integrity. There are some compromises he might make in business deals and networking connections, but he wouldn't be a part of human trafficking. That's going too far."

"Not even for his daughter?" Zu asked.

She met his gaze steadily. "If that were the reason I'd been kidnapped, he'd never have gotten me back. There'd maybe be proof of life, but they couldn't ever set me free. If they did, my father would immediately stop cooperating."

"Maybe." Arin sat forward. "Maybe not. Once they proved they could take you, and sufficiently impressed upon you that they could, then all they'd need was the threat that they could do it anytime, anywhere. Your father might comply based on the threat alone."

"That is what it looks like happened with the family members of these two politicians." Pua pulled up pictures. "I found images of them in the emails, but neither of these individuals was reported missing to the police. There's no missing persons record or any kind of investigation initiated."

"It's different, then." Ying Yue stared at the screen thoughtfully. "Why would they have taken me away from Singapore if they were going to let me go again? My situation doesn't fit. If they had taken me, like the other family members here, then they would've reached out to my father right away and at least instructed my family not to contact the authorities. In fact, there was the press release to let the public know I was missing. That doesn't fit, either."

"True." Raul scratched Taz's ears as he pitched in. "So is the difference because of the way this third bad guy handles things, or is it something we don't see yet?"

No one had an answer.

Zu shifted his weight. "Let's keep going through what we know."

Pua nodded. "So once I had these points of interest, I was able to find contact between one of the dummy email addresses used by our bad guys and this person within Ying Yue's father's organization."

She pulled up a slide presentation, featuring a few email screenshots prominently on the screen.

Ying Yue stared at Pua. That was a lot more sleuthing than any of the law enforcement or her father's people had been able to do. Ying Yue was impressed.

Raul cleared his throat. "You put this together this morning?"

Pua lifted her chin and glared at Raul. "Look. I was effectively trapped inside my own office with a bomb outside my door. Presentations and spreadsheets give me Zen. Back off."

Raul held up his hands in surrender. "You did great, Pua."

"Incidentally, I checked on the police activity." Pua

tipped her head to the side. "They disarmed the bomb and confirmed it would've been enough to do a lot of damage on that floor but not take out the overall infrastructure of the building. They disarmed the claymores you found in the stairwell, too. No one was hurt. Officer Kokua wants statements from us by tomorrow."

Ying Yue frowned. "He seems to be very forgiving. He didn't want us all at the station right away?"

Pua gave her an enigmatic look. "They've seen a lot of us lately."

Todd barked out a laugh. "More likely he doesn't want a bomb at his doorstep. Officer Kokua is a smart man, and he knows we're good guys. We'll provide our part of the paperwork, but it's less strain on his resources if we aren't bringing trouble right into his office."

Ying Yue rubbed her upper arms. It was more than unsettling to know they were deep in the kind of trouble even the police didn't want to be involved in. When she looked up, Zu had left his spot at the back of the room and come to stand by her at the couch. She shifted over a bit, and Buck and Taz tumbled off the couch. He wedged himself into the corner of the couch and gathered her against his side. Immediately, the heat of him seeped through her clothes and dispelled the chills. She breathed in slowly, taking comfort in the earthy cinnamon scent of him.

Pua had a silly smile on her face, but she pushed on with her presentation. "Back to this man. Those were the email contacts, and this is our guy, based on his email and IP address."

She brought up an employee photograph along with a name, address, and multiple phone numbers.

Ying Yue sat forward. "I know him."

Everyone was looking at her now.

She sat back, slightly embarrassed at how excited she felt to finally have a face, someone who might be directly responsible for the chaos and fear she'd suffered. "He's definitely employed in my father's company and involved enough to have been at a few of the business events I've attended with my family. He's introduced himself to me in the past."

Had this man known the last time he'd approached her at one of her father's events? Had he smiled and expressed pleasantries and known then what he would be involved in doing to her?

"He's a mid-level manager in one of your father's businesses here on Oahu." Pua brought up his resume and company records. "I'm betting he's not even that high up with the human trafficking ring. Because of him, though, I do have a partial name for this new bad guy. Mr. Lee-Smith."

Arin groaned.

Raul sighed. "Jason is going to be disappointed his favorite undercover name is surfacing here."

Kenny shook his head. "Those are two of the most common surnames in the world. Hyphenated."

"What else do we know?" Zu pressed.

Pua shook her head. "Only that this guy got information on Ying Yue for Mr. Lee-Smith, including her address in Singapore and a couple of up-to-date pictures. He also had a very recent exchange in which he said he'd arrange for the subcontract deal to the private contract organization of Mr. Lee-Smith's choice."

"So we have him involved before and after Ying Yue was kidnapped." Raul let out a low whistle.

"And he's also here, on Oahu, as part of Mr. Jiang's

business group." Pua switched to a new slide with the hotel information.

"We need to talk to him." Zu pulled out his phone. "I'll contact Officer Kokua."

Ying Yue reached out and put her hand on Zu's before he initiated the call. "But if the police bring him in for questioning, won't that tip off this Lee-Smith person? Would it be better to draw this mid-level minion out and see what he knows first? Otherwise, won't Lee-Smith cut connections?"

Zu studied her. "Possibly."

She was crazy. Maybe. She felt like she was balanced on a tightrope, and if she tipped too far to one side or the other, she'd fall into terror and anxiety. There was no way to go but forward.

"I've interacted with the man, and as far as he knows, I'm not privy to his involvement. It would be tempting for him if I reached out, asking for help...say with getting a few things for my job in alignment while I'm remote?" Ying Yue wasn't sure it would work, but she was exploring the possibilities as she went.

Zu remained silent, his face very closed off and neutral. At least he wasn't laughing or sneering at her. Not that he would. She just didn't know what he was thinking in this moment.

It was Arin who spoke. "It could be advantageous."

Ying Yue addressed Zu, because Arin seemed to be supporting her idea. "It exposes me, yes. But isn't it me they're after anyway? Instead of continuing to hide until they find me or flush me out into the open, let's be pro-active. The only certain thing in any of this is that I can't run forever, and they seem to be willing to do more and more to find me."

A bomb was a serious escalation. Innocent people could have been hurt. Ying Yue looked at Pua, then back at Zu. The thought of them coming to harm hurt more than the fresh waves of fear brought on by thinking about her kidnappers or why she'd been taken in the first place. She would do anything to end this chain of events centering around her. She bit her lip, waiting for him to respond.

Zu rose to his feet and offered his hand. Tension eased and she placed hers in his, letting him pull her up, too. He addressed his team. "Put together a plan."

Then he led her from the living room, down the hall, and downstairs to a lower level. It was a sort of rec room area. But he didn't stop there. He continued across the common area to another room tucked in the back. It was a simple bedroom, small and cozy. He shut the door and faced her.

"Just for a minute, then we can go back upstairs if you want." He cupped her face in both hands. "I won't stop you if you want to do this. It's your choice. I just want to give you quiet time, when you're not in front of everyone, to think it through before you commit."

She placed her hand on the outside of his and leaned into his palm. He could've fought with her, used his leadership over the team to forbid them from letting her do this thing. But he didn't. She loved him for that.

It was a realization she wasn't ready to share with him yet. This was too new. Too intense. Maybe she was mistaken.

He leaned forward until his forehead touched hers. "I don't want to put you in the path of danger, Ying Yue. It scares me to the core."

Ah. But if this wasn't love, she didn't know what was.

Her heart ached with it, reveled in the emotion saturating his words and his touch.

"Say it again, please?" She whispered her request.

"It scares me." His voice cracked, vulnerable.

Her heart expanded. She could wrap him in this feeling she'd found growing inside her. Maybe neither of them was safe, but they could hold each other in the time they had. It was a different kind of protection.

She shook her head. "Say my name."

One hand slipped to the back of her head, his fingers threading into her hair. "Ying Yue."

She tilted her head up and closed her eyes as she pressed her lips to his.

CHAPTER SIXTEEN

Zu pulled into the parking spot, tucked into a sheltered nook out of sight of the road. Once they'd agreed on plans for the next day, they'd left the Millers' home at the same time. They'd all driven in different vehicles, scattering on the major roads and highways heading in various directions. The entire team would spend the afternoon into evening in various locations on the island, none of them going home.

Pua had gone with Kenny, since Kenny was probably the best of them all at staying on the move and hidden. A person didn't find Kenny if Kenny didn't want to be found. Besides, Kenny and Pua together made a formidable IT specialist combination.

Zu had driven Ying Yue north and made certain there'd been no followers on the long road before turning east and circling back to the beaches.

"If we're not going back to your house, where will we stay for the night?" Ying Yue looked out the windows at the empty stretch of sand and the ocean waves.

Zu shrugged. "It's been a while since I camped on the beach, and this loaner truck can be comfortable, if you're game. Technically, a permit is required, but the local authorities don't disturb people on the beaches unless they've got an open fire."

She raised her eyebrows. "Camping?"

"Have you ever been?" he wondered. He had a basic idea of what her childhood had been like and some of her current life, but there was a lot he didn't know. He was curious.

She laughed. "No, actually. My mother had a strong preference for well-appointed hotels. I like all sorts of hotels and B&Bs, but I've never been camping. I always thought it could be fun, though."

"Well, this might be roughing it for some of you." Especially dealing with personal needs. Zu could do a few things to make it more comfortable, but it was still going to be something of an experience for Ying Yue.

She shrugged. "It's just for the night, right? I'll need some place to freshen up tomorrow before I meet with this contact."

True. "The meeting place we have in mind is not far from here and off the beaten path. I can probably arrange for you to get access to their facilities to take care of necessities, but we shouldn't get there too soon ahead of the meeting time."

"No?" She tilted her head. "What if there are people waiting there to ambush us?"

"Arin will be in position there in advance, so that possibility is covered." Zu smiled. He liked the way Ying Yue thought critically and drew conclusions from what made sense to her. "I want to minimize your proximity to any of those potential threats, so we go in later."

"Ah." She sighed. "I'll think of this as an adventure."

He was thankful she was willing to do so. Actually, she was incredibly flexible and adaptable. He wondered if he'd have been able to adjust as quickly had their roles been reversed. To be honest, he'd like to think he could, but he wasn't sure he'd have managed to remain as positive as she had through all of this. "You're an amazing woman, Ying Yue."

She smiled at him. "I'm glad you think so. I find a lot to admire about you, too."

He wasn't used to this, the warm feeling of contentment those words gave him. Hot words said in passion, those he'd traded with partners in the past. These expressions of care ran deeper.

She leaned in then and brushed her lips over his jaw in one of her butterfly-light kisses.

"Before I get distracted and do my best to distract you, too, let's call this middleman in your father's company." He was very, very interested in clearing her mind of anything but him. But they had a plan to carry out, and she'd committed to being a part of it. He didn't want to get in the way of anything she intended to do, so long as he could do everything possible to keep her safe while she did it.

She nodded, suddenly very serious. "Yes. Okay."

She pulled the small notepad she'd borrowed from Kalea out of the glove compartment. She'd made a few notes on what she planned to say while discussing the plan with the team before they'd all split up.

"Try not to read directly from your notes," he cautioned. "When you read aloud, you have a different cadence than normal conversation."

She nodded. "Thank you. I wondered which would be better. I've given presentations, but this is more like acting.

I have bullet points so I don't forget something important, but do you think I should go for confident? Or something more hesitant?"

Good questions. "Be the you he's seen at those holiday parties. It might get under this man's skin to have you seem unperturbed after what he's helped put you through."

If Zu had to guess, the man might be frustrated with her as a symbol of things he couldn't have or status he hadn't achieved. There could be a big dose of misogynistic bias in there, too. It would become more clear once Zu had a chance to listen in on the phone call. "Don't worry about managing him. Just make your request. I'll give you my impressions on the interaction after, if you want them."

"I do." Her attention was on her notes. "A lot of my soft skills have to do with building rapport with people. From what I remember about this man—and it's not much—he just didn't make an impression on me. He wasn't particularly off-putting, but he also wasn't likeable in any way. I want to understand what you see when you look at this man. Maybe I'll learn to recognize my enemies before they can hurt me."

Reading people was an important skill, applicable across just about any career or industry. "Will do."

"All right." She sat up straight and nodded to him. "I'm ready."

He handed her the satellite phone. "Keep it under the timeframe we discussed. I'll give you a one-minute warning. If there's any chance he's got something in place to trace the call, we'll end it before he can get a fix on our location."

"Got it."

Zu glanced back at Buck, where he lay in the back seat. "Buck should be good for the next few minutes. Even if he does give an alert bark, it shouldn't be a surprise you're with him."

She nodded. Then she referred to her notes and punched the number into the satellite phone. When she was done, she lifted the handset to the side of her face.

The volume was turned high enough for Zu to hear the ring. After a moment, a polite woman answered the call. "Mr. Chen's office."

"Hello. This is Jiang Ying Yue. I would like to speak with Mr. Chen."

There was a shocked pause. "Miss Jiang, of course. One moment, please."

The wonders of the corporate office environment. One could almost always expect to be put on hold. Zu thought it took the fight out of a caller.

But Ying Yue spoke before the admin could put the call on hold. "I haven't much time. If this will take long, I will have to ask Mr. Chen to take my call another time."

"Oh. Of course. My apologies." The admin was flustered. "Mr. Chen is in his office. I will transfer you immediately."

Chen must've been aware of the call. Zu would've given his next meal to have seen whether the admin had been wildly gesticulating to get her boss's attention when Ying Yue indicated she might hang up.

"Miss Jiang. It is an honor." A man picked up the line, speaking with a clear US English accent. "To what do I owe this call."

"Mr. Chen." Ying Yue's voice dripped with formality and polite interest. "As you may know, I find myself in Hawaii at the moment. If I recall, you have some oversight on the contracts made for my father's main business interests. There is an unsigned purchase order awaiting finalization for the Search and Protect Corporation regarding private personal security for me while I'm here on the island. I'd like to personally review the statement of work and perhaps arrange for a master service agreement to ensure they can work with any of my father's companies again in the future. It's the least I can do when they've done such a good job."

"Yes. I'm happy to hear that, Miss Jiang."

No. The man definitely wasn't happy. He said the right words, but his tone was all off. Strained.

"I could forward the requested documents to your company email for you to review." Chen was seething, and he wasn't doing a good job of hiding it in his tone. Did he think people didn't notice?

"Ah. Unfortunately, I don't have access to a laptop." Ying Yue paused.

"I am here on Oahu." Chen offered, grudgingly, "I could print the documents and leave them at the front desk for someone to pick up."

"Oh, but that wouldn't be very secure." Ying Yue pitched her voice to hint at disappointment. "I'm surprised you would leave such sensitive paperwork in anyone's hands outside of my father's employ."

"What was I thinking? Of course not." Chen was starting to brownnose. If he'd been in person, he'd have fallen over himself. "I could bring them to you. Where are you staying?"

"Oh, it changes every few hours." Ying Yue let out a short laugh. "I'm enjoying my tour of the island."

She was getting into her role, maybe too comfortably. Zu tapped the outside of his wrist. It was getting close to time.

"They're taking me to see a lovely location tomorrow."

She gave Chen the address. "Perhaps you could meet me there for lunch?"

"Absolutely." Chen suddenly sounded very happy for a man who was going to have to drop everything he had planned to come over on hour outside the city to meet someone unexpectedly. "I'll have the documents ready for your review, and you can ask me any questions you might have over lunch."

Ying Yue smiled, slow and catlike. "Perfect."

* * *

Ying Yue stared at the menu but wasn't really taking in the offerings. She peeked over the top at Zu. "Are we really going to be ordering food? Will we be here long enough?"

Zu shrugged. "We might be. If you don't want to look suspicious, do what you'd do if you actually came here to enjoy lunch. The sticky ribs look good, especially with the green papaya and ginger salad."

"You and your team seem very food oriented." She looked around the restaurant. It was a pleasant atmosphere, managing to encourage relaxation in the midst of lush surroundings. A whole side of the restaurant was open to the rain forest and mountains. "You surprised me."

"Because we like to eat?" His face was mostly neutral, but she caught the twitch at the corner of his mouth.

"I'm used to most businesspeople proving how professional they are by only ever talking about the business they do." Actually, Ying Yue wasn't sure why she'd said they surprised her, only that they had. She found her thoughts coming together more clearly as she talked it through. "You and your team are relaxed. You all stop and take joy in the things around you, like good food. But it doesn't come across as a lack of focus. Your easy air of competence instills confidence, at least for me. It's more that you all perform at a high level of excellence and don't make a big deal out of it. As if to say, of course it should be this way."

He gave her a wink. "It can be."

She huffed out a short laugh. "Take where we're seated, for example. My father's staff would've made a fuss to be sure we got a table set in some sheltered nook or at least against the wall where our bodyguard could sit with his back to the wall. You requested a table in the middle of the room. And you positioned our seats so we could enjoy the view."

It was absolutely lovely, too. Breathtaking in a different way from the ocean scenes she'd been seeing since she'd been with him. The restaurant was partially open air with an expansive outer deck. Their table was still sheltered inside the restaurant proper, but she could see out and below to lush tropical gardens and lily ponds. When they'd arrived, she'd gotten a few pretty views of the Ko'olau mountains.

"First, I can see all the potential entrances and exits from where I'm sitting." Zu didn't lean forward but he did speak in conversational tone to blend with the general chatter going on around them. "If not directly, then there are enough mirrors to give me line of sight via the reflections. Second, we have resources in positions to have line of sight on any areas I do not."

"Trust me, my spot is nowhere near as comfortable as yours." Arin's voice came across the comm. Ying Yue was excited to have her own earpiece. Now she was privy to the chatter during the team operation, a part of things. It buoyed her to have the feeling of being part of the actions they were taking rather than just swept along. "The views are arguably more impressive."

"It seems unfair that we get to enjoy a nice lunch and the rest of the team are assigned other tasks." Ah, she wasn't as good as Zu at carrying on a conversation without letting on the side discussions going through the comm. She wondered how much practice it had taken for him.

"I have onigiri," Arin answered, unfazed. "I make them for myself all the time. Easy to pack, satisfying, and can last all day wherever I go."

"Okay, then." She skimmed the menu. There were a lot of nice options. Even the salads were tempting, each with a unique twist rather than the standard fare to be found on most menus. "If you're going for the sticky ribs, I'll try the pulled pork sliders."

Zu nodded. "Sounds like a plan."

He placed his menu down in a decisive gesture and she did the same. A waiter immediately appeared and took their order. She caught herself glancing around a couple of times even as she tried to appear relaxed. She wasn't but wished she could at least look it.

It was sinking in, what she'd done. She'd deliberately let human traffickers know how to find her. Here she was, giving them a very significant opportunity to get hold of her again.

"Ask me a question."

She jumped in her seat, realizing Zu had been staring at her for at least a few minutes. "I'm sorry?"

He shook his head. "Don't be. But let's give you something to think about. I like your questions. Ask me."

She stared at him. He was still relaxed and calm and appeared to be very in control of his environment. This was why she'd stayed with him, and with Buck. "Why are you not trying to be less conspicuous? Is it because you're the leader?"

He shifted in his chair, and several people glanced their way. He smiled. "I work with what I have. Nothing about me is inconspicuous, from my size to the color of my skin to the scowl I generally wear because I don't actually like people, present company excluded. Buck is always with me, but I don't think he makes me stand out much more than I already do. If anything, he makes me seem more approachable."

"He does." She shifted her foot under the table and a puff of hot air followed by a cool nose touched her ankle. Buck was lying quietly at their feet, so well behaved that most of the restaurant guests didn't notice him there. "He's a big dog, but he still changes people's attitudes just by walking by."

"Why do you think that is?" Zu asked, taking a sip from his water glass.

"People like dogs." She reached out and touched the stem of her own water glass. "Well, a lot of people do. And even people who don't like dogs understand a service vest. They recognize a dog working to help a human."

"I agree." Zu shrugged. "And if Buck is a working dog, doing his job, then I must be a human partner also doing my job, which is presumably good."

"I could play devil's advocate and point out a few cases where breeds of dogs had bad reputations as attack dogs." She enjoyed exploring different perspectives and liked the way Zu explored those topics with her. "Taz and King are German Shepherd Dogs, right? They used to be feared because they're also used as guard dogs. Other working dogs can be any breed, but some of them have to be big to provide the help required to be with their human. I've seen some pit bulls and Rottweilers working as service dogs. It seems those breeds would cause a negative attitude at first."

"You raise a valid point about breeds and public opinion, but people are not usually so thorough about thinking things through. They see the service vest first. Impressions are made in seconds, and those are what we're discussing, not the true nature of dog or person." Zu didn't move, but suddenly he was more intimidating. Like all of his formidable potential had been stuffed away somewhere before and now—well now, she was more aware of him being there specifically to protect her. Regardless of how she'd been the reason they were here in the first place. "For example, our target is here, and the first thing he saw was you, relaxed and enjoying yourself. Unafraid."

Was that what they wanted?

"Miss Jiang."

She turned and looked up, making sure her most pleasant smile was in place. "Mr. Chen, thank you for coming all this way. I imagine Mr. Nilsson might have been annoyed to lose you for the meetings around the lunch hour."

"Not at all." Chen's response had a brittle quality to it. His smile seemed forced, and his movements had seemed jerky as he approached.

She thought maybe she'd hit a nerve. Her father's aide may truly not have needed Mr. Chen for whatever meetings they had today. "Please, have a seat. Would you like to order something?"

"Oh, I don't know." Chen did pull out a chair and sit down with a nervous glance at Zu. He didn't greet Zu at all.

Of course he wouldn't. Most of the businesspeople she'd met tended to treat security like they were invisible, discreet employees who were supposed to be perpetually vigilant but blind and deaf to what their employers' private business might be.

"Here is the paperwork you requested." Chen handed her a dossier. "I can answer any questions you might have."

"Thank you." Well, if that wasn't the perfect segue, she wasn't sure what would be. "Could you please tell me who is paying you for information?"

Chen froze, color leeching from his face until his skin looked like thin parchment. "What? I work for your fa—"

She smiled, and this time she used the cold expression she'd practiced in the mirror when she'd been too new, too young, to be acknowledged or respected without it. "Do not try to hide at this point, Mr. Chen. You were quite involved in my kidnapping. I have the emails to prove it. I want to know who else in the company is working for Lee-Smith."

"I…" Chen started to look around wildly.

"Don't get out of your chair." Zu had leaned forward and clamped a hand on Chen's wrist. Chen looked down, past the surface of the table, and Ying Yue realized Buck had sat up and placed his muzzle right at Chen's groin. "Just answer the lady's questions."

CHAPTER SEVENTEEN

Zu preferred the straightforward approach, so as interrogations went, he was happy with how Ying Yue decided to get this one started. Chen was caught by surprise, and there was a good chance he'd come out here with a single objective in mind, to betray Ying Yue. The man's flustered babbling indicated he hadn't been prepared for Ying Yue to know he was a traitor.

"Miss Jiang, you must be mistaken." Chen tried to break Zu's grip but failed, miserably. "I have worked for your father's company a long time."

"Truth." Zu kept his grip, with his thumb over the man's pulse point. Honestly, his grip was too tight and the erratic nature of the man's heartbeat under the strain of the situation meant Zu wasn't likely to be able to accurately determine if he was lying. Chen didn't know that, though, so it couldn't hurt to allow the man to think Zu could detect a lie. In a lot of ways, it was more effective than an actual lie detector.

Chen gulped audibly.

"See?" Chen looked to Ying Yue, his tone imploring. "I only came here as you asked, to bring you the paperwork you requested."

"Lie."

"No, no, no." Chen's panicked expression basically gave him away.

Ying Yue sighed. Zu hadn't told her he would be doing this, but the added pressure on Chen might make this go faster.

She continued smoothly despite the change in plans. "Mr. George Chen. Your name is clearly featured in the email exchanges I've seen. It would be best for you to stop lying and answer my questions."

"Why?" Chen slid a glance at Zu, which then turned eager when he refocused his attention on Ying Yue. "You could make me a better offer. Then you can be sure I would tell you what you want to know."

She shook her head. "I have more faith in the police than money. You will tell them, even if you don't tell me now. But I wanted to give you the opportunity, if you have any honor left at all, to tell me to my face what part you've played in causing me harm."

The man went silent for a moment and Zu thought it was a lost cause. They'd exposed Ying Yue for nothing.

"You know." Chen spoke in a quiet voice, filled with shame. He looked at Ying Yue directly. "I gave Mr. Lee-Smith your address, photos of you. You are right. I should tell you directly what I've done. No matter what happens next, I should do this."

Zu thought the shame might be real, and a second ago he'd been ready to call it a fail, but this reversal was too much, too easy. There had to be a reason he was giving it all up so soon. Zu and Buck weren't putting that much pressure on the guy.

"Not a lie, but he's hiding something," Zu growled.

Chen glanced at Zu again and away. Maybe the man was afraid to look at Zu for too long.

"Alpha, this is Charlie, I heard that," Arin murmured through the comm. "Nothing on the perimeter yet, but I've alerted Officer Kokua to move in slow. If this is an ambush, we're not going to give them the chance to get the jump on us."

Ying Yue didn't give any indication she'd heard Arin. "What is Lee-Smith trying to accomplish in kidnapping me?"

Chen shook his head. "I do not have access to all the plans, but I was also asked for information on the manufacturing sites your father owns and which ones are operating with a tighter profit margin. Those are the ones for which Mr. Lee-Smith would like to bid on to supply temporary workers for at a lower rate of pay. It would be mutually beneficial."

It sounded fairly benign, but Zu didn't buy it. "How much lower would the rate of pay be? And who would see those wages? I don't think it'd be the workers."

Chen froze, then spread his hands with a shrug. "They would have food and lodging, clothes."

"Only enough to keep them alive," Zu growled. "You're talking forced labor. Lee-Smith would make a profit from those people and have a place to hold them temporarily before shifting those assets elsewhere. Or he could leave them there if necessary."

Chen shrank back in his chair. "It is business."

Ying Yue was sitting straight up in her chair. When she spoke, her tone was low and fierce. "Those are people."

"Alpha, this is Charlie. Two threats approaching. Requesting permission to neutralize."

Ying Yue looked at him in alarm.

"It's okay." He said the words to Ying Yue, but it was Arin who responded.

"Roger."

"So he wants to hold me hostage to guarantee my father will cooperate with putting his people in those manufacturing sites." Ying Yue's voice shook with anger even though she managed to keep her volume down.

A whiff of sweat and too much cologne came off Chen as he tried to shift in his seat. Buck growled.

"I only know these two things. Yes, he wanted you taken. Yes, he wants to put his property to work in your father's manufacturing sites." Chen laughed, and the sound of it was high pitched, not quite sane. "Your father isn't a virtuous man. No one as successful as he is could be. He will do this thing and perhaps not even suffer that much guilt when it is done. He is sensible. He will accept what cannot be changed and move forward."

Zu didn't like the sound of those statements. He had a gut feeling, a sense of urgency to move. Chen obviously believed Lee-Smith would achieve both his objectives.

"We're leaving now." Zu shifted his grip to catch Chen under the elbow. "You can come with us and be handed over to the police, or you can run. I'm sure Mr. Lee-Smith will not appreciate what you've shared and ensure you get what you deserve for your lack of discretion."

Chen babbled something unintelligible, but Zu was only half listening.

Ying Yue rose smoothly and fell in beside Zu. She stayed reasonably clear of Chen. Buck also kept himself between Chen and Ying Yue. They moved toward the entrance, then a few feet short, Zu gave Chen a shove out the front door and herded Ying Yue back through the kitchen door.

Behind them, the sound of sirens blared just outside the restaurant. Raul stood in the kitchen with Taz, holding a takeout package. "Time to go."

Ying Yue took the takeout and followed Raul and Taz.

Zu nodded to the chef and the waiter, then followed with Buck. "Charlie, this is Alpha. We are exiting."

"Roger," Arin acknowledged calmly. "Two threats neutralized and being taken into custody by police."

They left in a police vehicle, one of multiple nondescript, window-tinted vans. Twenty minutes and another vehicle swap later and they were back on the road.

"That worked out." Ying Yue was alert and excited, and her speech pattern made her sound like she'd had a quadruple espresso in under twenty minutes. He opened his mouth to respond, but she continued, "We got the information we needed, and we can make sure my father is aware of Lee-Smith's intentions. With me safe, there's no way my father will enter into the proposed business deal."

Zu nodded but aborted his original response, concerned. She was high on adrenaline, he thought. He'd heard this before in other people, this eagerness. It had made people seek out dangerous situations unnecessarily. He didn't want that for her.

She frowned. "You could celebrate with me a little."

"You're still in danger while Lee-Smith thinks you're useful to him." Even to himself, he sounded distant, even if he was within arm's reach, right there in the driver's seat. A growing sense of foreboding twisted his gut.

"I'm with you." Maybe she was too naïve in having faith.

She sounded young and too sweet for what was happening to her. She believed in Search and Protect because Zu and his team hadn't given her any reason to doubt them. Especially Zu.

He nodded. "We continue to be successful because we don't allow ourselves to stay in a steady state too long. We don't get complacent. It's too early to celebrate."

"And that means you have another plan?" She was slowing down and had phrased her question with caution, maybe. He at least hoped she was picking up his hesitation. "Let's talk about it."

"I have some thoughts," Zu admitted. He looked at her briefly, then turned his gaze back to the road ahead. "Ying Yue, what exactly is the nature of your father's business here in Hawaii?"

"It's been planned for months." She drew the statement out slowly, defensive. "He's meeting with potential business partners regarding some of the electronic devices he manufactures. It has to do with technology and software."

Zu nodded. "But you don't know exactly what he's doing here or why he has such an extensive security contingent with him. He didn't tell us when he came to Search and Protect, either. He's also got a significant number of business leads here, too. Whatever this is, it isn't a normal business deal."

"You're suspicious of my father."

"I think his business is worth looking into, but it's not my job."

Ying Yue's voice took on a defensive edge. "Then what's your point?"

He was provoking her, and he was sure it was necessary. It'd be for the better. "This is not as clear as good guys and bad guys. You need to get past your naivete."

"My father would not be a party to human trafficking."

Zu shot back, "I think he is."

* * *

Ying Yue closed her eyes. They were about to have a significant difference of opinion, and she didn't want to. What was worse, she felt like Zu was driving them both to it. "No. He's not. He's done so many things to preserve the well-being of his employees, no matter what level they are. He wouldn't do all that and be party to human trafficking."

"There are different levels of involvement in any kind of operation." Zu wasn't backing down, either. She hadn't expected him to, but maybe she'd hoped.

"Please clarify." She wanted to be fair. She wanted to hear him out. But she felt this awful fist of anxiety tightening inside her midriff.

"You work with financials as a part of what you do. Investors can provide financial support while being conveniently ignorant of the details of any given operation." Zu tapped his fingers on the top of the steering wheel. "Your father could agree not to scrutinize the personnel once he signs a contract to allow Lee-Smith to staff his factories. It's all completely plausible, and all your father would have to do is not look too closely. Maybe Lee-Smith doesn't need you to convince your father to do it, just to work with Lee-Smith exclusively. With you used as leverage, your father could even dismiss any crisis of conscience."

Ying Yue laughed harshly. Zu settled into the driver's seat more firmly, and the air between them felt several degrees cooler. "My father built his empire from the ground up. You don't succeed that way if you're not a control freak. He oversees every detail humanly possible and only ever delegates once a person has dedicated their life to proving to him they're worthy of the trust. Employees like

Mr. Chen get in because someone lower than my father needs to learn better judgment. Your theory doesn't take into account who my father is."

"I know people." Zu made the statement like it was carved in stone, it was such an inarguable fact.

"You know types of people and what most people will do," Ying Yue shot back, frustration adding fuel to her growing anger. "But you look for the worst, and people have to move heaven and earth to get you to acknowledge the best in them. Not everyone can be heroic. Sometimes, they're just decent."

Despair threatened to surge up and drown her then. She hadn't ever been anyone's savior. She was normal, with her fair share of flaws and struggles. Compared to the way Zu and his team had saved her, the best she had to offer was being a decent human being. What if that wasn't good enough?

"You're not wrong," he said, finally. His voice had gone deep, and he gripped the steering wheel and then released it, alternating like he didn't want to break something. "Search and Protect isn't the first team I've put together. I had another private contract organization and a business partner. He was the person who worked with people, the relationship builder. He did our networking, our schmoozing, and put together all our contracts. I managed our team and kept the training standards high. It was a balanced partnership. I didn't step into his territory, and he didn't step into mine."

Ying Yue listened, trying to hear and absorb what he was saying despite being very angry with what he was implying.

"It hit me like a bullet to the chest when I realized he was taking contracts without worrying about how many innocent people would be harmed. He turned us into the worst kind of freelancers, the ones that make the word *mercenary* a curse. We were making huge amounts of money, but at the kind of cost you only pay back in hell." Zu growled out his words. "And it went on a while before I opened my eyes and looked and admitted what was happening. By the time I did, he owned enough of a controlling interest in the organization that I had to walk away with almost nothing. You need to look at your father, maybe see what you don't want to see. And you need to stop being so excited to be a part of what we do. Both those things will just get you hurt or worse."

Her breath came ragged as she tried to keep the shreds of her calm. She waited, but he didn't continue. His face was deeply etched in a scowl, and he wouldn't look at her, but part of her wanted to reach out and wrap him in her arms as best she could. He was opening up to her, making himself vulnerable, and sharing his mistake with her. And yes, he intended to help her.

But intentions didn't make a person right.

And no, she didn't want to reach out with empathy in this moment. She was too tired, too angry to. Because he was, in his own way, being patronizing as hell. "Are you trying to imply that because even you compromised and looked the other way, every person would? You weren't a saint, so no one can be? I'm just too naïve to see what my own father would do?"

"You are too naïve." Zu replied sharp and fast, with more heat in his voice than she'd ever heard before. "You haven't seen the shit people can do to each other. You think you've been through things, and yeah, they were bad, but you know they could've been worse. So much worse, Ying Yue. You just don't know."

It was her turn to let silence fall between them, and she felt what they'd begun to share between them straining, both the revelations here in the car and the relationship that was growing between them. They were too new. But here was the reality. They didn't truly know each other. He wasn't just questioning her judgment; he was assuming she was too ignorant or inexperienced to know evil in the world, and he was wrong.

Whether he was right or not wasn't the actual problem. His attitude meant they weren't on equal footing in this relationship, and she would not tolerate it. But she couldn't beat him over the head with her own qualities. She had to lead him to it, if he'd follow.

"What is it you're attracted to about me? My sweet innocence?" The sarcasm in her own voice was thick. She was getting ugly, but she couldn't stop herself. She might regret it later, too, and anxiety churned in her stomach, but if she kept the words inside, she feared she'd be replaying this conversation for the rest of her life. If they were going to have it out, she'd say the things she had in her mind and heart and not let them sit inside her and fester. "I'm not some ingenue from a fairy tale or epic adventure story."

"Are you sure?" he asked, and the words dropped like stones in her gut.

Oh, he was definitely dipping heavy into the sarcasm, right along with her.

Her heart was breaking. This wasn't something they were going to overcome. She hated herself for it, but she couldn't back down even though part of her wanted to. Her jaw ached from clenching her teeth together.

"That's how you see me." She said it as much to herself as to him. "I was a damsel in distress when you found me. I still am now. Not only did you get to be my knight in—let's face it—somewhat dented armor, but you get to continue to be my valiant protector. Nothing I do will bring me side by side with you as a partner or person equally capable."

He didn't tell her she was wrong. That was okay. She wasn't.

But she couldn't be happy in that relationship dynamic. She'd lose any self-worth she had. The tension in her chest tightened, and she had to admit, she was already losing it now.

Tears ran hot down her cheeks, and she wasn't sure when she had started crying. "What will you do when I pick up my life again, and I start doing what I do best? I gather money for a living. I convince people to donate. How can you ever believe I am doing my work with the highest of integrity when I use my PhD to help companies minimize tax impact when they transfer assets to the causes I work for?"

"You aren't..."

She didn't let him finish. "Your entire argument is based on the premise that people are susceptible, even driven, by greed. Some people give in to it by turning a blind eye. I get that. I appreciate you implying maybe my father would be one of those, but you were pulling your punches some, weren't you? Anyone as successful as my father can't possibly be that blind. He has to know, which makes him worse than you. But even you were blind to it, once upon a time. Do not preserve me as the sweet, innocent, blameless damsel by assuming me incapable of making the same mistakes."

Zu had hit the accelerator on the car, and he took a moment to ease off, slow them down. "You're a victim in this."

Her skin burned and she tasted salt. Yes, she was totally

crying, and she didn't care. Let him feel bad. She wasn't going to bottle this up or try to hide this from him. "A victim isn't all that I am. Don't make it all I can be inside your head."

"I'm not."

She almost screamed she was so frustrated—with him, with herself, with the situation that wasn't over yet. She would have to start all over again proving to everyone around her that she was a competent, autonomous, talented person capable of being something other than someone's daughter... or someone's precious damsel to protect.

"When this is over, you do not get to wrap me up in soft cloth and place me someplace safe."

"You need to understand this could take a long time to resolve..."

There it was. The patronizing tone. She heard it, and it made her nauseous.

"Stop," she said cold and calm, cutting into their fight and shutting it down. "Right here, right now, we are not discussing this further."

"There are..."

"No." She was done.

He started to try again, but his phone rang, broadcasting through the car.

He hesitated, letting it ring.

"Go ahead. Answer it." Ying Yue pitched her voice sweet and wiped her face. "I guarantee you this conversation is over."

Zu sighed, which only kept her temper burning. "Alpha here."

"Boss." Pua's voice chirped across the line. "We've got a communication in from the FBI. They want Ying Yue to come in for questioning about her kidnapping."

CHAPTER EIGHTEEN

Zu pulled into the visitors parking area in front of the office building currently maintained by the FBI. It'd been a long, quiet drive once they'd received the message from Pua. Ying Yue's words still hung heavy in the air between them, and neither of them had broken the silence. It wasn't so much what she'd said as the hurt he'd heard in her voice that continued to cut into him. He'd been open and honest and very sure he was telling her what to expect for her own good.

Ultimately, she'd been right about the way he thought of her as a damsel in distress. He wasn't sure she was as correct about his perception of her remaining that way moving forward.

It was important to stay focused on the here and now, maintain hyperawareness of where they were and what was around them. He could think a few steps ahead when it came to countering their adversary, with the objective to keep her safe.

But he hadn't given thought to what would happen to them when the mission was over.

Truthfully, did he ever think about life between missions? Or was the time between one contract and the next only an exercise in acquiring and preparing for the upcoming work?

He didn't know how to be just him outside of a mission. The concept of a relationship wasn't something he'd considered even as he'd savored every moment with Ying Yue. He wasn't sure if he had any kind of chance to repair the damage the argument had done the both of them, but he had better damn well think on it, hard.

Once he parked the car, she waited for him to let Buck out of the back and then come around to the passenger side and open the door. She didn't accept his help getting out of the car. He let his offered hand fall to his side and simply escorted her to the front security booth. It felt petty to be irritated with her. She'd followed procedure. He'd had other clients blatantly ignore his instructions and just get out of the car themselves before he and Buck had come around to their side of the vehicle. It left those people exposed. Even if she wasn't taking him up on the courtesies, she also wasn't endangering herself to make a point.

Shit, he was irritated with her anyway.

They approached the gate, where two men in suits were waiting. Interesting. Normally, a security guard would take their IDs and let them in the gate to walk the rest of the way across the paved front walkway to the actual building. Then they'd enter the building and wait in the small reception area there. Zu hadn't had much interaction with the FBI, but he'd been to a few of their offices on the mainland. The buildings differed in age and design, but the procedures were generally consistent from facility to facility.

"Miss Jiang?" One man stepped forward. He was a white man of average height and build, with medium brown hair cut in a simple style a hundred thousand other men in suits might wear. He didn't have any features of note, really. Nothing to help a person remember him. The only thing that kept him from being the ultimate forgettable agent was his eyes, a steel gray rather than nondescript brown. "I'm Agent Vella, and this is my partner, Agent Jain. Thank you for coming to meet us."

Zu stood back a step as Ying Yue shook hands with each of them.

Agent Jain was a brown man who could pass as a number of ethnicities with minimal effort, also of average height. He maybe had an inch or two on his partner but was a slighter build. His hair was a touch longer on top, but otherwise, Jain had the same quality of being eminently difficult to describe in any way that would be useful for someone trying to identify him.

Way off in a distant corner of Zu's mind, he chuckled to himself. He'd never have done well as a government agent. He was too notable in physicality and not good at maintaining the pleasantly polite, don't-be-alarmed demeanor each of them exuded. At the moment, he wasn't inclined to fade into the background, either, since both of them were working so hard to ignore him and Buck.

"If you'll come with us, we'll sit down and discuss your recent experience." Agent Vella indicated the building beyond the gate. "We'll just pass through the security booth instead of having the boys open up the entire gate."

Zu moved to follow as Ying Yue walked with Agent Jain toward the booth. Agent Vella stepped directly into Zu's path. Zu considered running him over, but it was better to play nice with the FBI whenever possible.

"Mr. Anyanwu, isn't it?" Agent Vella held up a hand and did a reasonable job of not leaning back far in order to look up into Zu's face. "We don't have a need to talk to you. We received your organization's statement from the local police. You and your dog aren't needed for this interview."

Ying Yue turned, honestly startled. "Mr. Anyanwu and Buck are my private security."

Agent Vella smiled, not bothering to turn back to her as he spoke over his shoulder. "Miss Jiang, you don't need private security while you're with the FBI."

Agent Jain tapped a sign stuck to the outside of the gate.

WARNING

RESTRICTED AREA

IT IS UNLAWFUL TO ENTER THIS AREA

USE OF DEADLY FORCE AUTHORIZED

Agent Vella jerked his head toward the visitor parking area. "If you're going to wait, make sure to keep your distance."

Asshole.

Zu didn't waste his time in a staring contest with the tiny man. Instead, he looked at Ying Yue. She appeared to be conflicted, wavering between following Agent Jain and staying with Zu. Fight or no fight, she wasn't comfortable with being away from him.

"Miss Jiang, we do need to speak with you. Please follow us inside." Agent Jain had put a little force into his request. "Unless it's your intent not to cooperate, you should really come with us."

Well, now they'd gone from pissing contest to barely veiled threat. They didn't have to say "or else" to have their meaning come across.

For her sake, he kept his temper leashed. Any argument he made would just bait these agents into making things more difficult. He didn't want to make this worse for her. He could repair what was between them once she'd

finished this interview. He locked gazes with her over
Agent Vella's head. "We'll be here for you. Doesn't matter
how long it takes."

She nodded and gave him a tiny smile. Then she turned
and followed Agent Jain. Agent Vella didn't even bother
to thank Zu for his cooperation. The little man just turned
on his heel and followed Ying Yue into the security booth.
Zu stood there, watching as they paused to speak to a
uniformed agent in the booth.

Another uniformed man stepped out and approached
Zu. "Sir. We need you to move away from the entry gate
now."

"I'm keeping line of sight on my client." Irritation lent
an edge to his voice. What the actual hell? At his side,
Buck let out a low growl.

The man's jaw jutted forward, and he actually dropped
his hand to his sidearm. "Now, sir. Walk away and maintain
a distance from the gate. The visitor parking area is fine
for waiting."

The idiot might actually be threatening to shoot either
Zu or, worse, Buck. If he opted to shoot Zu, Buck would
be on the man faster than the man could defend himself.
There was no way it could end well for Buck, who would
be quarantined or even destroyed for attacking the man
who, for all intents and purposes, was doing his job. It was
on Zu as Buck's owner to protect Buck by not putting him
in a situation where the dog would have no recourse but to
act in accordance with his training and instincts. They had
to back away.

Frustrated, Zu caught sight of Ying Yue as she watched
him nervously from inside the booth. Agents Vella and
Jain still spoke to the other uniformed guard, apparently no
longer concerned with Zu. He tried to give her a reassuring

smile, then he headed back to his car before the uniforms got too trigger-happy.

Pua answered his call. "Hey, boss."

"I want all the information you can find about why the FBI is now involved with Ying Yue's kidnapping." Zu didn't like this. Not one bit. "I also want to know anything you can find on agents Vella and Jain here in Oahu. I want to know if they're stationed here permanently and, if not, when they arrived, and whether we know anyone who's encountered them ever."

* * *

Ying Yue resisted the urge to run after Zu and Buck as they walked away. Logically, she shouldn't be worried. They would be about a hundred yards away in the parking lot. She was with the FBI. It wasn't as if she was unprotected.

But the urge to run after them didn't come from fear of being exposed or in danger. She'd said harsh things, and Zu hadn't responded. Arguments like the one they'd just had created a chasm between people. Maybe there was no coming back from it, but if they didn't try to communicate to close the gap right away, it only got wider and wider. They hadn't had a chance to even express to each other whether they wanted to address the issue, and she didn't want them to end this way.

She thought from Zu's expression just before he'd left that he cared. He'd smiled. For her. He never smiled in front of anybody, as far as she knew. That had to mean something. She was sure it did.

The security guard returned to the booth with his hand still on his gun. He was grinning wide and had a nasty look in his eyes as he spit on the floor. "Idiot walked away. He's actually headed back to his car."

"He's too good to be baited by small people like you." The words popped out before she could think better of them. The man might be under federal employ, but he was still just a security guard manning a booth at a gate. There were only a handful of cars parked within the walls of the facility as far as she could see.

All four of the men present laughed. A chill crackled across her skin as she stared at each of them in turn, two agents and two security guards. Why were they so antagonistic toward a private contractor? She knew there tended to be friction between professionals, but Zu and his team had such a positive relationship with local law enforcement, she hadn't thought the FBI would be so abrasive.

Agent Vella jerked his head in the direction Zu and Buck had gone. "You have no idea how pissed off he and his friends have made some very powerful people."

This was wrong, all wrong.

Her heart rate kicked into overdrive, and she mentally locked down all of the thoughts scrambling around. From this moment forward, she wasn't going to give them the satisfaction of seeing her frightened or feed whatever power trip they planned to go on with her. "I'd rather not be here longer than necessary. What questions did you have for me?"

Agent Vella widened his eyes. "Us? None. But we do represent someone who has questions for you."

Agent Jain shrugged. "Well, maybe he doesn't have questions. He's definitely got plans."

The disgusting security guard with the spitting problem leered at her. They didn't bother trying to dissemble anymore.

Enough. Zu. She screamed.

A hand clamped over her mouth, smothering her, and she was pulled roughly back against someone, restrained before she could even think to try to run. The other security guard. She'd lost track of him, and he'd gotten behind her.

A gray sedan pulled up next to the security booth on the inside of the gate. That was all she could make out as she was forced out of the booth and into the back seat of the car. Agent Jain got into the passenger seat, and Agent Vella got into the back with her. It wasn't until the doors were closed and they were moving that the hand came away from her mouth.

The gate was opening, and they were pulling through, leaving the facility. They were going to drive right by Zu and Buck.

Agent Vella spoke to the man struggling with her. "Hold her down. Don't let her see out the windows."

The windows were tinted anyway. How was Zu going to see her? He had to be watching the gate area. She knew he was going to be suspicious of any car coming or going, but maybe he wouldn't follow this car if he thought she was still inside the building. If he couldn't see her, how would he know?

Think. Everything she was coming up with relied on Zu. She needed to do something.

She purposefully went limp so suddenly that her captor cursed, alarmed.

Agent Vella didn't care. "That's it. Be a good girl."

No.

She kicked out hard and bucked until she got a hand free. She reached for what she had a chance of getting to, the window button. The window opened a crack and she screamed with everything she had.

"Did you fucking think you were going to make it out the window?" The security guard laughed as he wrapped his arms around her. "Your bodyguard didn't even see you try, stupid bitch."

"What a waste of fucking energy." Vella leaned past them both to hit the window button and close it. "Get the window closed, just in case."

But he was too late. Hope washed through her and brought tears to her eyes. Barking, she heard barking.

Maybe Zu couldn't see her, and she never thought she'd be able to open the window enough for him to catch a glimpse of her.

But Buck had heard her.

CHAPTER NINETEEN

Zu had been watching the car leave the FBI facility. With the tinted windows, he couldn't see much, only a driver he didn't recognize and nothing to give him any hints as to who else was in the vehicle. He was in the process of noting the license plate when Buck went wild.

Zu looked up into the rearview. Buck was focused on the leaving car. Zu didn't wait for any other sign. He fired up his car engine, reversed out of their parking spot, threw his vehicle into drive, and proceeded after the gray sedan. He also hit the Call button on his phone.

"Boss? I don't have—"

"License plate HNG728. Gray sedan. Call it in to HPD. Stat." Zu barked out the order.

"On it." Pua didn't ask questions. She also didn't drop the line. He could hear her calling Honolulu Police Department via a different phone.

As he heard her state the reason for the call, he added context for her. "Jiang Ying Yue has been kidnapped. Repeat. Kidnapping in progress."

Pua repeated his information to the police. Her voice grew strained.

The car ahead of him had made the turn onto the main road and was getting up to high speed. He had to stick with them until Honolulu Police closed in. He put on a little more speed to close the distance. He wasn't going to lose Ying Yue.

He heard the blowout only a fraction of a second before the steering wheel jerked out from under his hands. His vehicle started to spin, and he heard the screeching sound of bare metal on the road. He kept his foot on the gas pedal, maintaining speed as best he could to prevent the car from spinning further out of control. Once he got to the side of the road, it was everything he could do to keep the vehicle headed forward as it decelerated. Another impact hit the car, and the car jerked, rolling over on its side.

Luck, or not, but the car didn't roll farther than upside down.

"Buck." Zu struggled to assess the damage to himself and his partner.

Buck whined and rustled, crawling across the hood of the car to lick Zu's face. One small blessing. Unrestrained in the car the way he had been, Buck could've suffered serious injury.

Zu located his phone on the roof, now below him. Then, he reached to the side and opened the driver's side door.

Dirt flew as a shot fired hit the ground right next to where Zu's head would've been, had he immediately tried to exit the car. Zu yanked the door closed and considered his options.

Shit. Shooter outside. He and Buck were pinned inside unless he could come up with some way to get out safely.

Zu freed himself from his seatbelt and caught himself on his hands and knees in the overturned vehicle. There was a ridiculously small amount of room for him to maneuver if he stayed in the vehicle. Also, it was only a matter of time before the shooter decided to try taking a shot at something on the exposed underside of the vehicle to force Zu to exit or go up in a ball of flames.

Zu reached into the back, past Buck, for his go bag and pulled it to him. He yanked open the zipper and grabbed a smoke grenade.

"Buck, *af.*"

Buck flattened himself against the roof of the car. Zu pulled the pin and threw the grenade out the shattered driver's side window, then turned to cover Buck as the grenade burst with white smoke.

One one thousand, two one thousand.

Zu opened the driver's side door again and rolled out of the vehicle, bringing his go bag with him. Buck followed, and the two of them made for cover in the trees along the side of the road. Zu had to hurriedly clip enough of the chain-link fence to let himself and Buck through, hoping the white smoke was enough to obscure the shooter's vision. Once they were through, he tucked them behind a few trees growing close together with a good amount of underbrush to further conceal them.

He waited, his firearm ready, for several long minutes. No more shots were fired. They'd managed to confuse the shooter, and hopefully the shooter no longer knew exactly where they were. He retrieved his phone from his shirt pocket. "Still there, Pua?"

"Boss! That was a lot of noise, and I've been on mute here freaking out."

"Update Officer Kokua. Possible shooter in the vicinity."

"On it." There was a pause, and then Pua whispered, "Please be okay."

"We're good, Pua. Buck and I are good."

"Oh, sweet pies and cookies, thank you. I know I'm supposed to wait for you to tell me and listen for the key information and pass it on, but I was so scared, boss, and I really needed to know you two were okay. Sorry. HPD confirmed. They're taking measures. Officer Kokua says they're coming in to your smoke signal."

Well, it'd been for other reasons, but it was good the smoke had served multiple purposes.

Minutes later, Officer Kokua arrived with an armored SWAT vehicle and an ambulance.

"Zu!"

By then, Zu had shrugged into his own armored vest and helmet, plus he had checked Buck over and gotten him into his K9 tactical gear. They'd gotten lucky. Crazy lucky.

Zu stood and Officer Kokua headed toward him, relief evident on the other man's face. "We need to get you to a hospital."

"No. I need my team. They took her."

* * *

"You're going to pay for that. We could've just driven away. No one the wiser. But no, you had to go for desperate measures."

Ying Yue narrowed her eyes at Agent Vella—probably not an actual FBI agent, or maybe he was. She had no idea what people Lee-Smith could have on his payroll at this point. She wanted to look defiant, brave. Hard to do it with duct tape plastered over her mouth and her wrists now bound behind her back. They weren't taking any more chances with her.

She was doing everything she could to think through the fear tightening her chest and churning her stomach. She'd heard gunfire and the sound of screeching and metal crunching. It was hard to tell what had actually happened, and she had only caught a glimpse of Zu's SUV rolling over at the side of the road in the rearview and side mirrors. Maybe she'd seen a silhouette tossed around inside, or maybe it'd been her imagination gone wild with her worst fears. And Buck hadn't been secured in his crate.

"Your bodyguard is buried in the wreck of his car, and it's your fault," Agent Jain snapped out. "If you'd have just stayed quiet, he'd still be sitting like an idiot back in that parking lot."

Of the two agents, Jain seemed more worried about the consequences as things got more and more complicated. He kept checking his watch and wiping perspiration from his forehead. They were trying to meet a timeline, and he was nervous.

"You know what?" Vella was much more calm, even cheerful in a psychopathic kind of way. "You did us a favor. He was a major pain in the ass, and now he's no one's problem."

No.

Zu wasn't gone. She didn't believe it.

Vella laughed, the sound of it ugly. "I'm not going to have the driver circle back for you to see it with your own eyes, but no one crawled out of that wreck. Even if he did, we had someone waiting to put a few bullets in his head."

Agent Jain must've drawn some confidence from his partner. "Bottom line: he's not coming for you."

She wasn't sure if someone could walk away from a car wreck like that. But Zu was a professional. Not only was he a professional, but he and his team were some of the most competent people she'd ever encountered. He had to have the training to handle the situation. And if he managed to survive, he was going to come after her. Even if he didn't care for her—and she believed he did—she was his client, and he made his job the primary focus of all his energies. She respected that about him, loved him for his integrity, even.

If he survived, he'd come after her.

If he didn't...

"Don't hope for the rest of his team, either." Vella was watching her. Maybe he was reading her expressions. She needed to develop the blank, neutral face she'd seen Zu and Arin and Raul all adopt. "We've had eyes on all of the Search and Protect people, and we're maintaining a close enough watch to keep them all moving around, jumping at shadows. None of them are anywhere near enough to come after you before we disappear. They can look for you, but they don't have the resources to find you."

There were so few of them. It was just Arin and King, Raul and Taz. As far as Ying Yue knew, Todd and Kalea Miller didn't go into the field. Todd might, but he was only one additional resource. Pua would be working her technical magic getting them intel, sure, but they needed to keep Pua protected as well. Pua had already been endangered once because of Ying Yue.

Despair crushed her so hard, she closed her eyes and tried to breathe against the weight on her chest. She couldn't wait and try to survive just on faith that someone would come get her. If there was one thing the Search and Protect team—Zu especially—had taught her, it was that a person could keep surprising the enemies around them.

She was going to have to watch, keep her mental faculties sharp, and be ready when a chance presented itself. She was going to have to get creative and find a way to save herself. She didn't have the skills any of the Search and Protect team had, but she would do her best. Even if she couldn't be a knight in shining armor, she could at least get herself out of the situation she was in and meet the cavalry on its way to her.

Maybe?

She would. She wasn't going to give up.

CHAPTER TWENTY

Zu stepped into his house after a long, circuitous route to get home. It was the last secure location he had for the Search and Protect team. The one place, so far, Lee-Smith hadn't managed to discover. It would have to be the staging area for his team to regroup and plan decisive action. Lee-Smith wasn't just a distant threat anymore, or a target. He was an active aggressor against the Search and Protect team, and now the man had Ying Yue.

Raul and Taz were waiting for him. They'd been the closest and also the first to arrive at the property, even after all the team members took precautions to lose any potential tails. Raul didn't say anything, only gave Zu a nod as he entered. Raul was perched on one of the stools by the breakfast bar, not the one Ying Yue had used when she'd been working there. The loaner laptop she'd been using was still at her place, neatly closed and waiting for her.

Taz rose to sniff noses with Buck. Raul's black-faced German Shepherd Dog was easygoing, but still dominant in personality. But this was Buck's territory, his scent everywhere, so it wasn't a surprise when Taz backed off and went back to lie at Raul's feet. Dominant dogs were always testing each other, establishing the hierarchy. But the dogs of Search and Protect were well trained, so they kept their challenges subtle and responded immediately to any command from their owners to leave off. Today, Buck and Taz hadn't needed any correction from their handlers. They could no doubt sense the tension in the air, the preparation.

The dogs were getting ready to work, and any personality differences would be set aside in favor of doing their jobs.

Arin arrived next with King, the two of them materializing from the beach area. Her huge German Shepherd Dog partner's legs and belly were wet from wading through the incoming waves. She carried a long pack strapped across her back. She'd brought her rifle in addition to her regular gear. It might come in handy, or it might not. It was hard to say until he had more information.

"Boss, you're okay!" Pua rushed in the front door with Todd Miller close behind her. Speaking of information...

Pua skidded to a halt, taking in Arin and King, Raul and Taz, Zu and Buck. She looked at Raul. "How'd you get here?"

Raul leaned back hands open and up. "Wait, why are you just asking me? What about Arin? And for that matter how did you get here?"

Pua tipped her head to one side. "Because Arin is always supposed to get where she's going, and we're not supposed to ask how she got there. The whole sniper thing, right. Or maybe ninja? I don't really know. But she gets where she's going and she's here and King's wet and I want to know but I'm not going to ask. But me? Todd drove and I napped."

Raul was shaking his head through her stream-of-consciousness declaration, then he stared at Pua. "Wait. You napped?"

Pua nodded, completely unrepentant. "Of course. Nap when you can, so when you need to act, you're ready. I learned that from Arin."

Zu coughed into his fist. Raul was rubbing the top of his forehead as Pua's commentary left him flummoxed, and Zu thought Raul might be wearing his hair thin.

"Arin, queen of speed napping, it's good to see you again." A new voice joined the chatter. All three of the Search and Protect dogs were on their feet, and their handlers turned to face the living area open to the ocean.

Out of the gathering twilight, a man strode in, hands loose at his sides and obviously not carrying any weapons at the ready. He was dark-haired, brown-skinned with a gold undertone, and brown-eyed. He was tall—taller than Raul, maybe, but not quite able to stand eye to eye with Zu. This man was a fighter, given the way he moved and assessed the room, and not just a soldier, either. He was a brawler. He had bruises across his knuckles and darker skin across his shins from recent training. At the man's side was a German Shepherd Dog, not as big as Arin's King and more tan in the face than Raul's Taz.

"Alex Rojas." Raul's greeting was the signal for them all to relax, even the dogs. Though Zu had corresponded and even spoken on the phone with the professionals of Hope's Crossing Kennels, only Raul had met them face-to-face. "You and Souze decide to swim off the jet lag?"

Alex shrugged. "Could be. Water's warm here."

Despite his commentary, Alex was only wet up to his knees, and he'd rolled his pants up high enough to save himself from standing around too damp for too long. Still, Zu considered grabbing extra sweats for people and throwing a load of sea-soaked clothes in the laundry.

Buck gave a warning bark as all three of the Search and Protect dogs turned to look toward the front of the house.

"Some people decided to go around the long way. The rest of us decided to catch a ride, then jog in the rest of the way like the land-loving creatures we are," another man stated from the entryway. He'd come in silent, and at his side stood another dog. The man had blue eyes and bronzed skin and wore a tank top that exposed his regiment of tattoos. The dog was equally stoic. More black than tan, he was the smallest dog in the house but probably fierce as hell. Belgian Malinois tended to be used in tandem with SEAL teams and could do a hell of a lot more than most people ever dreamed a dog could do.

Raul turned and gave the man an equally friendly grin. "David. Good to see you and Atlas, too."

David nodded then looked to Zu. "Azubuike Anyanwu. Permission to enter."

Formal. Zu nodded. "Granted and be welcome."

Buck sat, keeping a watchful eye on the newcomers, but Zu wasn't worried. None of the canines would attack unless given a command by one of their respective handlers. The dogs weren't about to cuddle up in a pile of friendly snuggles either, but that was fine.

David strode the rest of the way into the room with a pointed look at Alex.

"Hey, I figured since we were invited, and the house was wide open..." Alex looked at Zu.

Zu shook his head. "It's all good. Where's Brandon Forte?"

David Cruz and Alex Rojas were two of three men Pua had called in as reinforcements. They were most recently trainers at a kennel on the mainland called Hope's Crossing Kennels. In fact, these men had trained Raul's Taz. Raul's first assignment had been to go to Hope's Crossing Kennels and build ties with the trainers there in the case of this kind of need.

They were all men of honor. Raul had confirmed, backed by Arin, who'd gone over to the mainland to help out with a situation there. These men could be trusted, and they owed the Search and Protect team. It was time to call in the favor.

Alex pulled a phone from his pocket. "Forte had to take a later flight. I left out of Philly International and Cruz left out of Newark. Forte left out of JFK, and that airport is a hellmouth. He was due to land close to the same time as us, but he might've run into some delays."

"You didn't have too much trouble getting through inspections with the dogs, obviously." Zu figured Pua would've helped with the documentation needed and arrangements at Honolulu International Airport. Search and Protect already made those arrangements for their dogs, especially since Hope's Crossing Kennels specialized in training military working dogs.

"They took one look at Haydn and passed him through with his paperwork." One more voice joined as another man stood in the entryway.

Zu motioned for him to come inside.

He was a white man, tanned by time spent outdoors, with brown hair and hazel eyes. He was dressed casual in a T-shirt and jeans, but wore worn combat boots. At his side was a jet-black German Shepherd Dog standing proud with a left front prosthetic limb. "It's good to meet you in person, Anyanwu."

"Call me Zu." Zu motioned for Pua to head into the living room. He touched a panel, bringing down the walls to fully enclose his house. "Pua, we're going to need to bring everyone up to speed. Start with what you've got, and I'll supplement with what happened most recently. Every minute we spend here is one less Ying Yue has, so let's make it count."

* * *

The problem with taking action was that it needed to be carefully planned to actually work. Zu stalked the length of his bedroom and back again as he waited for Pua and Kenny to set up an ops area downstairs. Kenny had showed up after the debrief with impeccable timing. The man would've been ridiculously suspicious if he hadn't proven over and over he was a friend and an ally to Zu and the rest of the Search and Protect team. Someday, he was going to learn Kenny's story. He thought that if Ying Yue had been there, she'd probably have told Zu that once he found out what he wanted to know about Kenny, he was going to want to get incredibly blackout drunk and forget it all, or Kenny would likely have to kill him.

Zu chuckled in spite of himself.

It'd been happening all evening into the dark of night. He'd be deep in the debrief or discussing strategy with Brandon's team from Hope's Crossing Kennels, and his brain would invent what Ying Yue would've likely said to him.

She'd been a part of his life for only a few days, but she

was in every thought, every breath, every moment, waking or sleeping. Every room she'd explored in his house echoed with her questions, her laughter, and, here in his room, her sweet sighs of pleasure. She'd been a dream beyond any he'd ever hoped for. He definitely didn't deserve her.

He and his team had reached a point where there was nothing more he could do, no more planning any of the strategists among them could manage, without more intel. And so Pua and Kenny were working in tandem in the kitchen. Pua had kicked them all out and claimed the refrigerator and all the snacks in Zu's pantry for her and Kenny while they worked.

The Hope's Crossing Kennels team was bedded down in the guest rooms, and his own team was in the living room, all of them taking the precious moments to rest so they could be ready when there was something they could do. The jokes about Arin's napping were fun, but the skill was real. The lesson she'd taught Pua was one that could make the difference between surviving or making fatal mistakes. Zu should be flat on his back, getting what sleep he could, too.

But his house wasn't his anymore.

The feeling wasn't about the two teams who'd assembled here. It wasn't about opening up his private space to them. These were people he trusted. Eventually, he'd have come to a place in his life when he'd have been ready to welcome his friends, his chosen family, to this place.

It was about his heart and the way he'd given it to a woman he'd never seen coming. She'd been taken, and with her, his sense of home. Even though he was standing in a building he'd designed and she'd been here for a fraction of the time this place had existed, without her, it was achingly incomplete.

This was what Arin meant by "what-if," and it left him gasping for something so like air, he didn't know how to breathe past it. This would've happened if he'd let Ying Yue go back to her life. This would've happened because he hadn't even known himself well enough to know he needed her this way.

Now, he needed to find her, and when he did, she might choose to leave him. And that would be okay, because it would be her choice. He refused to accept anything else. He wouldn't acknowledge the outcome at the hands of anyone else. Not Lee-Smith, not her father, not anyone.

They'd find her. There was no other option. Until then, he would miss her from every corner of his house.

"Boss?" Pua's voice came floating up the stairs, barely a whisper.

Buck rose to his feet and padded to the door of the bedroom. Zu stepped past him and started down the stairs. "What've we got?"

Pua looked up at him, dark circles under her liquid brown eyes. In her own way, she was the staunchest of them. "A couple of things. We've got a call in from the mainland I think you're going to want to hear. I've also got a couple of possible leads, but I need a little more time to pull it all together."

"One step at a time, and each of them takes the time it takes." He wanted to scream at her to hurry, but that was his fear talking, and it wasn't the voice they needed to save Ying Yue. So he kept the monster on lockdown and gave voice to the real thing they all needed to believe in. "We do what we need to do to find Ying Yue. We make her safe... and we eliminate the danger."

Anger raged inside his chest, incinerating any of the weaknesses that might endanger that objective. He'd take a particular joy in the process of elimination. That was the part of him Ying Yue had never seen, maybe should never see. It was the reason he didn't deserve her. Because he, like the other men and women who'd assembled to help in this mission, had been an excellent soldier.

He intended to erase Lee-Smith and anyone else involved in hurting Ying Yue from existence, and he didn't plan to be merciful. He did intend to be decisive, violent, and devastatingly efficient.

CHAPTER TWENTY-ONE

As Zu came back downstairs, he realized Pua had assembled everyone from both Search and Protect and Hope's Crossing Kennels. He must be truly losing his edge if he hadn't heard the others head down to the living room. Of course, if it'd been one of his people and not himself, he'd have pointed out that the recent car crash and use of a smoke bomb at fairly close range might've caused temporary hearing loss. But this was him, and he wasn't willing to give himself the leeway. So as he entered last into his own living room, he was scowling deeply.

David Cruz was standing in the middle of the room in front of the wall they were using as a screen. A temporary webcam had been set on a tripod. A white man with the creases of age and long years of the strain of command etched into his face was staring at them from the wall. The man was obviously waiting and definitely not the type of person used to it, if Zu was going to go by his uniform.

David nodded to Zu, then turned to the webcam. "Sir,

I'd like to introduce you to Azubuike Anyanwu, leader of
Search and Protect. Zu, this is Captain Jones, US Navy."

Zu stopped beside David, giving the webcam time to
focus on him. He stood upright, in the position of attention
out of habit. Pua had slipped past him and tapped a laptop set just below the image of Captain Jones, where the
image of David and Zu was displayed for their benefit.
It always helped to know what the person on the other
end of the video feed was seeing. Captain Jones could see
the whole room and all of the people assembled, plus the
dogs, though Brandon Forte's Haydn was a shadow in the
low light. Black German Shepherd Dogs apparently had an
excellent built-in stealth mode.

"Sir." Zu nodded to Captain Jones.

"We're going to make this quick, Mr. Anyanwu."
Captain Jones stared straight into his camera, giving the
impression of making eye contact. "And let me be clear,
this conversation never happened."

Zu shot a look at David Cruz, figuring this particular
conversation was courtesy of Cruz and his connections.
Cruz gave him a neutral look Zu chose to interpret as
"Go with it."

"Understood, sir." This was not the time for witty commentary, and humor wasn't Zu's forte anyway.

Captain Jones looked relieved. "It's my understanding
you are looking into a situation involving the father of
Jiang Ying Yue. While I don't have intel specifically regarding Miss Jiang, her father is a person of interest to the
US government."

Honestly, it wasn't surprising. Most businessmen with
global influence at the level of Jiang's would be on several
government watch lists. Zu waited. This was the sort of
intel best received uninterrupted. He might not get to ask

questions at the end of it, either. He was going to get what Captain Jones intended to give him, and this most definitely constituted a favor down the road. Ying Yue was worth it.

"Mr. Jiang holds the contracts to manufacture several lines of high-end, exceedingly popular smartphones," Captain Jones said. "It would be extremely valuable to any number of interested parties if specific software were to be installed and present on the phones even if the phones were wiped or reset to factory settings."

Of course Captain Jones was choosing his words carefully, even on a secure video conference. He was referring to a backdoor, either installed via software or even coded into the firmware of the hardware on every phone manufactured by Jiang's sites. If Captain Jones was giving Zu and his team this information, a US government agency—maybe more than one—was involved with the meetings Jiang was having on Oahu. It made a lot of sense, considering Hawaii's strategic importance to the US and globally.

"It would be problematic if any US government agency was involved with a factory or manufacturing site enveloped in accusations of forced labor, indentured servitude, or even below-standard work environments. Such circumstances would trigger a closer look at exactly what the factory or manufacturing site was doing for those US government agencies. If Mr. Jiang is under pressure from an external party, the US government would need to ensure any possible points of leverage were secured," Captain Jones continued. "To that end, I'm giving clearance to your technical analyst to work with multiple nearby contacts to access satellite intel on the island of Oahu specifically. Find your client, Mr. Anyanwu, and report back to me immediately. Meetings cannot proceed until we are assured Mr. Jiang has no further external pressures clouding his judgment as these deals proceed."

Zu nodded. Military satellite data could help them locate almost anyone on the island, given a skilled technician and enough time. Time was the critical value in this case.

"Mr. Jiang also received an encrypted message recently. I am having that decoded and sent to your technical analyst also."

It was probably the ransom demand. Between that and the satellite imagery, they'd be able to pinpoint where Lee-Smith's people were going to meet Jiang for the exchange. It was enough to find Ying Yue.

"Thank you, sir." Zu thought quickly. "Is there any intel on the initial contract calling for Jiang Ying Yue's original kidnapping?"

It seemed moot at this point, but something about the lack of any context for who had ordered her kidnapped in the first place bothered him. They could assume it was Lee-Smith, but if so, why had the man put her on a container ship headed to Oahu alongside inventory managed by someone else? They were missing too much and filling it all in with assumptions or educated guesses. He didn't like it.

"Not at this time." Captain Jones cleared his throat. "It is in the US government's best interest to supply your team with pertinent intel, so I am also willing to arrange for your technical analyst to have access to intelligence files on Lee-Smith's background and activities over the last six months."

Pua piped up. "Awesome, but if you know about him, why let the human trafficking operation continue to come back over and over again?"

It was a good question. Captain Jones's eyes narrowed, but Pua was off camera. Zu kept his own expression neutral.

"Human trafficking is just one aspect of Lee-Smith's business," Captain Jones said, finally. "As the Search and Protect team has experienced, you can keep taking the business out over and over again, but until you burn out the root, it will just keep coming back. We've had a watch on Lee-Smith from a broader perspective; considering not just human trafficking, but the other angles through which he monetizes his illicit activities in order to formulate a strategy to take him and his associates down permanently."

Zu glanced at Pua. Her eyes were wide, her mouth shaped in an *O*. She shook her head. No more questions.

Captain Jones sighed. "I have a daughter, Mr. Anyanwu. I sincerely hope you and your team will bring Miss Jiang back unharmed. However, the key person of interest to the US government is Mr. Jiang. I will be deploying resources to ensure he comes through this in one piece. Miss Jiang is outside the scope of their orders. While my resources will not provide support to any effort to retrieve her, they will not obstruct your team's attempt. I'll also have a word with HPD. I believe you coordinate with them regularly, and it makes sense for that to continue."

Meaning Zu and his team, plus the Hope's Crossing Kennels people, were Ying Yue's best chance. They could communicate with Kokua for information and planning as well. He could work with those circumstances.

"Understood, sir. Thank you." Zu wasn't active duty, wasn't even military anymore, technically.

Captain Jones nodded, then looked at David Cruz. "David."

"Sir," David responded.

Zu was very curious as to how David Cruz was on a first name basis with Captain Jones. Now was not the time to find out.

That was it. Captain Jones signed off.

Pua whistled low and stood up. "Well, that was intense. Whose dad is he?"

* * *

Pua had access and the decoded email ready for them in minutes. Based on the instructions detailed in the communication, she had grabbed the appropriate satellite images for the location of the drop point. From there, she stepped away as the rest of the team studied the images and developed their strategy.

Meanwhile, she and Kenny started digging through Lee-Smith's intelligence files.

Coffee was flowing like water for the entire team. Zu had pulled leftovers from his freezer and started heating them up in a big pot. It was the easiest thing he could think of to keep people fueled.

He handed out bowls of the soup, piled high with chicken pieces, and thought about how Ying Yue might've been interested to try it. Maybe she'd had this dish before, or perhaps not. Either way, pepper soup was highly variable, and every cook made the recipe their own. She'd never had his.

Kenny was first to try it, and the man's face lit up with pure pleasure. "Dis soup broke da mout, brah."

Zu nodded his head to acknowledge the compliment. He wasn't sure everyone would like it, but it was a high-protein meal and had the kind of flavor to wake up tired people.

Alex absentmindedly took a spoonful of the rich broth

with a tender chunk of chicken in it. As he chewed and swallowed, he sat up. "Damn, Zu. This is good. Spicy as hell, though."

Zu raised an eyebrow. "Too spicy for you?"

He took a sip for himself. It was always possible the soup had gotten too strong after being frozen and reheated. Flavors swept over his palate, intense but going well together. If anything, they'd had time to meld the way any good soup or stew did, getting better on the second and third servings. It had heat on multiple levels from garlic and ginger with a healthy hit of truly spicy peppers to burn away fatigue. The chicken meat was meltingly tender, falling off the bone.

Arin reached across Alex and nicked a brilliant orange pepper out of his bowl. "Let me take that."

"There's a chicken foot in here," Raul commented, but he didn't stop eating.

"I use the whole chicken," Zu continued. "Feet and wing tips add to the richness of the broth. It's all about the collagen."

Arin shrugged. "I make gang kiew wan gai the same way. It's a kind of Thai green curry using chicken pieces."

Zu nodded. "This doesn't use curry paste, but there's hot pepper, onions, garlic, ginger, and some other stuff."

The sounds of single-minded eating filled the room. Ying Yue definitely would've wanted to taste this.

"Some other stuff." Arin snorted. "I get most of the flavors in here, but there's something...nutty? Not peanuts. Not almond flour. Something."

"Njanjsa." Zu shrugged. "It's not easy to find, and I don't have it all the time. I use it when I can for flavor and to thicken the soup. It's a family recipe."

He wanted to have this conversation with Ying Yue.

He wanted her to know about this facet of him. He could cook, and he wanted to share some of his favorites with her, dishes he'd grown up with and learned to make so his memories of family were close even if his actual family was far.

"Family." Pua set her bowl down, empty of all but a few cleaned bones. She'd demolished her serving. "Oh. Family. Yes yes yes. Totally. That's what it was."

She rushed back to her laptop and started punching in commands at lightning speed.

Raul looked into his soup. "And thus food is inspiration."

He wasn't kidding.

Pua lit up, showing Kenny, who was still sucking on a chicken foot. He spit out a few delicate bones. "Right on. I see where you're going."

The two of them dove back into the world of data and forgot about everyone else.

Raul edged up to them and snuck their bowls out of the way, emptying the bones into the compost and placing the bowls in the sink. David didn't say a word the entire time, only headed back to the pot for seconds.

Minutes later, Pua bounced on her stool, almost falling over in her excitement. "I found you, you little turd."

As curses went, it was almost ridiculously mild considering the present company.

"Pua, language." Arin's laughing tone took the edge off the commentary.

Pua glanced up and blushed. "Okay. We've been wrong. All of us. Totally wrong with a very specific assumption. Everybody to the living room. Be prepared to drink information from a fire hose because once we knew what to look for, Kenny and I hit jackpot."

She hopped over two different dogs on the way to the

living room and would've tripped over King, but the huge dog turned his head into her hip to steady her. Kenny followed, picking his way around the various dogs and muttering, "It's a good thing I didn't bring Laki. One of these mainlander dogs woulda tried to eat him, fo shua."

Pua didn't even acknowledge Kenny's commentary, though she gave King an absentminded pat. She just inserted the cable for the projector into her laptop and started presenting. "We've all been working on the assumption that Ying Yue was kidnapped to be used as leverage against her father, because her father is a VIP. And that kind of is why she was targeted, but there's more to it than that. The reason for her being the target isn't what we were expecting."

Kenny took over the laptop as Pua stood up and started pointing at the projection on the wall featuring a man's face.

"Sure, she's really well known because of who her father is. And that's how this man reached out to her. He's a business associate of Mr. Jiang's and a longtime friend." Pua pointed to the image of an older Asian man. "But their business interactions have nothing to do with Mr. Jiang's factories or manufacturing sites or anything. This man is donating huge amounts of money to nonprofit organizations and working with Ying Yue on the distribution of those funds."

"Why?" Brandon and Zu asked at the same time.

They exchanged glances. With two leads in a room, it was bound to happen.

"Because she's outstanding at what she does." Pua didn't pause. She was on a roll and gaining more momentum with every word. "Ying Yue doesn't just have a PhD in international tax law—the way she explains it makes it sound so everyday and average. Oh no. She's a freaking genius. She excels at minimizing tax impact on the transfer of international assets, monetary or otherwise. She told us, but she downplayed it. The reality is so much better. She's one of very few people who can do what she does at all. Legally, that is. Well, even not so legally. But Ying Yue is unquestionably sound in terms of her professional integrity. Her ethics are snowy white and strong enough to withstand a full-on bombing. Figuratively speaking."

Kenny tossed a few graphs up on the projection. The dollar amounts were staggering, and Raul let out a low whistle.

"That's why she was asked to handle these funds, because her integrity is impeccable." Pua was bouncing. Literally bouncing. "This man is entrusting his life's fortune to her to distribute to deserving charities, and it is not sitting well with his nephews and nieces. There's one man in particular, an enterprising young entrepreneur with an especially abysmal investment history, who recently put out a contract on the shadiest of shady networks to make a specific finance person disappear. The contract was picked up by Lee-Smith."

Pua balled her hands into fists in front of her. "Ying Yue was targeted by a greedy little turd out to get his uncle's fortune, and it put her on Lee-Smith's radar. Lee-Smith probably picked up the contract and figured he could get himself a two-for-one, using her to pressure her father while he was at it. That's the gap. Ying Yue wasn't part of Lee-Smith's nefarious plan from the beginning. This whole thing rose out of opportunity because Ying Yue is too damned good at what she does and too damned honest to be convinced to give turd boy the money."

It was Kenny who picked up the next point of logic.

"Lee-Smith isn't going to give Mr. Jiang back his daughter. It's never been about that when it comes to her. He might draw this out, blackmail Jiang for an extended period of time. But the longer anything like this goes, the more chance there is for it to blow up in his face. Lee-Smith has been in the game too long. He's going to get what he wants from Jiang, then he's going to tie up loose ends to finish the outstanding contract."

Zu wanted to smash his fist through a wall or throw a chair through a window. He wanted to pick things up and slam them into the ground. None of it would do Ying Yue any good. The reality was, Lee-Smith was going to eliminate Ying Yue as soon as he had what he wanted from her father.

He turned back to the satellite images they'd been reviewing on various laptops. "We've got a ticking clock, people. Let's get this plan into place and move out."

CHAPTER TWENTY-TWO

Zu, this is Officer Kokua. Jiang has arrived and will begin the ransom drop-off. Your team should move now."

"Roger." Zu acknowledged the communication and placed the satellite phone back on his harness. He'd be using his comm for the coming mission here, in the rain forest, where Pua and Kenny had identified Ying Yue was being held. "This is Alpha, all units proceed."

Based on Kokua's surveillance, they'd been right. Lee-Smith hadn't brought Ying Yue with him to the ransom exchange. The bastard had no intention of returning her to her father. And so they were here, in the deep tropical rain forest portion of Oahu, ready to extract her while Lee-Smith's resources were split between guarding her and escorting him.

Alex's voice came over the comm ten minutes or so into the mission, lighthearted and falling into the same kind of banter the Search and Protect team adopted on a mission. "This is Papa; we're almost a mile in, and Souze doesn't want to slow down yet."

David chuckled. "C'mon, Papa, you're not telling me you're admitting you've developed a dad bod, are you?"

Alex rose to the bait. "Look who's talking, Oscar. Everyone can hear your wheezing over the radio."

Zu rolled his eyes as he crept through the dense underbrush, following Buck. Off to their right, Brandon Forte, current designation Hotel, was making his way on their planned course following his Haydn. They needed the dogs in the lead because the area was almost inhospitable to humans coming in or out either on foot or via vehicle assistance. The rain forest was too dense.

"Well at least Atlas is leading the way, otherwise Souze would have no idea where to go," David continued in a joking tone.

It made sense for Atlas to be making headway faster. The Belgian Malinois was a good ten pounds lighter than the German Shepherd Dogs, more compact. His smaller size gave him an advantage in the dense undergrowth.

Brandon Forte decided to join the chatter with a quiet comment of his own. "Lead? Souze is smart and prudent. He's got a nose for trouble and the wisdom to proceed with caution. If we encounter any IED, it's Haydn who will sniff it out. We all know Atlas and Souze are waiting for a target to attack."

Of the dogs, Atlas and Haydn had seen active combat overseas. Atlas had been deployed with Navy SEAL teams before his handler was killed in action and Atlas was retired from military duty. Haydn had been an explosives detection dog and was caught in a secondary explosion, losing his front left leg. The black German Shepherd Dog was moving through even the rain forest with little to no trouble, able to keep up with all of the other working dogs on the team. Souze was a former guard dog, Schutzhund trained, initially, rather than military. He was still a formidable aggressor.

This was why the Hope's Crossing personnel were in the lead, Brandon and Haydn paired with Zu and Buck, Alex and Souze paired with Raul and Taz. David and Atlas were on their own as Arin had gone to high ground with her sniper rifle. King would be hidden near her perch, standing guard. The Search and Protect team dogs specialized first and foremost in scent detection. Their added training would come in handy once they engaged the enemy, but it was wiser to let the primary military working dogs take point.

Raul joined the fray. "This is Bravo. I hear a lot of talk and a lot of heavy breathing. You all sure you have the stamina for this?"

"Boys." Arin's voice came across the comm, dry and husky. "Would you please remember we're on a serious mission?"

"And?" Five male voices responded in unison.

"Well, this is going to be all sorts of fun." Arin sighed. "Alpha, this is Charlie. I am in position and have clear line of sight on the structure."

The comm went silent as the banter ceded to more serious communication.

"Charlie, this is Alpha. We've been on course for a decent amount of time; do we need a course correction?" Zu was reasonably sure they'd remained on course, but having Arin positioned on high ground could give them the visual check they needed.

"Negative, Alpha," she responded. "You and Hotel are almost to your initial position. Proceed on current course. Papa and Bravo are doing fine. Oscar, course correct to one o'clock."

There was a muttered curse from David as he realized he and Atlas had strayed from their intended path. It took a few minutes for Arin to confirm they were all in position.

Once they were all in position, Zu took a moment to check the satellite phone. No further communications from Kokua, so no nasty surprises yet. Lee-Smith was still occupied with Jiang in the ransom exchange. Their plan was simple and decisive, and they should be able to pull it off as long as they maintained the element of surprise.

Over the comms, a dog barked, alert and aggressive at the same time. There were sounds of a shout and a struggle before the comms went silent again.

Zu crouched, poised on the balls of his toes, waiting and listening.

"Alpha, this is Papa. Souze is exposed, but still operational," Alex said. "He's leading an enemy fire team in a crappy truck away from the compound. He'll likely lose them in a mile and circle back."

Zu breathed a sigh. "Roger. All the tennis balls in the world for that dog. You're keeping eyes on?"

Alex huffed, the sound of his labored breathing loud in the comms. "Working on it."

Arin cut in. "This is Charlie. Lights are coming on in the compound. Based on where they're swarming out from, I've got a clear picture of Ying Yue's location."

They were treating the enemy base like a major assault target, but in reality, the building was small, with limited personnel, and there were only a few entrances or exits. Identifying which room held Ying Yue was doable, especially with the quality of the night-vision scope Arin was using on her rifle.

"This is Charlie. Confirmed just over twenty combatants, just like Pua said." Arin sounded satisfied.

Zu nodded to himself in the dark. "This is Alpha. Update on weapons and locations?"

"Point one and three from your approach. Small arms. No vehicles." Arin referenced their pre-identified points from their hasty plans. The satellite images Pua had been able to access had given them all a chance at making this work.

Brandon Forte grunted. "Easy enough if they didn't have the damn spotlights."

Zu reached out, running his hand down Buck's back, feeling the slight roughness of the ridge of fur running in the opposite direction along Buck's spine. "Agreed, but luckily we've got nonhumans on the team."

* * *

"Bravo and Papa, move out." Zu issued the planned commands to coordinate timing of execution. They all knew what they had to do. "Oscar, proceed."

Zu made eye contact with Brandon, and the two of them moved forward. From Arin's point of view above, they were fanning out in a four-pronged frontal assault with the dogs in the lead and heading toward the edges, the humans moving steadily toward the center with weapons live. When they engaged, they wanted the enemy ahead and outward, so they could shoot at an angle to the actual target building and avoid any potential backdrop weapons fire connections with the building itself.

Too soon, floodlights flared ahead. Alarms cut through the night. Enemy fire peppered the trees and undergrowth.

Arin muttered across the comms. "Somebody was spotted."

No one answered. Here and there, enemy threats fell as

sniper fire took out shooters attempting to target the dogs. They may not have spotted the humans yet, but it wasn't hard to figure dogs in tactical gear meant human handlers were out there in the night somewhere.

They were close, so close, Zu could smell the building. It was out of place in the rain forest. The bite of gunpowder hung in the air along with the residual reek of cigarette smoke from patrols that'd used the opportunity to take a smoke as they walked the perimeter of the building. Humans left an imprint wherever they stayed for any length of time.

A female voice rang out in the night. She gave counts of remaining enemy forces and their general position before her shouts were choked off. Ying Yue.

"This is Charlie. Those reports were accurate." Arin's voice held a note of respect. "She's loose, and they're confused trying to deal with whatever hell she's giving them. Now's the time to move."

Ying Yue had waited for him, for them. His gut tightened and he surged forward after Buck. She still had faith in them. She'd given them useful information and beyond the distraction she was providing, Zu also knew there was at least one enemy still inside with her, and said individual was too slow to have stopped her in the first place.

Haydn darted toward the building, a dark-furred shadow barely discernible from the shadows cast by the blinding spotlights. Zu fired a few warning shots upward at an angle in a random succession and rolled to the side as return fire came back, panicked and uncontrolled. Brandon Forte send four bullets toward that locale, silencing the enemy in that sector.

David and Atlas moved as one toward the front gate on

a zigzag course to one side of it. As they reached the wall, David kneeled and presented his back to the sky. Atlas bounded forward, and as the Belgian Malinois sprang upward off his handler's back, David surged to his feet, giving his dog an extra boost. Atlas cleared the two-story wall with ease and tore into the enemy targets positioned on top of the wall.

"Damn it." Arin's voice sounded strained. "I can't cover Atlas and Alpha's approach at the same time. Ying Yue is in the farthest room along the north corridor."

The jump had been unplanned, but damned impressive. It was also extremely effective in causing mass confusion among the remaining enemy guards. Zu could improvise. He prepared to go forward without cover, but Brandon materialized from the underbrush at his side.

"This is Hotel, I'll provide cover for Alpha."

"Roger." Arin went silent.

Brandon didn't look at Zu, only raised his weapon. "Go."

"Roger." Zu ran forward and entered the main entryway.

"This is Oscar, right behind you, Alpha." David entered behind Zu and began clearing the hallway and rooms in the opposite direction as Zu headed directly for Ying Yue.

Once Zu reached the farthest room, he fired shots at the base of the central door, then moved to one side.

There were no returning shots.

"Ying Yue?" he called out, a part of him deep inside freezing as he waited for a response and went through the worst-case scenario.

"Took you long enough!" It was Ying Yue's voice and she sounded pissed.

Pissed was good. In fact, she sounded gloriously angry.

Ying Yue opened the door. Ropes hung from her wrists and she was disheveled but otherwise unharmed.

Zu carefully checked the room behind her to find one guard, unconscious on the floor.

He looked at Ying Yue.

She held up her hands. "He stepped in front of me when all the gunfire started going off to check the door. I used these to choke him until he just...stopped. I checked. He has a pulse. But I dropped a crate on his head just in case, so I think he's going to be out for a while."

Over the comm, Arin let out a low whistle. "Is the man's head caved in?"

Raul responded, "She said he had a pulse."

"That was before she pulled a roadrunner trick and dropped something on the coyote's head." Alex paused. "Look, my kid is into old-school cartoons and stuff from overseas."

Buck headed into the room and did a quick circuit, then returned to Zu. No alerts.

"This is Alpha. The room is clear. I have the package."

More accurately, the package had come to him.

He pulled Ying Yue into a fierce, quick hug, then set her on her feet. "Stay with me. Follow as close behind as you can. If you hear gunfire, get low and let me shield you. I'm wearing Kevlar. You are not."

Ying Yue only nodded affirmative.

Good enough.

They emerged from the room and gunfire rang out immediately. Zu shoved her back into the room as he got low and prepared to return fire.

Buck charged out and down the hallway. As he did, another streak, this one black and tan, hurtled into the group of shooters from the side.

Buck and Atlas had both shooters by the forearms, the men dropping their weapons in a panic.

"This is Oscar, move move move!" David appeared, taking out both of the shooters before they could disengage from the dogs.

"This is Charlie. Come south out the front door," Arin said as they ran down the hallway and emerged from the building.

As they continued to run, Buck joined them, then Brandon and Haydn. In minutes, all of the Search and Protect and Hope's Crossing forces had withdrawn and melted back into the night, headed back to their checkpoint where Todd Miller was waiting with their vehicles.

Zu got on the satellite phone as they ran. "Officer Kokua, this is Zu. We have Ying Yue. Repeat. We have Ying Yue and she is safe. Take Lee-Smith."

CHAPTER TWENTY-THREE

Zu was back at the Honolulu Police Department building again, but this time for a very different reason than the last time.

Zu stood in the darkness, observing Lee-Smith's interrogation as the detectives took turns questioning him. Zu had to admit, Lee-Smith was cool under pressure and confident. He sounded like he believed everything he said, even if there was evidence of his lies. The man was a masterful liar and very skilled manipulator.

Zu didn't envy the attorneys responsible for prosecuting the man. If Lee-Smith ever went to court before a jury of his peers, he'd have most people believing anything by the end of court session. But taking him to court and prosecuting him weren't Zu's job. Bringing him to justice hadn't been Zu's job, either. It'd been Kokua's and his men's.

The Search and Protect and the Hope's Crossing Kennels teams had brought Ying Yue to safety, but the nightmare wasn't over. Kokua had called Zu once the police had Lee-Smith. The higher-ups at the police department and the FBI had asked for Ying Yue to face the man who'd ordered her kidnapping to see if their meeting would result in Lee-Smith revealing information. But she'd never met Lee-Smith, and she didn't have the training to conduct any kind of interrogation. They'd just be fishing, waving her in front of Lee-Smith as bait. When Zu had offered to come instead, she'd thought hard on it, then accepted. He was better suited for this.

Besides, he wanted to meet Lee-Smith face-to-face.

Kokua joined him in the darkness. "You ready to go in there and see if seeing you shakes a few ill-advised comments loose from this guy?"

Zu nodded. "He's steady under pressure. I'm not sure seeing me will throw him off-balance, but I've got a few ideas to damage his calm."

"You preferred going in there yourself rather than expose Ying Yue to the man." Kokua might be nudging Zu a little hard. "While you damage his calm, try not to do too much physical damage to him, even if you're here to look him in the eye after all he's done to Ying Yue."

He'd try.

Ying Yue had been taken, tossed around some, but handled gently compared to the majority of captives Lee-Smith was responsible for trapping into forced labor or indentured servitude. It didn't stop Zu from seeing red when he'd seen the dark circles under her eyes and the bruises at her wrists and on her upper arms from being pushed and dragged along.

"I'll go in." Zu stepped forward and put his hand on the doorknob, then paused. "Any word on the two dirty minions posing as FBI agents?"

"Yes and no." Kokua crossed his own arms and tucked his chin low. "Unfortunate on both counts."

"How so?" Zu waited. He didn't plan to go in without more information.

Kokua mumbled a curse under his breath. "It turns out they were both agents for the Federal Bureau of Investigation. Legit and apparently on Lee-Smith's payroll. The bad news is they've gone off the grid. We can't find them or even determine whether they've departed the island."

"Let me guess, the FBI is taking over the investigation when it comes to those two, not doing a joint effort." Zu scowled more, if that was possible. He was beginning to assemble a very secret, very personal file on people who'd done irreparable harm to him or his. Vengeance wasn't a healthy obsession, but certain things could be very good for the soul in low doses.

"That's all we've got for now, but we'll keep you posted as we can." Kokua's word choice was careful enough to bring a blip of amusement up on Zu's radar. There was likely a world of commentary Kokua would love to express, later.

Zu nodded. "Let's see what Lee-Smith has to say to me, if anything."

He turned the doorknob and strode into the interrogation room, closing the door behind him. After a pause, he moved to stand a few feet into the room, but not close enough to impinge on the space of the two detectives handling the interrogation.

"You." Lee-Smith focused on Zu immediately.

It seemed like a good bet Lee-Smith had a personal issue with Zu—and by extension, Zu's team. Burning a person's business to the ground, not once, but twice, could have those kinds of results among more than one interested party. Zu would do it again in a heartbeat. "Azubuike Anyanwu, head of Search and Protect. I see my reputation has preceded me."

"Ha." Lee-Smith sneered. "You and your people are a thorn in my side."

Zu nodded. "We've each put in a lot of time honing our particular skill sets. I can see how the application of any of those could get a little painful for the target."

"Do you even understand the extent of my influence?" Lee-Smith stared at Zu. "You can put me behind bars, and it won't matter. My business will continue running without me and will be waiting for my return. I'm a patient man by nature. You and your team aren't worth the time and effort anymore."

"No?" Zu wondered what the last statement was supposed to mean. He might get the answer, or he might not. Either way, the response could inform some of Zu's planning for the growth of the team over the next several years.

"Of course not." Lee-Smith shook his head. "At first, you were an annoyance. Ruining the plantation caused an unfortunate delay in my business activities. Then the second encounter between my most recent protégé and your people at the hostess club was a mistake. He had a penchant for hanging on to plans for the principle of the thing. He should've cut his losses and run, but he'd underestimated what you and your team could do."

"And this time we took down your little fort out in the forest." Zu allowed the corners of his mouth to turn up in a hint of a smile.

He wanted to goad Lee-Smith a little. He was also genuinely satisfied. Search and Protect and the Hope's Crossing Kennels teams had managed to extract Ying Yue from a stronghold guarded by greater numbers with nonlethal force. It took far more skill to manage that than to leave piles of bodies in their wake.

Anger sparked in Lee-Smith's eyes, more emotion than he'd displayed at any time during the earlier interrogation. "You all were like children, smashing a toy fort simply because you'd been excluded from the important business deal. In truth? You don't want me to play with Jiang? I don't have to. There are plenty of other businessmen like him, and I can cut more profitable deals elsewhere, rather than deal with him and his insufferable personal aide."

The man sighed. "Unfortunately, your temper tantrum resulted in the loss of a recent acquisition, a woman needed to fill a separate contract. She was interesting, really. I liked her, to an extent. If anything, I enjoyed her spirit far more than the disrespectful attitude of the boy who wanted her to disappear. Since that young entrepreneur has managed to mishandle finances one of my direct reports loaned him, I'm not inclined to carry out his contract anymore."

Zu considered Lee-Smith's blasé attitude while maintaining a blank expression. Truly, Lee-Smith might not realize what he was saying. Or it could be a ruse. Zu decided to roll his shoulders and turn his head until he got a couple of good pops out of his neck. Lee-Smith might've been trying to coax Zu to come after his people. Hard to say. So let Lee-Smith think he was getting to Zu's temper. Either way, both detectives were sitting back and doing their damnedest not to move and distract Lee-Smith from his discussion with Zu.

He decided to talk as if his team's primary concern was Mr. Jiang. Lee-Smith wouldn't be expecting the truth, but how much of the lie could the man identify? "You were planning to make a certain successful business professional's life a lot more complicated. Really, a ransom drop-off? Could you be any less subtle to prove you and your minions are very bad people?"

Lee-Smith actually laughed. "I will cede the point to you. I was surprised you would have knowledge of Jiang's manufacturing sites or even what value they could contribute to my operation. Bravo."

Of course, Lee-Smith had to make it sound like a praise phrase that dog trainers used. *Braaf*, good boy. His insults were potentially the most layered, nuanced, complex things to come out of his mouth.

"Last night's demonstration showed you Mr. Jiang has more security around him than you can afford to throw resources at, considering the finite value he represents to you. He owns only a fraction of the manufacturing sites. Are any of his other business ventures really a fit for your interests?"

Lee-Smith surprised Zu by nodding, drooping his shoulders slightly. "There really has been far more loss than gain in this little experiment to kill two birds with one stone. I'd thought the initial contract to make one Jiang Ying Yue disappear dovetailed well with a father who controlled businesses that might so conveniently fit into my plans. I normally would've washed my hands of it as soon as she was rescued the first time, but you see, I couldn't resist a chance to crush your team under my heel when you involved yourselves."

Zu stilled, giving Lee-Smith a hard stare. Ying Yue had endured all of her additional suffering because of the deeds of his team, because of him.

Lee-Smith leaned forward. "Yes. Wallow in it, o noble soldier of fortune with the truly pathetic knight in shining armor complex. Take your misguided attempts at chivalry and consider them for what they were. Endangerment of the very innocents you so idealistically attempt to save."

Those words hit their mark, and Zu's already smoldering

rage burned through his lungs as he forced himself to continue breathing evenly in and out. Lee-Smith was right. Zu hated the man even more because he wanted to refute the bastard. But what made Lee-Smith so frustrating to prosecute wasn't simply that he lied. He wielded the truth like a weapon turned against its owner. Nothing Lee-Smith had said to Zu was actually untrue.

"You hate people like me because you can't vanquish us." Lee-Smith lifted his hand, palm upward, and closed his fingers into a fist. "The universe and karma don't work the way you think they should. We move at a higher level, while you scramble around trying to make life bearable for innocents. They're too blind, too entitled to appreciate the protection you provide and don't deserve any kind of existence besides making money for people like me. Even my being here won't give you the satisfaction you want. I have been ahead of you at every step, forcing you to react. People like me manipulate law enforcement, government agencies, massive corporations—all exponentially bigger than you."

Truth used to support lies again, but Lee-Smith was also grasping at whatever win he could grab in his greedy paws to carry him through the days he was facing in prison. Nowhere in his dramatic evil villain speech was there any statement that could let Lee-Smith go free.

Zu smiled and watched the passionate conviction in the other man's eyes dim. "You deal in bureaucracy and greed. You weren't prepared to encounter us. You won't ever understand how to counter what my people can bring to the field, and we will still be out in the world, damaging your bottom line. So go to prison and rot there."

* * *

Ying Yue stood in the middle of the hotel suite, using one of the hotel notepads and a pen to make to-do lists for when she got back to Singapore. She couldn't settle in any one place in the room. It wasn't the same one she'd stayed in a couple of days ago. Had it only been a couple of days? It seemed like weeks, forever even. Here she was, back in a luxurious hotel suite with security guards hanging out in the sitting room area. None of them would speak to her, and when she tried to get to know them, they looked at her as if she had two heads.

Of course. Why would she try to know anything about the people responsible for protecting her?

She missed Pua's chatter and Arin's occasional dry commentary. She missed King wandering around the hotel suite and lying in the middle of the floor like he was a piece of furniture. She missed Raul and Taz coming in and out. Most of all, she missed Buck's steadying touch nearby whenever she had even the slightest moment of insecurity and the solid, warm, incredible presence of Zu.

A knock sounded on the bedroom door, and she jumped.

"Miss Jiang." She recognized the voice as Julian Nilsson and told her racing heart to calm down.

"Come in."

Julian stepped inside with a handful of shopping bags from high-end stores. "Since you'll be here on the island for an additional night or two as the police investigation is wrapped up and the authorities meet with you for your statement, I took the liberty of ordering a selection of clothes for you. Please keep anything you'd like, and we'll take care of returning the rest."

"How thorough. Thank you." She stepped forward to take the bags, but Julian had already set them down on a low bench at the foot of the bed. Of course, everything in its place.

"I'd like to express how relieved we all are that you are here with your father, safe." Julian's gaze found hers, and he was, as always, unreadable to her.

Before, she'd have murmured something appropriate and equally as empty. But she wasn't the same person anymore. Or maybe she was but unwilling to tuck herself away for the comfort of the people working for her father. "I'm not actually with my father."

Julian's eyes narrowed slightly. "No. But you are staying in the same place as him, and he has every intention of joining you for a late breakfast when there is a reasonable break in his meetings."

"I see." Meetings carried on, of course. Perhaps she'd have been bitter about it before, but now, she had a different perspective, and she wasn't absolutely sure how she'd gotten here. "I'd like access to a secure laptop if possible."

"Why?" Julian didn't sound against the idea, only curious.

Good. She was weary and felt adrift. She wasn't sure she had it in her to argue with him. Funny how even arguments with Zu had left her energized and looking forward to future conversations.

"I had begun getting my finances and business affairs in order after my disappearance. I do have a job to get back to, I hope. I'd like to leverage the time before meeting with my father doing that. Then I can be fully focused on the time he has to spend with me." That was the change in her reaction, the lack of bitterness or resentment. She valued the things she had to do and her own time, so coordinating to meet with her father had a different kind of meaning for her now.

"I see. The Search and Protect team provided you with access to one of theirs?"

"On a secure VPN, of course. They had several protocols in place to facilitate my needs while still keeping me safe." She started to poke through the bags of clothes to see what she might be able to wear to meet her father. She was looking forward to it, actually. She'd like to feel out this new perspective face-to-face with him.

"They failed." Julian's statement was flat and factual.

"Only when actual FBI agents called me in for questioning and abducted me." She straightened and glared at Julian. "Are you saying you or the security teams here would've done anything different faced with the same scenario?"

Julian was silent.

"I understand the anger my father harbors and where it stems from. He was afraid for me. He trusted a team to keep me safe, and mistakes were made. I refuse to declare an entire team persona non grata simply because they were put into a situation no one had a chance of recognizing as a trap." Her face heated as she continued to vent her frustration. If it wasn't for the Search and Protect team, people who'd become friends and at least one who'd become something so much more, she'd never have been found at all. She'd have been worse than dead. "The reality is that same team executed an extremely difficult rescue mission while my father took a bag of money to a drop-off location and would've negotiated for my release. He did what he could, and the Search and Protect Team did what they could."

"From the start, their members have made our staff appear inadequate." Julian tugged on his shirt cuffs. It was perhaps the most agitated she'd ever seen him.

"They were when it came to protecting me." She sighed. "We've been through this, and it is beneath my father and you to continue to be hung up on it. The short-comings of your security team were clearly demonstrated at the airport. In moments of danger, I was left standing outside the protection of the security team, exposed. You all left me."

There'd been more emotion behind her last statement than she intended. She backed away a step or two and gave herself a minute to clear her head. She wasn't yelling at Julian specifically anymore. She wanted to know where Zu was, why he'd rescued her again and left her at the hospital overnight. Why hadn't he come to talk to her?

"It's not my job to consider you." Julian bit out the words, but remained facing her rather than turning away. "I am first and foremost focused on your father and his best interests. As far as I was ever concerned, you were more than capable of looking out for yourself or acquiring the help you needed on your own. I wasn't wrong."

She blinked. It was the first time Julian—or anyone—had stated she was capable. "Then what is your problem with the Search and Protect team?"

He hissed out a stream of air between his teeth. She had never heard him, or anyone, do that before. "They have literally been camped out in the lobby and patrolling the property since you returned from the hospital. They are making sure our team is constantly aware of their presence. But they have not, at any moment, crossed the line and entered any area we've secured. They're all just...out there."

She stared at him. They were all here? Zu and Buck were here. Her heart kicked into overdrive. "Thank you, Julian."

He looked extremely disgruntled. "You're welcome, Miss Jiang. I'll make sure you get a laptop."

As he left, she considered the room around her. She was safe, truly. The people involved in her kidnapping were in police custody, and she had no reason to remain in hiding. She would have the means to put her life back together, and no one seemed to be standing in her way. Sure, there was security here with her, but she realized she could walk out of this room. They'd have to figure out how to accompany her, but they couldn't keep her in here.

The question was, what did she want to do?

She wanted Zu. But that wasn't any kind of action plan. That was a driver. Their argument seemed trivial, almost erased by her second kidnapping. But the problem had been real, and she wasn't going to pretend it wasn't there. She needed to decide whether she would try to mend the gap between them and work with him on building a relationship between equals.

Yes. Absolutely.

She dove into the bags. Things had changed, and she was no longer a damsel in distress. She also didn't plan to be a dove in a gilded cage. They were out there, making themselves obvious.

He was waiting for her.

Because he understood she could come to him on her own, if she wanted.

Oh, it was convoluted and maybe crazy. It was completely possible she was reading too much into the whole situation. But she'd been making lists all morning, or trying to, and none of the tasks on them made her happy at all. They were all things. Do this. Get that. Set up another thing.

She'd finally given up and simply doodled a list of things she wished for this very moment. They'd all been things like eating malasadas with Pua. Get hibiscus tea.

Figure out where Buck gets the barbecue Zu enjoys. The farther she went into her whimsical list, the more she wished for things like a long soak in Zu's hot tub, walking along the beach at Zu's house, swimming in the pool in Zu's backyard, stealing all of Zu's pillows...

Singapore was her old life, and it wasn't the place that she wanted back. What she wanted was her career and the fulfillment she got from working in a position where she did so much good. It wasn't the city or her apartment. As good as the food and culture was in that city, she hadn't ever taken the time to fall in love with it.

No. Singapore wasn't home. It was a place where she lived. And love?

He was not in Singapore.

CHAPTER TWENTY-FOUR

Zu and Buck waited in the breezeway of the front lobby. They'd taken up a position out of the way of the valets and arriving or leaving guests, in a small seating area where they could see all approaches from either the street or the large corridors. It was a big resort, though, and Arin had found a vantage point from which to view the hotel from a different angle. Raul and Taz had simply opted to stroll through the shops in the center of the resort village.

They were here. If there was a chance, if he had a chance, then Ying Yue would be able to find one of them.

If not, well, he had new contracts to consider and a team to continue building. The Hope's Crossing Kennels team had returned to the mainland. He'd extended an open invitation for them to join the team permanently at any time, but Brandon Forte had a different vision. He and his friends were committed to the place for second chances that was Hope's Crossing Kennels.

Search and Protect was a place for restarting, too.

For all of them except Pua, the Search and Protect team was a third or a fourth or a fifth chance at building a life. Happiness was one aspect, but they all wanted more. They wanted a career and profession they could take pride in, with the faith that they'd never be forced to make the difficult choices that haunted all of them from past service. None of them could say they had no regrets, but all of them wanted to move forward free of creating new ones.

So he was here. Because he didn't want to regret letting Ying Yue go, and because he would be haunted by what-ifs for the rest of his life if he didn't try to ask her to give a life with him a shot. At the same time, he couldn't just go climbing the tower, because her angry words had sunk in. She wasn't a damsel, waiting for him to come rescue her. She was a lady, and he'd come to wait at her doorstep, figuratively speaking, until she decided to come see him.

He figured the lobby was about as halfway as he could make it and still make this whole abstract concept clear.

Abstract concepts were really not his forte.

Buck rose to his feet, leaning forward slightly. The big red dog didn't pull on his short leash, but he trembled ever so slightly with eagerness and even issued a soft, gentle woof. Zu stood too, following where Buck was looking to see a very familiar, incredibly precious figure walking toward them.

She was dressed in a white tank and pants, the fabric flowing loose around her legs. Her hair was swept back and gathered low at the back of her neck, and she had a flower tucked behind her right ear. He watched her approach, and all he could think about was how happy he was that she was staring right back at him, smiling.

When she got to them, she reached out to scratch Buck behind the ears. But she was still staring at Zu. He drank in the sight of her. She looked well, her skin luminescent and touched with a faint blush at her cheeks. There were still shadows under her eyes, but they were much better than when he'd first met her. She'd gotten a chance to rest a little.

After a long minute, he realized maybe he should say something.

"Hey."

"Hi."

She laughed.

He hesitated. He was here and she'd come, and he hadn't thought out what he could say because he figured he'd make a mess of it. But in retrospect, not having any kind of plan at all was also a tactical error.

"What are your plans from here on out?" His question came out awkwardly, but it was what he wanted to know. He could ask how she was feeling, but then he might have to confess he'd had Pua nick the medical reports from the hospital. That hadn't been quite legal, and it definitely was questionable from an ethical standpoint.

Ying Yue tilted her head. "Brunch with my father in a bit. Then my schedule is flexible through the afternoon and evening."

He liked the confidence in her voice, steady. She had a new self-assurance she hadn't had while she'd been in hiding with him. A pang of regret hit him in the chest, but he pressed on despite it. "Your schedule?"

She nodded. "You and Pua helped me get started putting things back in order when it came to my life. I've still got a lot to do."

"Ah." He was glad she was diving into her life again,

but he also mentally swatted at the wistful sense of feeling left behind he had. "That's great."

But what about them?

"You?" She put the question out there, and it might have been a nicety, but there was a warmth to her tone. The question really was from her to him, and not just what one asked next.

"Well, a lot has changed in the last several days." He shifted his weight from one foot to the other, unsure how to do what he was about to do, but stating the truth was always a good start.

Her face fell. "I'm sorry about..."

"No." He hurried to clarify and maybe even felt a little bit panicked. He didn't mean to cut her off, but he didn't want her thinking that it was bad or she had a negative impact on anything in his life for one second longer. "Good things."

"Oh." She stared up at him, wide-eyed.

Yeah, he was breaking all records for awkward one-on-one communication here. "I walk through every room in my house and realize I've been searching. Someone is missing. I look in my refrigerator and my pantry and realize I never cooked for you. I wake up, and I miss trying to get my pillows back from you. I go into the office and stand by my desk and remember what it was like to have your lips touch my cheek."

He swallowed hard. There. He said the things. This vulnerability hurt and left him lighter at the same time. At least she knew.

"Every minute of the day is different," he added. "I'm different. And I don't know how to ask you what is possible between us."

Her lips parted, and her eyes filled with tears.

Panic stabbed him and he stepped back. "I'm sorry. I didn't mean to make you upset."

She shook her head, dashing her tears away with the back of her hand. "I think that's the longest set of words you've ever said to me."

A laugh burst out of him, surprising him. She laughed, too.

"How did we get so far under each other's skin in just a couple of days?" she asked.

"I don't care." He reached out and brushed his thumb along the curve of her cheek. "I'm glad we did."

"So what do we do next?" She leaned into his touch until her cheek rested in his open palm.

"I'm not sure." He really had no idea. Happiness flooded every fiber of his being just being allowed to touch her, and all those words were lost in a maelstrom of hope. "I'm just glad you're willing."

She turned her head and kissed the inside of his palm. "I'm glad you didn't hide back in your headquarters and make me stage a raid to get you to talk to me about this."

He raised his eyebrows. "Well, if you were considering staging a raid in this outfit, maybe add some body armor over it. That'd be something I never knew I wanted to dream about."

She narrowed her eyes.

"I have all the confidence in the world you could plan and execute the actual raid, mind you." He tried to look innocent, but he was pretty sure his face didn't do innocent. He widened his eyes anyway and smiled, for her. "Especially since most of my team would help you."

"Damn straight." She lifted her head proudly, then her expression softened. "But I'm better at my day job."

"A genius, from what I hear." He let his hand fall away

from her face, but she caught it and held his hand in both of hers.

She shrugged, a blush spreading in a soft shell pink over her cheeks. "I'm very good."

He nodded. "You make a difference for a lot of people in need."

"Not so different from you." Her gaze fell to their hands, and she squeezed his gently.

He tightened his hand around hers in return. "How do we explore what we can do together? We've each got our own profession, but the rest is adjustable, I think."

"Well, to start, I don't need to live in Singapore to do my job." She sounded thoughtful, her tone light. "I could work remote, or even bring quite a bit of my business here to Oahu."

He hesitated. "It's not fair to make you move your home."

She shook her head. "It's a place I lived. It's not home. The Search and Protect team showed me what a real home was. Pua first, then Todd and Kalea, but mostly you."

The warmth in his chest expanded until he thought it might burst.

She continued, "You are the person I've come to with my troubles, not because I expect you to make them disappear, but because the load is lighter when you understand me. You are my safe space, the person I don't have to do anything for. I can simply *be* when I'm with you. And I want to be all those things for you, too."

He folded her into his arms, then, holding her to his heart. "It's too soon to say this, but I'm going to spend every day you let me proving to you that I mean it. I love you."

She wrapped her arms around his waist, turning her head so she could hear his heartbeat. "I love you. I don't care how long it's been, just so long as we have whatever days we can from here on out."

Buck leaned his head against both their thighs.

She laughed and freed one hand to scratch his ears. "You too, Buck."

Raul's lucky to have the best partner a man could ask for: a highly trained, fiercely loyal German Shepherd Dog named Taz. But their first mission in Hawaii puts them to the test when a kidnapping ring sets its sights on the bravest woman Raul's ever met...

See the next page for an excerpt from *Total Bravery*...

How can I help you?" The man on the other end of the call didn't laugh or crack a joke in response to Mali's request for help. Honestly, it'd come out as a plea, and she'd been half expecting him to dismiss it. He didn't ridicule her or tell her he'd get her sister to call her back when she returned.

He was paying attention, and he was absolutely serious.

She swallowed against a fear-parched throat, relief and hope trickling in past the constriction in her chest. "There's someone—several people—chasing me. I think I lost them in the crowds at the big shopping center."

"Are you safe where you are?" His tone was calm but managed to convey urgency, too, and it helped her focus.

She glanced around her. "Maybe? Probably not. I walked fast, but I walked, didn't run. So they might not have seen me leave the mall area. I tried to blend in with the tourists."

The moment she'd seen her pursuers, a childhood memory of her sister's voice played through her head, telling her to never run from immortals—or predators in the real world—because running attracted their attention. So she hadn't. Random, maybe, but here she was with a chance to evade some very scary people. She'd take advice in whatever form it came.

"Can you get to the Search and Protect office building?"

She laughed, the sound harsh to her own hearing. "That's why I was near the Ala Moana Shopping Center. I was trying to get there."

God, had she even said the name of the place right? She was so not a local. This guy didn't sound like one either. Would he even know how to find her?

Taking a deep breath, she fought for calm. "I took a taxi there first, trying to get close to the office building. But then I spotted the people chasing me waiting nearby and left."

They hadn't been standing right out in the open, but they'd been dressed in suits. In the heat of the day, not even the office workers actually wore full suits as far as she knew. Not on Oahu or any of the other Hawaiian islands. It'd set off alarms in her head, and she'd veered off, falling into step with tourists headed from the mall to the other shopping areas.

"Okay." His calm acceptance helped her settle. "If you walked away from the mall and stayed with the crowds, are you near the beaches now?"

"Yes." *Hurry.* They both needed to communicate faster. "Around the big hotels. I figured there'd be more security near them."

"It's mid-morning, still cool out. Good time for shopping until people get hungry and start looking for places to eat lunch." His words were coming quicker, too. "There's always catamarans over there, launching from the beach for a sail out to deeper water. Vendors sell tickets to tourists all up and down the streets. They go out for an hour, maybe two. Do you see any signs for those? You can buy tickets right on the beach."

"Yes." Once he'd told her to look, she spotted one or two right away. "There's one right between two of the big hotels with boardwalks."

"Good. I know where that is." His tone took on a crisp quality, full of confidence. "Get on one of the catamarans. Don't drink much but do what you need to, to not stand out. That'll take you out of reach until I can get to you. I'm headed there now. When you get off the cruise, I'll be at the ticket booth waiting for you."

"How will I know it's you?" She'd never seen any of her sister's friends, not from the military or whatever Arin did now.

"Look for the guy with the service dog. I've got a GSD."

"A what?" Even as she asked, she hurried toward the ticket booth and fumbled for her tiny change purse where she kept her cash, one credit card, and ID. She struggled to juggle it and her phone while she tried to keep aware of her surroundings. The thing was cute but it was a pain in the ass to get what she needed out of and back into it.

There was a sigh on the other end. "German Shepherd Dog. He's big, black and tan, a lot like Arin's partner. We probably won't blend in with the crowd."

That was okay though, right? Once he came to get her, she'd be safe. No one was going to just grab her with some badass mercenary.

"It'll be okay. Get on the catamaran." His voice was soothing and sounded so good. She wanted to know what his lips looked like shaping those words.

"I'll get a ticket." And maybe she could take the time on the waves to reassemble her scattered mind.

"Go ahead, Mali. I'll be there as fast as I can." He ended the call.

She tucked the phone into the back pocket of her shorts. When she reached the small booth, her heart plummeted. The catamarans went out at the top of the hour. She had at least a forty-minute wait. Buying a ticket and a floppy hat to protect her dark hair from the sun's heat, she tucked the ticket into her change purse and tried to maintain a casual attitude as she scanned the area around her.

Suddenly, being between the big hotels didn't seem like such a good idea. The streets between them were more like alleyways, shadowed by palm trees, with lots of random doors and archways to get pulled into. There was nowhere to run on the narrow boardwalks, and it wouldn't be easy to jump over the waist-high walls into the private pool areas. Maybe a hot action movie star could vault those retainer walls and sprint across the hotel grounds to lose his pursuers, but she was a skinny postdoc who could at best be described as vertically challenged.

She'd left the sidewalks along the street thinking it'd be harder to grab her and stuff her into a car, but was the beachfront area so close to the hotels much better?

Every man walking past her seemed to be staring at her through his sunglasses. Every woman seemed to be looking the other way. The women who did look in her direction could've just as easily been after her, too.

She rubbed her palms together. It was the beach, though. She'd spot suits a mile...

Cold fear washed through her, and her stomach twisted hard as the distinctive black fabric of men wearing ridiculously hot suits appeared at the far end of the boardwalk.

They were so far away that they were barely more than dots but they stood out in stark contrast to the sane people wearing light colors and airy warm weather wear.

They were still trying to find her. They had to be. They couldn't know exactly where she was because they'd have made more of an effort to sneak up on her. Wouldn't they? If she could see them coming so easily, she still had a chance to fade away before they spotted her.

Time to walk in the opposite direction. Removing her light-colored hat so it wouldn't catch the eye as she moved, she held it close at her side. She forced herself to move at the pace of the people in front of her, only passing tourists on the narrow boardwalk when others were. There were the occasional picture takers halting to capture a memory here and there. She slipped around them and counted each as one more obstacle between her pursuers and her.

Her heart raced as she tried to catch sight of the people behind her in any reflective surface. Suddenly, every person wearing sunglasses was a rearview mirror. She didn't dare bring attention to herself by looking over her shoulder.

Her memory of her big sister's advice came back to her again, echoing in her ears over the harsh sound of her own breathing. She even remembered the childhood movie that'd inspired her sister. The lesson had been simple. There'd been two things to remember. Don't run. Don't look back. These weren't immortals and she wasn't a unicorn, but they were definitely predators, and she didn't want to attract their attention if they hadn't spotted her yet.

The boardwalk ended, and the beach spread out in front of her. Too many people stood idle on the path ahead. Her thoughts crystallized almost painfully as it occurred to her that the men behind her could be dressed so conspicuously to drive her into an ambush ahead of her. It'd been a miracle no one had grabbed her yet.

She couldn't keep walking. They might have others ready to meet her where the path led back to the street. Getting shoved into a car would end her chances of being rescued by Raul Sá and his GS—whatever.

He'd told her to do what was needed to keep from standing out.

Her gaze passed over the beach dotted in sunbathers. The awesome thing about Waikiki was the way some people came prepared with towels and beach bags, but others just showed up on a whim and laid out on the sand using nothing but their shirts.

She began unbuttoning hers.

In moments, she'd slipped up close to a scattered collection of local girls, all laying out. Some had shirts, some didn't. They were all gorgeous. The best Mali could do was be thankful she'd always tanned easily and had been on the island long enough to develop summer color. Her Southeast Asian heritage gave her dark brown skin with golden undertones, not quite the same but similar to the local islanders. She wouldn't stand out as tourist-pale among them.

Wearing a bikini under her clothes had been a regular thing for the last several days as she and her fellow post-docs took advantage of the locale to enjoy the beaches every bit as much as their research. She was leveraging the habit to hide in plain sight.

Dropping her shorts, she laid them out and spread her shirt over the sand. She stretched out on her belly quickly, hiding her dark hair under the floppy hat, and watched the feet of passersby. Hopefully, people couldn't see her trembling.

* * *

"Damn." Raul fumed at the delay as he and Taz threaded their way through the crowds on the sidewalks. Even in late morning, traffic headed into the Waikiki area—or "town," as locals called it—was insanely slow. On the island of Oahu, it seemed like it was tourist season year-round, and Waikiki was overrun by them.

He headed down the side street he thought would bring him out at the beach closest to his destination. It was a risk because he was going by memory from a vacation years ago. He hadn't had time since he'd arrived to refresh his knowledge of the area.

Hopefully, Arin's little sister was going to see him coming and give him a sign or he was going to be screwed trying to spot her right away. Hawaii, especially Oahu, had a huge number of Asian visitors and locals with some Asian ancestry, so it wasn't as if the woman was going to stand out in the crowd just based on physical features. He could spot Arin in a heartbeat, even in a crowd, but Arin had told him that she and her sister didn't share a strong physical resemblance. It was a family joke. Beyond that, Arin didn't talk much about her family besides how incredibly smart her sister was. Intelligence didn't help when Raul was trying to recognize her on sight. And considering the places he and Arin had served in, neither of them had carried pictures of family or those close to them.

His best chance had been looking in the hallway closet. He'd traded instant messages with Arin the night before, the way they did a couple nights a week. Arin had told him how she'd met with her sister for dinner. How it was funny her sister was on the island for some sort of research thing and Arin hadn't known ahead of time. Mali had simply texted her out of the blue. Mali had forgotten her jacket at dinner, and Arin was holding onto it, expecting to meet with her again.

There'd been one jacket in the closet that looked like it belonged to a young woman. It was more of a lightweight hoodie in teal. Arin rarely wore anything outside of a monochromatic black and white color scheme so Raul had grabbed it, guessing it belonged to her sister. The rest of the core members of their team were male, and Miller's wife was of a completely different build. No way did the hoodie belong to her.

As he and Taz came out on the beach, Raul headed straight for the catamaran booth where tickets were sold. The catamarans came back up on the beach in right about the same place. To his left and right, big chain hotels rose up and towered over the beach.

No one else was waiting around the booth. The next sail wouldn't go out until just before sunset. A quick scan up and down the boardwalks extending in either direction revealed no suspicious characters. Of the people out and about, he and Taz were actually the most conspicuous. Then again, there weren't a lot of big dogs on the island, and Taz was wearing a service dog harness.

Stealth wasn't one of his objectives today. In fact, if his presence scared off whoever was after Mali, all the better.

There were a bunch of women wandering past. Several of them glanced at him with interest, but there was no flash of recognition. None of them approached him. Just about every female in the area was with a partner, friend, or group of friends. No lone woman anywhere, much less one looking nervous or waiting for someone.

"Taz."

His partner looked up at him immediately, ears forward and ready to work. If they'd been working alone, he wouldn't even need to use the dog's name. But here, in a crowded place, it was best to make it clear he was addressing Taz.

Raul retrieved the baggie containing her hoodie from the small backpack he'd slung over his shoulder. He held the plastic bag open for Taz, showing him the scent article inside and allowing his partner to sniff it liberally. "*Zoek*."

Track. Taz was trained to respond to Dutch commands, one of the standard languages used to train working dogs, and this was his primary skill set: finding people.

His partner went to work. The big dog ranged back and forth in front of Raul, sniffing first the ground and then lifting his nose to catch additional airborne scents on the breeze. Taz proceeded forward once he'd systematically checked everything within the current grid, from the sand to the side of the booth to a nearby retention wall. In a few minutes, Taz froze, his stillness deliberate.

He'd found a trail.

"*Braaf*." Even as he praised the dog, Raul's heart pounded. Just because Taz had hit on the trail didn't mean Mali was safe. It just gave them something to follow to her, so long as the trail remained clear and wasn't disrupted farther ahead. Raul also didn't know if Mali had left the area of her own free will. If she'd been taken or if she'd had to run, there was no way to tell from the ground around the booth. The loose sand and the passersby left no hints. All he knew was that the woman he'd come to help wasn't where she was supposed to be, and his partner had a trail that might be hers. He needed to assume the worst and hurry as best he could. "*Zoek*."

Excited by the trail, Taz surged forward to the full length

of the six-foot lead. If this had been a sanctioned search and rescue in coordination with local law enforcement, Raul would've let Taz off leash. In this case, he kept the GSD tethered. If they were stopped by police or other security, he wanted to be with the dog when they approached so he wasn't mistaken as lost or without a handler. But considering the urgency, Raul let Taz set the pace.

They moved at a fast walk. Taz followed the trail along the narrow boardwalk past the huge hotel. Despite the heavy foot traffic, the big dog proceeded with confidence. He was locked into working mode and wasn't allowing anything else to distract him. They paused once or twice as Taz sniffed the ground and the railing before continuing.

She must've paused in each of those places.

A few minutes later, they were moving out onto the broad expanse of Waikiki beach. It was getting to the hottest part of the day, and Taz was panting now between sniffing the air to catch scents. Heat rose up off the hot sand.

Raul called Taz to a halt and gave the big dog a quick drink, making sure his nose got good and wet. The water served two purposes. Taz's well-being was paramount. A handler always thought of his dog before anything else. The second reason was the impact of the harsh sun on the bare sand of the beach. As the area dried out from the morning, scent particles would be harder to catch unless the dog was well-hydrated. Taz's panting, the increased saliva, and a wet nose maximized Taz's ability to keep and follow the trail.

It took only moments and Taz was back on the trail. The dog veered away from the path. Mali must've decided not to go back toward the street. It was a smart choice, but where had she gone? Raul saw nothing but sunbathers and tourists lounging out on the beach.

His partner wasn't relying on sight, though. Taz weaved his way through tourists and locals.

"Don't touch the dog, please." Raul smiled to diffuse the disappointment as people sat up or leaned toward Taz. "He's working."

Even with a service harness on, there were a lot of people who tried to pet a working dog. Though a decent number of people scooted away when they caught sight of Taz, too. At around eighty-five pounds of muscle, he was a good-size canine. His mostly black face, with only hints of tan, was intimidating.

Despite the reaching hands, Taz remained focused on his task, nose to the ground here and lifted to the air there. It was Raul's job as his handler to run interference so Taz could do his job.

They had a lady in distress to find.

In moments, Taz approached a group of girls. Raul hesitated, keeping his eyes on his dog, but Taz was all about the trail. The big dog sniffed right up to a petite sunbather with an amazingly shapely, tight behind and poked his nose right into her golden bronze hip, then sat, looking back at Raul expectantly.

"Taz." Raul was scandalized. Jesus, the hoodie must not have been Mali's. Instead, they'd ended up molesting some random girl...

The bikini-clad, dainty woman stirred and peered up at them from under a bright white, floppy hat. The face...

...was a ghost of Arin's, about five years younger, with a more delicate jaw and rounder cheeks. The biggest difference was in the eyes; the skin folds of the upper eyelids covering the inner angle of the eyes. Maybe most other people didn't see the resemblance, but he did.

Taz leaned toward the woman's face, sniffing, and then gave a soft bark.

No doubt about it, Taz had found his target. Raul pulled a well-chewed tennis ball from his pocket and tossed it to Taz as his reward, then turned his full attention to the woman. "Mali Siri?"

"My full last name." Her voice was hoarse. "You said you knew it."

Fair. Even if Taz was proof that Raul was the person she'd spoken to on the phone, she was smart to get confirmation that he knew her older sister as well as he'd claimed.

"Srisawasdi." He fumbled over the pronunciation a little. The *r*, the last *s*, and the *i* were almost silent but he tended to miss the correct intonation. Intonation mattered in the Thai language, he'd learned, and could completely change the meaning of the word. So he spelled it out for her, too. "It was strongly implied that it would be better for your parents to shorten their surname to something easier to pronounce when they immigrated to the United States, so it was shortened. But Arin never forgot the full name and the meaning behind it."

Mali closed her eyes then opened them slowly, her expression weary. "Neither did I, but she's always been angrier about it. It's a long story. I'm just...tired."

Raul looked sharply at her face. Her lips were cracked, they were so dry. "How long have you been lying here?"

He kneeled immediately and handed over a spare water bottle. Now that he wasn't embarrassed out of his mind about his dog poking a strange girl's butt with a cold nose, he took a more serious look at Mali Siri. Her golden bronze skin had a red undertone to it. She'd been in the sun long enough to burn. "Sip that slow."

She did as he advised, her movement sluggish and her hands trembling. She spilled some water down her chin as she sipped.

Muttering a curse under his breath, he scanned the area to confirm no potential threats were nearby and then he draped her hoodie around her shoulders. "Take your time. You're safe now."

ABOUT THE AUTHOR

Piper J. Drake is an author of bestselling romantic suspense and edgy contemporary romance, a frequent flyer, and day job road warrior. She is often distracted by dogs, cupcakes, and random shenanigans.

Play Find the Piper online:
PiperJDrake.com
Facebook.com/AuthorPiperJDrake
Twitter @PiperJDrake
Instagram.com/PiperJDrake

Looking for more romantic suspense?

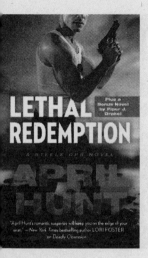

LETHAL REDEMPTION
by April Hunt

Top FBI profiler Grace Steele was just a girl when she escaped the Order of the New Dawn, and she swore never to return. But when Steele Ops needs her help extracting a young woman from the secretive cult's clutches, she's all in...even though the mission requires posing as an engaged couple with the man who broke her heart nine years ago. Includes a bonus novel by Piper J. Drake!

FOREVER STRONG
by Piper J. Drake

Ying Yue Jiang believed her kidnapping was a case of wrong place, wrong time, but she soon realizes that she has become a pawn in a dangerous game. When the handsome and mysterious Azubuike Anyanwu is hired to protect her, he discovers a traitor in her father's organization. As both tensions and attractions grow more intense, Ying Yue and Azubuike will have to test their allegiances and trust in each other in order to stay alive.

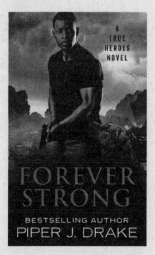

Follow @ReadForeverPub on Twitter and join the conversation using #ReadForever.

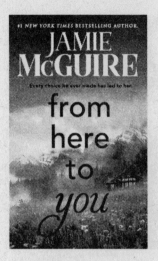

FROM HERE TO YOU
by Jamie McGuire

When Darby Dixon learns that she is pregnant on the morning of her wedding, she realizes that marrying her abusive fiancé would be the worst decision of her life, so she flees to the small town of Colorado Springs...and into the arms of Marine Scott "Trex" Trexler. Trex knows Darby is the woman he's been waiting for his whole life, so when her ex starts making threats, he'll do anything it takes to protect her and her unborn child.

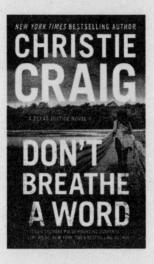

DON'T BREATHE A WORD
by Christie Craig

When special agent Juan Acosta meets his gorgeous neighbor, he knows she's hiding something. As he gets closer to the mysterious woman and her daughter, his investigation uncovers dark secrets that will put them all in danger. Includes a bonus story by April Hunt!